Kindred Spirits

Kindred Spirits

Allison Lane

Thorndike Press   **Chivers Press**
Waterville, Maine USA Bath, England

This Large Print edition is published by Thorndike Press®, USA and by Chivers Press, England.

Published in 2003 in the U.S. by arrangement with NAL Signet, a member of Penguin Group (USA) Inc.

Published in 2003 in the U.K. by arrangement with NAL Signet, a member of the Penguin Group USA, Inc.

U.S. Hardcover   0-7862-5580-3   (Romance Series)
U.K. Hardcover   0-7540-7322-X   (Chivers Large Print)

The text of this Large Print edition is unabridged.
Other aspects of the book may vary from the original edition.

Set in 16 pt. Plantin.

Printed in the United States on permanent paper.

British Library Cataloguing in Publication Data available

Library of Congress Cataloging-in-Publication Data

Lane, Allison.
    Kindred spirits / Allison Lane.
    Waterville, Me. : Thorndike Press, 2003.
        p. cm.
    ISBN 0-7862-5580-3 (lg. print : hc : alk. paper)
                                                        2003053717

For all the readers of *Devall's Angel* and *The Unscrupulous Uncle* who have begged me to write Jack Caldwell's story. Enjoy.

Chapter One

My honor is dearer to me than my life.
— *Don Quixote*

Colonel Jack Caldwell cursed as he limped along the derelict path. Undergrowth tugged at his legs. Vines tangled his feet and tried to snatch his cane. This was not a direction he would ordinarily choose, but none of the sites nearer the house would do.

His injured leg buckled, tossing him ignominiously into a bush.

"Damned French bastards!" he growled, then shoved his irritation aside. It no longer mattered that the leg was slow to heal. Weakness would add credibility to his accident. Everyone knew he was shaky. And everyone knew — or thought they knew — that he was anxious to return to duty. Why else would he exercise the leg from dawn to dusk, triggering cramps that made sleep difficult?

Climbing to his feet, he analyzed the evidence of his fall. The cane had skidded on a mat of dead leaves, digging a long gouge in the soil. His right foot had slipped in the other direction. The fall had broken two branches from the bush and flattened shorter plants.

Good.

Forcing the recalcitrant leg into motion, he limped onward, wishing that he could sit a horse long enough to scout the estate. But his injuries made riding impossible. While his shoulder, head, and side had long since healed, his thigh remained weak despite assurances from the surgeons that it would recover, leaving no trace of a limp — another reason he had to finish the matter now; once the limp disappeared, people would question a fall.

His tutor's voice suddenly swam out of memory. *Are you sure you have considered this thoroughly, Jack?* Reeves had asked that question a thousand times in their years together, usually when Jack was poised to make a mistake.

But this time even Reeves must agree that death was his only option. He could no longer face his eyes in the mirror, for his family's bad blood had finally overcome his long devotion to honor.

His family was the most disreputable in England. His father, the Earl of Deerchester, was the latest in a long line of spineless sycophants and dishonorable cads, each displaying some combination of brutality, cowardice, and irresponsible selfishness. His great-grandfather had disgraced himself at the battle of Blenheim. His grandfather had pledged allegiance to both sides in the Jacobite uprising of 1745, yet fought for neither. His father and older brother were worse. The shame had branded Jack at school and followed him into the army.

He'd spent a lifetime trying to escape the family legacy, first with Reeves's help and later on his own. But honor had been difficult. He'd had to be twice as virtuous as other boys just to be accepted. And sometimes even virtue wasn't enough.

He shuddered to recall the scandal that had nearly destroyed his career. Though eight years had passed, the memory could still freeze his soul. A cub had wagered recklessly at cards, losing half a year's allowance. To hide his poor judgment from the father he feared, the boy had cried foul — not against the gentleman who had won the most in that fateful game, but against Jack, whose family had been embroiled in scandal for generations and whose brother Wilcox was suspected of far more than cheating.

Taking a deep breath, Jack continued along the path. He'd been lucky that time. A friend had forced the cub to recant. Jack had never asked Devall about his methods, but it had taken him six years to repay the debt to his own satisfaction.

And for what? Though he'd been innocent of fleecing greenlings, blood always ran true in the end. As his had. Thirty-two years of honor, of serving others, of exemplary living wiped out in one day.

Waterloo.

He shuddered. It had been the blackest hell he'd survived in fifteen years of war, but the price of that survival had been his honor. And enough shreds of that honor remained that he could not ignore his crimes as Deerchester would have done. Nor could he laugh off the damage as Wilcox was wont to do.

Waterloo had proved that his façade of honor was too thin to control his breeding. He was as brutal as his brother, as cowardly as his father, as scandalous as any of his ancestors. Dedication to right hadn't worked. Nor had determination or scrupulous attention to every thought and deed. To protect society from his family's blood, he must die before he hurt someone else.

10

Only thus could he atone.

Yet even in death he could not add new scandal to the family name — which was why he could not confess and leave his fate to a court-martial. So his death must seem accidental.

Since regaining enough mobility to stumble through his front door, he'd forced his battered body outside every day to establish the habit of wandering the estate alone. No one would be surprised if he found trouble. Seacliff Manor had belonged to his mother's uncle, who had died just before Waterloo. Jack had never seen the place before inheriting it, so he couldn't be expected to know its dangers.

Unfortunately, those dangers were well hidden. Though the house was run-down from having stood empty for forty years — his great-uncle had lived in London — the land was in excellent condition, and the cliffs that had inspired the estate's name had long since eroded into gentle slopes. The stream was too shallow to drown anyone and contained no rocks that might knock a man senseless. Even the bridge was so low that falling off would only sprain an ankle.

So today he was exploring the woods to the west. Somewhere in that direction, cliffs still rose above the beach.

The path became more overgrown with each step. Unlike the path to the village, this one had not been used in a very long time — which raised the question of whether his body would even be found if he fell here. But, of course, the staff would have to mount a search when he failed to return. When they spotted that broken bush, they would press on.

He worked harder to leave clear evidence of his passage. Ten minutes later, the trees opened onto space.

Perfect.

The forest crowded the cliff, forcing walkers to the brink. A sheer drop ended on a rocky beach thirty feet below. No one could survive such a plunge. Wind and rain had gouged several bites from the edge and undercut other spots that were now poised to crumble. The nearest was twenty feet away, where a large shrub reached greedy fingers toward the sunlight, narrowing the path to a scant two feet.

Inhaling deeply, he murmured an apology to Reeves. The tutor had tried so hard to guide him to an honorable life. But even Reeves couldn't work miracles.

It was time.

He hobbled westward, leaning heavily on

the cane landing inches from the edge. Not all the weight was show. He had walked too far today. His thigh throbbed, and his knee tried to buckle with every step. But he would soon be free of pain. The ground would crumble, pitching him over the side.

To make the accident obvious to even the dullest observer, he halted by the shrub and used the cane to chip away the crumbling rock. The fresh gouge flared like a beacon in the sunlight. Bracing on his bad leg, he slid his right foot sideways to create a skid mark and —

"Jacques!" cried a female. "What are *you* doing here?"

Startled, he whirled, his feet sliding out from under him. The voice sounded joyful and welcoming. Who the devil was she, and what was she doing on his estate?

"Jacques!"

So intent was he on identifying her that he automatically grabbed the shrub as he skidded over the edge.

The woman screamed as the branch cracked under his weight.

Marianne Barnett wandered through the woods that protected her manor from Channel storms. It was a beautiful September afternoon, warm with only a hint of the coming autumn.

Autumn had always been her favorite season. Much had changed since she'd lost her family, but not her love of autumn. The vivid colors and biting air exhilarated her. Wading through drifts of fallen leaves was one of her greatest pleasures. If only —

Thrusting regrets aside, she concentrated on the forest. With no grounds staff to maintain it, it had run wild. Sheep kept Halworth's lawns under control, but the rest grew as it would.

The result was a fairy-tale world not usually seen outside of books. Dead branches littered the ground, half buried in decaying leaves and moss. Shrubs and vines grew thick along paths and clearings — anywhere they could find a little sun. It was a wild place, a private place, unwatched by servants, known only to her and the resident animals.

A squirrel bounded onto a tree trunk as she passed, scolding her for interrupting his work. This was his busiest time of year as he rushed to collect food for the winter. A flock of geese circled overhead, flapping and honking in unison as they practiced for the journey that would start in a fortnight. Something moved in the shadows. A fox, perhaps. They had made the park a refuge, for here they were safe. No one entered but her.

Marianne hadn't always lived alone, of course. Her childhood had been no different from her peers', with rules and governesses and plans for the come-out that would lead to marriage and children of her own. Only last night she had dreamed of her twelfth birthday party, attended by a dozen neighbor children. The air had rung with shouts and laughter as she and her guests engaged in fun — three-legged races run with arms wrapped around partners' shoulders, a tug-of-war that ended in a pile of giggling bodies, confidences exchanged with a neighbor whose bent head leaned against her own, hugs and kisses from friends and family . . .

How long had it been since she'd willingly touched another person?

She sometimes felt like Sleeping Beauty, locked in her castle while brambles engulfed it, blocking any escape.

But that would change on her next birthday. In the meantime, books appeased her curiosity about the outside world, knowledge substituting for experience. This year alone she'd climbed Swiss mountains, sailed to China, and explored Etruscan ruins and Greek temples. And if she longed to see through her own eyes instead of through others', she knew better than to question her uncle's decrees. He was her guardian, with absolute control over her person. Lest she forget, his secretary reminded her of the consequences of rebellion. Mr. Craven called at Halworth Park every quarter, his arrivals marking the low points of her year.

Still mad as a March hare, I see, he'd said a week earlier when she'd cringed from his touch. He'd backed her against the wall so he could breathe hotly into her face while his talonlike fingers skimmed down her arm and across her chest. A few seconds of his touch invariably incited hysteria. But at least screams brought her staff on the run, allowing her to escape with his usual reminder ringing in her ears. *Never leave the park or speak to others, Marianne. If anyone discovers your infirmity, Lord Barnett will lock you in an asylum with the other lunatics.*

Such threats made solitude acceptable — for another six weeks. That's when her trust would end, placing Halworth and her life in *her* hands.

Her exhilaration over her coming freedom convinced her that Barnett had to be wrong. She didn't feel mad. Granted,

Craven's visits sent her into fits, but those outbursts were the only ones she'd suffered in years. Her servants didn't incite terror.

Yet uncertainty remained. Craven was the only outsider she'd seen since her uncle's last visit eleven years ago. The servants were too familiar, having served Halworth since before she was bor—

She frowned. Hastings and his wife had been butler and housekeeper for nearly forty years. Both were past seventy and showing signs of age. Even the maids were on the shady side of fifty. What would she do when they retired? Especially Hastings. While she looked forward to consulting with her steward and visiting neighbors, the thought of a strange man living in the house raised tremors.

Perhaps that was why she was suddenly dreaming of yesteryear, conjuring vivid memories of the days when trust had been easy, when Halworth had been the area's social center, when life had been happy . . .

But those times were gone, she reminded herself. Erased in one terrifying moment. Parents. Siblings. Half a dozen servants. All gone. And she'd been helpless to stop it. Grief had long since faded, but the helplessness remained, raising fears that her uncle was right.

She hated being in thrall to emotions she could not control.

Shoving the memories aside, she traced the lacy pattern of a fern and forced her thoughts to the future.

It was time to send for more books — twelve years had committed most of her father's extensive library to memory, so she expanded it several times a year. The last several shipments had concentrated on agriculture and estate management, but she was as prepared to assume control of Halworth as was possible under the circumstances. This time she wanted to learn more about Davy's experiments with matter — his recent treatise in *The Edinburgh Review* had piqued her interest. And a book on topiary, perhaps. Until now, she had kept the gardens the same, loath to modify her mother's designs. But she needed a new challenge, one that would distract her from her growing dissatisfaction — as her day of freedom approached, confinement increasingly chafed her soul.

Solitude now grated, as it had never done in the past, but her uncle's guards would report any attempt to leave the park. She couldn't risk it, for the threat of the asylum was always there.

She was so tired of being at the mercy of others. Her trustees were almost as bad as her uncle. A year earlier, they had refused her request to examine the Halworth ledgers, insisting that no female could understand business — which was absurd, for the end of the trust would put everything in her hands whatever their reservations. When she had persisted, they had urged her to wed so her husband could take charge.

They must live in a fantasy world, for they knew as well as she that Barnett prevented her from meeting anyone. Though twelve years had passed, he would never forget her hysteria the last time she had faced a stranger.

The reminder revived earlier memories of the nightmarish return to England after she'd lost her family. Hiding by day. Stumbling through unfamiliar territory by night. Fearing everyone they met — even children might have betrayed them, and men would have done worse. Francine had protected her as best she could, but the maid had been too scared to think. If not for Jacques . . .

Melancholia swept over her. Perhaps Jacques had done her a disservice by bringing her home. The life she'd loved had ended that day, and even her imminent freedom would not restore it.

Frowning, she halted. She had first met Jacques during that period when strangers had sent her into hysteria, so why had she meekly accepted his help? No hysterics. No screaming nightmares. No kicking and clawing at the first touch of his hand.

You knew I would never hurt you, he murmured in her head. *We are kindred spirits.*

"How could I have known that? I thought you were French. You were wearing their uniform."

Intuition. You had good instincts in those days — you still would if you trusted yourself.

She shook her head free of his voice. Having no one with whom to converse, she had fallen into the habit of talking to people she had once known. Her favorite companion was Hutch, her old governess, but Jacques ran a close second. He was forever urging her to explore new horizons.

Now she pondered his suggestion. Her intuition had been right, for Jacques had not hurt her. Another proof that her uncle was wrong. If she had tolerated Jacques . . .

Not just tolerated. She had clung to him as to a rock in a stormy sea. From the moment he had joined them, she had known that they would survive. Jacques was magnificently heroic, remarkably capable, and the most honorable man she had ever met. Without him, she would never have escaped France.

Trust yourself, he murmured again. *Your old life may be gone, but you can build a better one.*

"Perhaps."

Test it. Go out and meet people. You can be so much more than you think.

"Soon, I promise. But you know I can't dismiss the guards until my twenty-fifth birthday. As long as they are here, I cannot leave Halworth. Nor can I deny entrance to Craven."

Start by writing letters. You will need a solicitor if you hope to be independent. Now is the time to find one.

She frowned. It was true. Ending the trust would be just the beginning. A solicitor could tell her of any responsibilities or restrictions she hadn't considered. While the Halworth library was extensive, most of the books had been added by her classicist father, so there were no tomes on legal matters. A solicitor could also recommend a good man of business. She would need help with the trust investments.

The trees thinned as she approached the one place she had always felt free. Here she could embrace the wind, glory in the view, and envy the birds swooping overhead. But as she lifted her face to the sun, she caught an odd movement out of the corner of her eye. A soldier was chipping the rock twenty feet away.

Recognition bloomed. "Jacques! What are *you* doing here?"

As if her thoughts had conjured him from thin air, he stood before her, hatless, his dark hair whipped by the wind. His shoulders seemed broader than she remembered, though his red coat hung loosely, hinting that he'd recently lost weight. Mud caked the gray breeches clinging to powerful thighs, and a long scrape marred one boot. At her shout, he whirled.

"Jacques!" she gasped as his feet slipped, spilling him over the side. He grabbed a shrub, but it was too fragile to bear his weight.

Screaming, she raced forward, heedless of the danger, terrified that she'd killed him.

You can't let him die! shouted Hutch. *He is your savior.*

"Give me your hand," she gasped as his walking stick clattered on the rocks below.

Pain, fear, fury, and a strange satisfaction

swirled through his gray eyes, but he finally thrust his free hand upward.

He was heavier than he looked. But caring for Halworth's gardens had given her unladylike strength. Bracing her feet against a rock, she pulled with all her might.

The rock sheared off, sliding toward the edge and taking her feet with it.

Chapter Two

Jack swore as the woman skidded toward the brink.

"I'm too heavy. You'll fall," he gasped, cursing himself for grabbing the bush. He couldn't have asked for a better conclusion — a clear accident, complete with a witness. "Let go!"

"Can't . . . owe you . . . life."

Her foot slid into a crack and stuck, giving her more leverage. Showing surprising strength, she grabbed his wrist with both hands and hauled him higher. Guilt twisted her face, clear even as she strained.

He surrendered. She wasn't going to give up. Sighing, he shifted his other hand to a sturdier branch and crawled clear. Letting her feel responsible for his death would ruin her life and add a new stain to his soul.

But her intervention infuriated him. "Who the devil are you? And what are you doing on my land?" he snapped, standing. Without his cane, he had to steady himself on her shoulder until his thigh locked in place.

She blanched, switching her tone to the murmur women used to soothe obstreperous children. "Actually, these woods are on my land, Jacques. Their edge marks the boundary between Halworth Park and Seacliff. You did come from Seacliff, I presume?"

He ignored the question, even more infuriated that he hadn't known — one of the things his steward had been nattering about, he supposed. The name Halworth sounded vaguely familiar, but he'd paid little attention to Poole's lectures, too overwhelmed by his infamy to care about his estate. It would be someone else's problem as soon as he was well enough to die.

"Who are you?" he repeated, examining his nemesis. Wind tangled curly blonde hair that had never seen a maid's touch, and plastered her unadorned round gown to a slender body. It puckered the nipples clearly visible beneath the thin muslin. Yet despite her lack of stays and despite a tanned face that proved her bare head was a habit, her tone and grace proclaimed her a lady. Sunlight glistened from blue-gray eyes.

His loins stirred. After years in Spain

among weathered army veterans and dark Spanish beauties, he found the pallid complexions of English ladies insipid.

But fear tempered his rising lust. She was unaccompanied. Meeting her alone was scandalous.

He backed toward Seacliff, praying that she didn't have a brother or father ready to jump from the shrubbery and cry compromise.

"I'm not surprised that you have forgotten." She followed, relaxing as they moved farther from the edge. "It's been twelve years. You knew me as Marie. I never properly thanked you for helping us escape from France."

Jack stared, mentally removing six inches in height and all of her curves, then plumping her cheeks and turning her eyes slaty with fear. "My God! It's really you."

His head whirled. It wasn't just the passage of time that had blocked recognition, though she'd been only twelve when he'd bidden her farewell. But the vibrant lady before him bore little resemblance to that terrified child.

His mind retreated to May of 1803.

He had been in Paris when the Peace of Amiens collapsed. With arrest orders out for all Englishmen, he'd stolen a French uniform and headed for the Channel, praying he could find a smuggler willing to carry him across.

Three days later, he'd happened upon two soldiers questioning a woman and child. Prudence demanded that he ignore them, but something about the child had touched his heart. Though her posture indicated passivity, intelligence had lurked in her eyes. And grief. And terror.

He'd ordered the soldiers away, then questioned the woman himself. Clarisse was a lady's maid and French émigré. Marie was her employer's daughter. They were also returning to England, so he'd taken them under his wing.

Marie had not said a word during the entire journey — hardly surprising, since she'd just lost her entire family. But seeing her today proved that he'd done one thing right in his life. She would never have made it home on her own.

"It's really me," she confirmed, meeting his gaze. "I should have thanked you for your help, Jacques. Mama's maid had no idea where we were or even which direction we should be going. I've often regretted my poor manners. Failing to thank someone for assistance is bad enough, but you were a true hero, not only saving our lives, but going far out of your way to escort us to Barnett Court."

"It was nothing," he countered stiffly. The reminder of how far he had fallen stabbed his conscience. "So you live here now?" Dorset was a long way from Essex — but she would have wed several years ago; she was long past girlhood.

"I inherited Halworth from my father." Pain flashed through her eyes.

"The estate remains yours?"

"Of course." Surprise changed to a blush. "I see what you mean, but I am not married. Save for a month with Lord Barnett, I've spent my entire life here." Her mouth snapped shut.

He wanted to ask how that had come about — a twelve-year-old would never have been put in charge of an estate, regardless of ownership — but she had closed the subject.

Yet manners could not muzzle his curiosity. Something wasn't right. Intuition rarely misled him, and it was screaming now.

Twelve years should have put paid to her grief, so why the pain when she spoke of her inheritance? And why had she not come out in London long ago? An estate made a handsome dowry, and Lord

Barnett was comfortably fixed. So why was she dressed like the poorest tenant lass? Dorset was one of the richest pasturages in England. Even if she had inherited only the use of the estate, the income should be substantial. When added to looks that stole his breath, men should have been flocking to her side.

Guilt rose to choke him. He should have stayed at Barnett Court until he was sure she was comfortable. He should at least have spoken personally to Lord Barnett. Instead, he'd turned her over to Lady Barnett, then left, taking Clarisse with him — Lady Barnett had taken one look at the beautiful Frenchwoman and glared daggers.

Now he wondered how the disapproving Lady Barnett had felt about housing her husband's niece, who even at twelve would have cleaned up well. Had she refused to keep the girl under her roof? That might explain Marie's return to her father's house.

Jack cursed. Again his breeding had distorted his judgment, allowing selfishness to overthrow duty. And he hadn't even realized it. A caring man would have made sure of the child's welcome. A few hours of delay — or even a day — would have made no difference. Yes, reporting to his regiment had been important, but it hadn't been *that* critical. He should have talked to Lord Barnett. He should have checked on Marie a month later . . . six months . . . a year. Accepting responsibility for her created an obligation.

But instead, he'd shoved Marie at Lady Barnett, informed the woman that Marie's family was dead, then left for London. When Lady Barnett had implied that Clarisse and Jack were lovers, he had whisked the maid to safety. But he'd never asked whether Lady Barnett could care for a grieving child. And he'd said nothing to Lord Barnett. Nor had Clarisse. They had left it to Marie to explain the circumstances of her family's demise.

Appalling! A twelve-year-old girl who'd said not a word in six days. How could he have been so stupid? He'd shirked his duty with a vengeance and now had to question how many other times he'd allowed base selfishness to lead him into dishonor.

Another ancient scold echoed. *It doesn't matter whether you meant to hurt Cook, Jack. You will be judged by the result. If you truly wish to embrace honor, then you must think before you act, no matter how insignificant that action might seem. You never know the true importance of an event until it is over.*

This time his actions had left Marie alone and grieving in the company of a harridan who lacked a heart. Another crime for which he must atone.

"This is a lovely spot," he finally said.

She nodded. "It is one of my favorites."

"Would you mind if I returned to enjoy the view? I need to exercise this leg if it is to heal."

Her eyes moved from his bad leg to the spot where he had fallen, finally resting on his face. "You are welcome anytime, Jacques, but I must ask that you be careful. The cliff is quite weak, often giving no sign of where the next collapse will occur. Remain near the trees at all times. I would not want you to suffer another accident."

"You can be sure that I will exercise more caution."

"Thank you."

"You are well?" he asked inanely while he sought a way to ask about her past. He had never been tongue-tied before, but today his mind was a blank.

"Quite well. My routine suits me," she added, apparently sensing that he was concerned about her situation.

He nodded, though there were too many signs of wrongness. But he couldn't find the words that would ask personal questions. Despite that six-day journey together, they were strangers. This was the first time he'd heard her voice. A very melodious voice, he admitted through another wave of heat.

"You are weary," she continued, recalling his attention. "Why don't you rest on that rock before beginning the trek home?" She pointed to a flat boulder tucked beneath a nearby tree. "I can see that you are in pain."

He nodded.

With a brief farewell, she left, breaking the spell he'd been under since recognizing her.

He collapsed on the rock and glared at his thigh. Damn her! He'd been so close! Now he must devise a new accident. He could not pay for Waterloo on Marie's land — she had suffered enough in her short life. Nor could he pay for it anywhere until he found out what was wrong with her.

And he must search his conscience for other signs of dishonor. Only after repairing all damage could he atone for murdering a man in cold blood.

Marianne frowned as she walked back to the house. Jacques was suffering, and not just physically. He had been preparing to jump when she arrived. Since she could not imagine him killing himself over a limp, there had to be something seriously wrong.

Jacques was the most honorable caring man she had ever known, even more than her revered father. So she had to help him. He must not waste his life so cruelly.

He was clearly in thrall to melancholy — as she had been twelve years ago. Hers had been triggered by grief, but she doubted that Jacques would be that weak. He wore a uniform, so he'd probably been injured at Waterloo, but a military man would be accustomed to death — unless it had been the death of a beloved relative or a wife.

Yet she could not imagine Jacques falling apart even over a wife's death. He was too strong, too honorable, too perfect. So why had he tried to jump?

Learning anything useful would be difficult. Her only correspondence was with her trustees, such as it was. She requested books. They sent summaries of her accounts.

Her uncle's orders meant that she'd seen no neighbors in twelve years. Her staff rarely discussed the outside world, unwilling to distress her by mentioning the life she could not enjoy.

Uncertainty again raised its ugly head. Was Barnett right? She might feel normal, but many fears had abated only because she avoided their causes — like closing her stables. Others remained. Nightmares still relived that month at Barnett Court. And the journey to Halworth had raised terrors that stalked her still.

Then how did you spend half an hour with Jacques just now? demanded Hutch. *Your only fear was that he would fall.*

"That's different," she snapped.

How? He's a man, isn't he?

"Well, yes." And what a man! Despite suffering from illness and injury, he had dominated the cliff. But she'd felt no threat. "Jacques has always been safe," she argued. "He risked his life to get us back to England, though we were strangers of no import. He could have traveled faster without us, but not once did he reveal frustration or regret. And though Francine was but a servant and no older than he, he treated her with respect. Other men would have demanded favors in exchange for protection."

But you don't know what happened after they left you.

"It doesn't matter. Jacques would never

34

harm me. If Papa miraculously returned from the grave, I could talk to him, too. It is others who raise fears — Uncle Barnett, Mr. Craven, every stranger we met on the road . . .”

She set her memories aside. Helping Jacques was more important. What would drive so good a man to take his own life? He was the most capable being she had ever known. No matter what they had encountered in France, he'd remained calm, competent, and logical. Those characteristics had permeated her conversations with him since returning to Halworth. His control tempered her hysteria. His exhortations had prompted her to study and remain active instead of wallowing in misery and regret. Had she misjudged him so badly?

She paused near the lake, staring blindly at the reeds that had sheltered three families of wood ducks last spring. She had to see him again, find out what troubled him, and validate her instincts. But despite his request, she doubted that he would return to Halworth. Men considering suicide cared nothing for the view. He would find a new location for his accident.

So how could she help him when he lived in the world and she did not?

You will have to leave the park, said Hutch with a shrug.

"I know, I know." She shuddered. As Jacques had just proved, it was possible to reach Seacliff on foot. The gatekeepers watched only the roads. After twelve years they no longer expected her to rebel. So as long as she didn't incite gossip . . .

But before slipping out, she must learn more about Jacques so she could ask the right questions.

And how do you expect to do that? You don't know his family name, his rank, or even his regiment.

"Well, fiddlesticks," she grumbled. It was true. His uniform looked military, but she had no idea of the specifics. She would have to do something she'd avoided for twelve years — ask questions.

Mrs. Hastings was waiting when Marianne reached the house. "Did you have a nice walk?"

"Very nice. A fox was abroad in the woods, and a squirrel chattered furiously at me for interrupting his nut gathering." Habit would send her to the library at this point, but today she forced an unaccustomed smile onto her lips and continued. "I noticed some odd activity at Seacliff Manor. Has the owner decided to visit?"

Seacliff had been vacant as long as she could remember. She hadn't looked at the house today, but it was possible to see one corner from the cliff.

"Actually, the former owner died last spring," said Mrs. Hastings hesitantly — everyone avoided references to death lest they revive unwelcome memories. "The new owner is his nephew, Colonel John Caldwell. Mrs. Stacey from the village said that he arrived a month ago to recover from wounds he suffered at Waterloo."

"What sort of wounds?"

Shock flashed across Mrs. Hastings's face, but she answered readily enough. "No one has seen him, but according to Mrs. Avon — she runs the bakery, you might recall — he took a hit in the side and another that broke his leg. They saved the leg and expect a full recovery, though," she added brightly.

"His family must be relieved. Has he children?"

"No. He's not married. And just as well. His father is that awful Earl of Deerchester — you must have heard tales of the man. The colonel is a decent gentleman, by all accounts, but folks don't want his relatives visiting hereabouts."

"If the colonel is as decent as you say, I

doubt he would allow Deerchester to bother his neighbors."

She'd heard of Deerchester all her life — he'd been the bogeyman of the nursery, in part because his seat was in Dorset, so he posed a real as well as a legendary threat — but details of his crimes were not given to children. Visualizing Jacques as his son stretched credulity. Jacques would never tolerate dishonor.

But Colonel Caldwell might, murmured Hutch. *You don't know what he's faced since France.*

"Never!" snapped Marianne, then blushed. This was another reason she avoided the staff. She was so used to arguing with Hutch and Jacques that she forgot others didn't hear them.

Mrs. Hastings smoothed her face to blandness, then straightened with brisk efficiency. "Are you ready for lunch?"

"Give me five minutes to wash up." Her hands were filthy and mud caked her half boots, but Mrs. Hastings would assume that she'd stopped in the hothouse or garden.

So his name was John, which meant he was probably called Jack. He must have used the French form while fleeing France, just as Francine had shortened Marianne to Marie, then changed her own name to Clarisse — she'd been terrified that someone might recognize her.

Knowing his name would make research easier. She received many newspapers and journals, having continued her father's subscriptions and added several more. They kept her attuned to the outside world.

She stifled a sigh, wishing she were normal.

Normal young ladies must study deportment and learn the arts that attract gentlemen, Hutch reminded her. *They aren't free to roam the woods unaccompanied. Nor are they allowed to read about politics or —*

"Quiet. I need to think."

If Jacq-Jack had recently lost a wife, no one knew about it. But Waterloo had been bloodier than the worst of the Peninsula battles.

Yet why would it push him to suicide? It took many years to achieve the rank of colonel, and Jack was young enough that promotion must also have required heroics in many battles. Even a fortune couldn't buy promotion into the higher ranks without the skills to support it. So there had to be something more. After lunch, she would seek information about him.

She had kept everything she'd read in twelve years. At sixteen, she had organized her father's papers and all the new material — with Hutch and her parents gone, she'd been in charge of her own education. Lacking a guide, she'd had to develop her own system for filing and cross-referencing. But it worked. She could now find anything easily.

Chapter Three

Jack cried out, bolting upright in bed, his heart pounding so hard he could scarcely breathe. Bile curdled his tongue.

Nightmares. They had plagued him since Waterloo, a constant reminder of his dishonor. Even in sleep he could not escape his shame.

Easing his bad leg to the floor, he poured wine and dragged the draperies back so he could see the moon-washed grounds of his prison.

Seacliff needn't be a prison, murmured Temptation. *Forget the past, and you can continue as before.*

"Never. I won't become another Caldwell blackguard." Which made Seacliff a prison. The only escape was death. Returning to duty would disgrace his uniform. Showing his face in society would encourage witnesses to denounce him. Visiting Deerchester Hall was out of the question. So he was trapped. Still. If only Marie had arrived two minutes later . . .

Which recalled his latest nightmare. This one had been different — no murder, no cowardice, no accusatory eyes, no drowning in his bad blood. Instead, it had relived that frantic journey to the Channel twelve years ago.

He had been just another visitor to Paris until he'd stumbled across Napoleon's plans to invade England. Honor demanded that he cut short his leave and deliver them to his superiors immediately.

He'd been packing when two French soldiers burst in. Napoleon was abandoning the peace accord. All Englishmen were being detained.

Desperate to reach his regiment, he'd fought, using tactics he'd learned from a Chinaman in Gibraltar. Two minutes later, he'd donned the officer's uniform, stuffed the plans into his jacket, then fled into the night. Since his imposture could only work at a distance — his accent was unmistakably English — he'd stayed off the roads and traveled by night, covering seventy miles before spotting Marie.

He still couldn't explain why he'd risked exposure to help her. At first glance, she'd been unprepossessing, caked in dirt from head to toe. Her expression had accepted whatever Fate had in store. Yet despite being clearly in the woman's charge, Marie had seemed utterly alone.

Perhaps that was what had touched him. It was as though a wall separated her from the world, something Jack had endured his entire life. His family's scandals had always stood between him and others.

He shook his head, hoping to dislodge the childhood memories, but he was too weak to hold them at bay.

Deerchester had inherited a full measure of the Caldwell cowardice, which turned his dishonor sneaky and limited his brutality to those who could not fight back — like his despised younger son.

Deerchester's heir, Wilcox, had dodged the family cowardice, becoming a vicious bully who thrived on blatant dishonor. Cheating was second nature, but few dared complain, for he found painful ways to avenge any insult. By sixteen, Wilcox had been a brutal degenerate who relished inflicting pain, even on those with whom he had no quarrel.

The only bright spot in Jack's childhood had been his tutor, the son of a neighboring vicar. Reeves had insisted that Jack pursue honor, and he'd protected Jack from the consequences of trying. Deerchester and Wilcox had derided Jack at every turn, calling him a milksop for caring what anyone thought of him and berating him for betraying his family. Without Reeves, Jack might have died from Wilcox's efforts to turn him into a man.

Stay away from him, Reeves had said the day he'd found six-year-old Jack in tears from one of sixteen-year-old Wilcox's attacks. *He hates you because he knows you are already a better man than he is. Something broke in Wilcox's head when he was born. But you are whole and need not follow his disreputable example.*

It was a nice thought, but breeding, not accident, determined a man's character. Effort might soften a bad trait or enhance a good one, but it couldn't turn a sow's ear into a silk purse.

Jack refilled his glass.

Childhood had taught him to hide the pain of Wilcox's scorn and Deerchester's rejection behind a mask of indifference. Thus he'd recognized the look on Marie's face that day in France. She had stood motionless, one hand clutched in Clarisse's, but she saw nothing. Her mind was miles away.

The drunken soldiers were demanding sex from Clarisse, who seemed reluctant, so Jack had stepped forward and ordered them off. He'd nearly fainted when they'd actually left.

Not being castaway, Clarisse had spotted his accent. But she, too, was fleeing France. So he'd taken them with him. Finding a smuggler who would accept three passengers had seemed impossible — he'd had little money, and Clarisse even less — but Marie's face had already haunted him. He'd never felt such instant rapport.

Tonight's dream had dredged up every horror from that interminable journey — the night he'd nearly been caught stealing food; being trapped in the open by a hailstorm; Clarisse telling an angry farmer that her sister was deaf and thus couldn't respond to his shouts . . .

Jack grimaced. Marie had been nearly cataleptic by then, walking wherever she was led, swallowing what was placed in her mouth, but responding to nothing. He'd been so focused on reaching the coast in one piece that he hadn't questioned her condition.

Oddly, Clarisse had barely registered on his mind, though she'd been a beautiful woman who would have done anything for him. It was Marie who had occupied his thoughts even after he'd returned to his regiment. Despite her silence, something about her had kept him aware of her at all times.

Limping back to the window, he watched a fox slink across the drive.

He should have paid closer attention twelve years ago. Losing her family could not explain the intensity of her shock, so leaving her alone at Barnett Court was even more dishonorable.

Little had changed.

Her eyes still demanded help. They were the most expressive eyes he'd ever seen, changing color with her changing mood. Relief turned them sparkling blue. He'd seen them gray with grief, slaty in fear, and icy when she was angry. A gray rim emphasized every shift. He wondered what color they were when she smiled.

Perhaps that bothered him most of all. He had never seen her smile. Twelve years ago, that lack had been understandable. She had just lost her family and was caught in a perilous trek across enemy soil. But she had not smiled on the cliff, either. Not even the meaningless smile the polite world bestowed on a minor acquaintance. And the joy of her initial greeting had not shown on her face.

He longed to entice a smile onto those

rosy lips, and not just for his own pleasure. He must make sure that she was safe. Only when he had discharged that duty could he address his own plans.

Marianne paced her bedroom. Though it was long past midnight, there was no point climbing into bed, for she could not sleep. Jack remained too vividly in her mind.

He'd been mentioned in dispatches after nearly every battle, making it easy to follow his rise in rank. His bravery was cited often — for leading charges against stiff odds or for whisking wounded soldiers from further harm. That habit had made him a legend after Badajoz, where he was credited with saving a dozen lives even as he led his men into the diversionary attack that let British troops breach the wall across town. He'd joined Wellington's staff a week later.

She'd been pleased that those he rescued were common soldiers as often as officers. It fit her memories of the man who had helped her in France. But validating her instincts raised new questions about his attempt at suicide. He was no stranger to battle or pain. Three times he'd been seriously wounded — in Ireland, on the Peninsula, and at Waterloo.

The papers also carried information — none of it flattering — about Deerchester and his heir Wilcox, Jack's father and brother. But stories about Jack had not mentioned the connection in ten years, indicating a rift. Did the estrangement weigh on him? An honorable man would yearn for family, even one like his.

But whatever the cause of Jack's melancholy, it had not yet reached his soul. Why else would he save himself while falling? So it wasn't too late to change his mind. Whether it arose from injuries or grief for fallen comrades or problems with his family, it was temporary. Given time, it would retreat, and he would again enjoy life. Keeping him occupied while time worked its magic would repay him for rescuing her.

She paused at the window, gazing across the park to the woods guarding the cliffs. She could keep him from jumping there, but that served little purpose. He would not choose her land again. No one of his heroic nature would leave an acquaintance to clean up after him. And while she could slip away to Seacliff for an hour or two, she could hardly spend every moment with him.

So she had to give him a reason to live.

His history and her own memories indicated that he needed to help others. Her best course was to request his assistance.

It wouldn't be easy. Asking for help would force her to admit facts few people knew. Baring even part of her soul risked drawing ridicule. Jack would have scorned Barnett's edicts, so he would think her weak for acquiescing. But it was all she could think of.

Her purpose was not entirely altruistic, she admitted. Though she was anxious to take charge of Halworth and institute some much-needed changes, doing so meant facing her steward. What if the confrontation triggered hysteria? Crane would never accept her orders if he thought her weak.

Doubts continued to plague her. No matter how normal she felt, Barnett's insistence that she was mad was difficult to ignore. Nightmares continued to plague her. And she couldn't touch others, even Mrs. Hastings, whom she had known for twenty-five years.

You grabbed Jack's hand to keep him from falling, said Hutch.

Marianne frowned. The gesture had been automatic — so automatic that she'd not recognized the import. And Jack had leaned heavily on her shoulder — he was the same height as Craven and much more solid, so he towered over her even more threateningly. That made her forbearance remarkable, hinting that her hysteria rose from Craven himself and not his actions. It was an exhilarating notion.

Be careful, warned Hutch. *Craven isn't your only problem. You met him long after Barnett diagnosed you as mad.*

Jack was hardly an adequate test of her sanity, for he had already rescued her and proven himself harmless. He'd resided in her mind for years, making him a part of her. But she could use her tolerance to distract him.

Biting her lip, she played with ways to phrase a request for help. She couldn't admit that Barnett thought her mad, so she must claim a lack of practice in conversation. And her goal would be to face others. Twelve years had passed since she'd last left Halworth Park. Twelve years since she'd spoken to tenants, walked through the village, discussed anything with real people beyond today's plans or next week's menus.

Expressing such goals revived excitement over her coming freedom. She shivered at images of facing Craven with poise and grace and paying calls on neighbors she'd last seen in childhood.

Don't lose track of your purpose, ordered Hutch. *Biting off too much at once won't work.*

"I won't." If she failed to keep Jack alive, nothing else mattered. Until she knew whether her tolerance extended beyond him, she would concentrate on his despair. And she couldn't risk doing anything that would anger Barnett.

In the end, Marianne managed three hours of sleep before dawn. Choosing a light cloak to hold the morning chill at bay, she headed for the woods.

It would not do to call at Seacliff. Aside from the utter impropriety of an unmarried lady calling on an unmarried gentleman, appearing at the door would cause talk. If the gatekeepers learned that she had left the estate, they would summon Barnett.

So she watched the house from the shrubbery just beyond the woods. A man as haunted as Jack would not quietly remain indoors.

From her vantage point, she could see the main entrance and two French windows that opened onto a terrace. The stables were on the other side, but she doubted he could ride far. His limp had been too pronounced. Yet that very fact would make a fall from a horse believable.

She bit her lip. Should she slip around where she could watch the stables? If anyone saw her, the news could reach her uncle in days. And even the sight of a stable sent her into a panic. She'd closed her own twelve years ago.

She was still frozen in indecision when the front door opened. Jack limped down the steps, a new cane gripped in his left hand.

Marianne's breath rushed out with an audible *whoosh*. Not only was he on foot, but he was headed in her direction.

"You look none the worse for yesterday's accident, Colonel Caldwell," she said calmly when he neared the woods.

He jumped. "Marie. You startled me."

"I suppose I did. Is your leg worse today?" She nodded at the cane.

"No." He frowned at the shrubs that sheltered her. "After your comments on the boundary between our estates, I am surprised to find you in my park. Do you come here often?"

"Never. But I had to make sure you came to no harm. I understand you are still recovering from Waterloo."

"Yes." His mouth snapped shut.

Marianne stifled a sigh. As she'd feared, the battle bothered him. Wellington had again cited him for bravery, but the newspapers described Waterloo as the worst battle in history — certainly the worst of the war against Napoleon.

"Why walk over here?" he asked again. "You could have sent a message easily enough."

"Hardly. My books on manners condemn writing notes to unmarried gentlemen. Besides, servants talk. How could I explain my interest?"

"But we are old friends. Even the highest stickler would accept an inquiry about my health under the circumstances."

She shook her head. "I am glad you consider me a friend, but no one knows of yesterday's meeting, and few know about France. So we must remain strangers who happen to own adjacent estates. However, I would not object to talking for a time. Would you care to walk? There is a lovely view of the lake not far from here."

"I would be delighted."

He looked surprised at his words, so she congratulated herself. Already she was distracting him from his melancholy. "Tell me about Spain," she began. "Not the war, for that is over. But what of the people? How does the land differ from England or France? The climate? The crops?"

"You sound interested."

"Always. I spend much of my time in study, but books rarely answer all my questions. You have traveled far and can give me firsthand accounts of other lands. Is it true that Spain is hotter than England?"

"Very. And the light is harsher. The air is clear, with none of the softening effects of our English haze, and the sun rises higher in the sky." He spoke eloquently, describing wooded mountains, searing plains, olive and orange groves that stretched for miles, and hot-blooded people who fit the land like a glove. He didn't stop until they emerged from the woods.

Grass sloped down to a crescent-shaped lake. Willows draped prettily into the water. A folly in the form of a Grecian temple rose on the inside curve.

"You are right," said Jack, a smile tugging faintly at one corner of his mouth. "It is beautiful. Do you come here often?"

"On the days I seek serenity. Sometimes nothing but the wildness of the Channel will do — or the challenge of the gardens. The lake offers peace." She pointed as two deer walked daintily to the shore for a drink. A mother and fawn, though the fawn was old enough to have lost its spots.

"Is this where you study?" he asked.

"Not as a rule. This is where I relax. I use Papa's library for study — not a lady-like activity, I understand, but Papa was a scholar and saw nothing amiss in female education. It is a peaceful life, but pleasant enough."

Jack frowned. "Most young ladies spend their time making or receiving calls."

She drew a deep breath, recognizing the perfect opening. "Perhaps one day I can join them — with your help."

He raised his brows.

"I have lived alone so long that I can no longer tolerate people. Lately, this lack has begun to concern me. My inheritance is currently in a trust, but that will soon terminate, leaving me in charge. If I cannot deal with the steward and other workmen, Halworth will suffer. I am hoping that you can teach me how."

"I know nothing of estates," he objected. "For fifteen years, my life has been the army."

"That is not what I meant." His response demonstrated another problem. The voices in her head always understood her meaning, but real people could not read her mind. She must be more explicit when talking aloud. "I've read numerous books on estate management and agricultural experiments. Once the steward takes me seriously, I can hold my own well enough. But I have lived secluded for so long that I can no longer relax around people. Nor can I discuss even innocuous subjects. You are the first outsider I have spoken to in some time. The practice will be good for me."

His eyes flared, almost in pain. Marianne wondered if she had crossed some implacable boundary with her request.

Jack started to speak, then shut his mouth. A full minute passed before he tried again. "I will be honored if you wish to practice conversation with me, but I am puzzled about why you have been secluded for so long."

"It seemed best in the beginning. Now it has become a habit." She had prepared this answer, for the question was obvious. But revealing that Barnett thought her mad might drive him away. She had to keep him close until he regained his faith in the future.

"Very well, Marie."

"The name is actually Marianne, Colonel," she said gently. "Like you, I used the

French version so we would not draw unwanted attention."

"Ah. Marianne it is, then. And I am Jack." He offered his arm, then led her on a circuit of the lake, chatting lightly about topics far removed from his life or hers.

Chapter Four

"Who owns the estate west of Seacliff?" Jack asked Poole that afternoon, surprising the steward into a jaw-dropping stare. Jack had ignored estate business since arriving from Belgium, often refusing to see Poole at all.

"Is there a problem?" Poole's shock gave way to trepidation.

"No, but it is time I learned about my neighbors." He steepled his hands, contemplating Poole's sudden nervousness. Had the man taken advantage of a disinterested employer to divert income into his own pocket, or was it Halworth Park that bothered him?

Jack had thought of little else since meeting Marianne that morning. Something was very wrong. A harridan like Lady Barnett might easily banish an unwanted niece, but why had Lord Barnett failed to provide a governess and companion? And the park showed few signs of maintenance — overgrown woods, a folly in desperate need of repairs, weeds choking a third of the lake . . . Where did the estate income go? Dorset was a prosperous county. She should have flocks at least as large as his own.

Poole shook his head. "The estate is currently owned by a Miss Barnett, the last surviving member of her family. I know few details, for she took possession before my time."

"The entire family is gone?"

Poole nodded.

"What happened?"

"Plague. Not here, you understand," he added quickly. "They were in some foreign place. Only the daughter survived, but that is all we know, for she refuses all callers. Anyone approaching is turned away at the gate."

"And people don't find that strange?"

"Not particularly. She's mad. Her guardian keeps her here so society doesn't learn of her affliction. Putting her in an asylum might draw attention to her state."

"Since everyone knows about it anyway, how does it serve him?" Jack snapped, instincts again aroused. He'd seen enough madmen to know that Marianne was not mad. A trifle untutored, perhaps, at least in the ways of the world, but she was sharp-witted and harbored an amazing store of knowledge. They had discussed her plans for when her trust ended. No madwoman would care about bettering the lives of her tenants or improving her estate.

"No one actually knows for certain," admitted Poole. "Madness is the most likely explanation for her seclusion. That Halworth's servants refuse to discuss her confirms that something is amiss. But we have no noblemen living nearby, so I doubt news of her leaves the area. Mr. Barnett was a scholarly younger son who married a vicar's daughter. Neither of them visited London, and I've heard no tales that they frequented Bath, either."

"Why do the villagers discuss the Barnetts with you?" asked Jack.

"They don't. I occasionally overhear comments when the Halworth butler or housekeeper appears, but most of my information comes from Halworth's steward. Crane is a friend — we accepted our positions at the same time. In ten years, he has never spoken to Miss Barnett."

"Who does he answer to, then?"

"The London banker who hired him."

Jack turned his questions to other neighbors, area villages, and the nearest market town, but his thoughts remained on Marianne.

Her situation was worse than he'd feared. She'd been imprisoned at Halworth for twelve years, denied her rightful place in society, and forbidden the supervision that every young lady required. Seclusion alone could fracture some people's reason.

But not hers. She was as sane as he — possibly saner — erudite, intelligent, level-headed, and capable in an emergency. Granted, she remained solemn, but if she never met people, that was no surprise.

Barnett had much for which to answer. He had taken charge of a grieving child, refused her any comfort, then banished her to a life of solitude. It was obvious that no one had cared a whit for her. Barnett had made no attempt to prepare her for entrance into society.

Such dishonor made Jack's blood boil.

But Marianne knew that Barnett had denied her a normal life, which was why she'd asked for help. Their morning walk had convinced him that she lacked confidence — understandable under the circumstances. Years of Barnett's manipulation had left her emotionally fragile.

But despite everything, she retained the core of strength that had helped her survive hardship and terror in France. He had seen it on the cliffs when she'd refused to let him fall. It had underlain her request for help. And how else had she prospered despite isolation?

So he had to help her. He had accepted responsibility for her welfare twelve years ago, and nothing had changed. He must rebuild her confidence and investigate Barnett. The man was no fit guardian.

Jack set his plans in motion the following morning, dispatching his batman Jones to Essex to learn what he could about the viscount. Then he limped toward the cliff.

For the first time in months he'd slept deeply and dreamlessly, awakening refreshed and eager to face the day. His body tightened in anticipation as he broke from the trees.

She wasn't there.

Cursing, he forced his leg toward the lake. She was in the folly, sketching. The tip of her tongue protruded as she worked.

"Good morning," he called.

Her eyes brightened when she spotted him. "Exercising your leg?"

He nodded. "I can't yet sit a horse for more than five minutes, so I must walk."

She set aside her sketchbook. "What do the surgeons say about your recovery?"

"Nothing to the point." He turned the

subject, for his purpose was to learn more about her situation. Was the house as derelict as this folly? "The library at Seacliff contains little beyond sermons," he began, hoping to extract an invitation. "Could I borrow some of your books on estate management? That is not a subject I've needed in the past, but now that I own an estate, I should learn enough to tell whether the steward is doing his job."

"An excellent notion. I can bring you a volume or two tomorrow."

He agreed, though her reluctance to invite him to the house bothered him. Perhaps she was more relaxed outdoors, where standards of behavior were less rigid than in a drawing room. But if she dared not let her staff see him, he could not approach them for information. Dropping his probing for the moment, he resumed yesterday's discourse on Spanish customs and how they contrasted with those of Portugal.

That marked the beginning of the oddest friendship of Jack's life. He met Marianne every morning, rain or shine. Their conversation ranged from estate management to politics to Roman history, Greek drama, and the latest scientific experiments. She rarely discussed herself. Personal inquiries drew vague replies followed by probing questions about his family or friends or military life. Since he was loath to discuss his own past, he could hardly press for hers.

His frustration grew day by day, for she balked at trying any of the things that might build her confidence. Conversation was all very well, but she needed to meet people. Yet she categorically refused to accompany him to the village.

As the weeks progressed, he admitted that his initial assessment had been incomplete. Lack of confidence was not her only problem. Learning at an early age how quickly life could change made her determined to enjoy every moment to its fullest. It might also explain why she avoided people and had never pressed for a Season. Marriage and children created attachments that would leave her vulnerable to new pain.

Yet that theory also had flaws. Her reluctance seemed more visceral than fear of future pain. Despite her enjoyment of the many small pleasures they found on their daily rambles, she never smiled. Not even when his limp disappeared.

She was obsessed with his leg, determined to see it whole again. To that end, she devised exercises to strengthen the muscles, massaged it to relieve cramps and stiffness, and marched him over miles of rugged terrain to improve its flexibility. Wellington could have used her on the Peninsula, for nothing deterred her from her self-imposed duty.

He cared little for the leg and feared that his bad blood might act on the lust her massage incited. But her pleasure at each improvement lightened the somber expression in her eyes, so he cooperated. She was the most unselfish lady of his acquaintance — quite an accolade, for his friend Lady Blackthorn was hailed as an angel by all who knew her. Marianne was even more giving.

But when nightmares jerked him from sleep, he cursed her regimen, for his improved condition would make it harder to stage a believable accident. And if word of his recovery reached Wellington, he would have to report for duty or resign — an impossible choice. Returning would disgrace his uniform. Yet resigning would bring Hooky storming to Seacliff to see what was wrong. The duke hated malingering — Fitzroy had returned to duty a fortnight after losing an arm — so Wellington would demand an explanation, probing until he found the truth. Jack couldn't face him.

Worse, he was beginning to crave Marianne's company. Not just the conversation, which stimulated his mind. But Marianne herself drew him. Her voice eased his despair. He yearned for her warmth, counting the hours until their next meeting. Even in sleep, she was with him, twice blocking his nightmares to bring him peace.

He cursed his need, for it served no purpose. She was no light-skirt, and he could never wed. His bad blood was too powerful to risk passing it to a new generation. Unless Wilcox had produced a child no one knew about — not impossible, for no one had heard from him in years — the Caldwell line would end with Jack.

But not yet. He still didn't understand Marianne's situation. She wasn't talking, and Jones had learned nothing useful.

Marianne glanced up when Jack joined her in the folly. "Did you finish reviewing Seacliff's books?" The calendar had ticked over to October, bringing a crisp chill to the morning air that brightened the autumn trees. Orange, red, and gold leaves already skittered over the grass. Soon it would be too cold to meet outdoors.

But soon he would leave. With his limp healed, he was as good as new, at least in body. She knew he could not postpone his return to duty much longer.

That terrified her, for he was far from healed in mind. As clearly as if he'd confessed, she knew he still intended to kill himself. Only his promise to help her had stayed his hand thus far.

The admission choked her. Despite a month of daily meetings, she had learned nothing about the cause of his melancholy. He refused to speak of his family, his regiment, or any future plans, living only in the moment. Whenever she raised those topics, he turned the subject to her life, asking questions that proved he saw more deeply than she wanted. Perhaps answering him would draw him further into the sunlight — if it didn't drive him away.

But she shied away from pressing him, for there was much she didn't understand. His regret sometimes slipped into an odd yearning that incited restless feelings in her stomach. Never before had such sensations assailed her. She could neither identify them nor discuss them. He always blanked his eyes when he noticed her interest.

Jack handed her the book he'd borrowed

on estate management, then settled onto the opposite bench. "Thank you. That made it easier to follow the ledgers. I'm fortunate to have Poole. He's done wonders despite my uncle's parsimony, though he claims we need new rams to strengthen the breeding stock."

"Undoubtedly. Inbreeding exaggerates any weakness. New blood dilutes problems and can even eliminate them. When was it last done?"

"Fifteen years ago." He shrugged. "My great-uncle lived in London and saw no reason to invest much in an estate that had run well for centuries."

"You are definitely lucky to have Poole, then. How do your tenants fare? Too many men support debauched lives by placing onerous burdens on their dependents."

"They are fine. My uncle wasn't greedy. He insisted that all necessary repairs be done, and he was as concerned as anyone when disease struck the flocks. But he saw no reason to change methods that worked. He wasn't a bad manager, just set in his ways."

She accepted the opening. "I know the sort well. My trustees are the same."

Jack nearly jumped, for it was the first time she had mentioned her trust in weeks.

"Your estate produces well according to Poole — he and Crane are friends."

"Probably because they both had to deal with absent, conservative employers. I've amassed a list of innovations I want to try when I assume control. I just hope Crane is receptive to modern ideas. I've never met the man."

"Why not discuss it with him now?" He held his breath, hoping she would answer.

She hesitated. "It is not that easy," she finally said. "The gatekeepers won't allow him into the park, and I cannot leave."

He could think of nothing to say. Despite his growing suspicions, hearing confirmation that she was a prisoner was a shock. "If no one is allowed in or out, why am I here every day?"

"I suppose I should explain, though I've enjoyed our talks too much to wish to jeopardize them." Turning her back, she leaned against one of the entrance columns and stared across the lake. "You already know that I cannot tolerate strangers — a legacy of that trip to France. But the truth is somewhat harsher than mere intolerance. A host of things drive me to hysteria — strange faces, physical contact, horses, stables . . . Initially my uncle provided gatekeepers so I could grieve in private.

Now they remain so no one discovers that I am mad."

"Poppycock!" He surged to his feet. "You are no more mad than I am. How can you believe such tripe? The only thing the gatekeepers have accomplished is to perpetuate the myth of your madness by preventing anyone from learning the truth."

"You do not know me, Colonel Caldwell."

He grimaced at the address. "I know you better than I know all but a few close friends."

"No." Inhaling deeply, she turned to face him. "You can't have been listening, Jack. I cannot abide strangers. That is bad enough, but I cannot abide family, either. I freeze if anyone approaches. I fall into screaming fits at the least touch. Trying to converse drives me to tears. Even people I've known for years trigger mad episodes merely by appearing on my doorstep. Often the fits last so long that I lose large chunks of a day from memory. I keep telling myself that I am sane, but in truth, everyone believes me mad."

"This is the first time I've seen anything that raises questions about your sanity, Marianne." He gripped her by the shoulders. "For God's sake, listen to yourself.

You cannot tolerate people. What am I? A dog? We spend hours together every day, yet you never show by word or deed that you find my company unpleasant."

"You are different. Safe. I know you would never harm me."

"Then you don't know me. I'm a warrior, Marianne. I've killed. I've maimed. I've done things that would make your blood curdle. I can't even claim honor, for even I can't live with some of my deeds."

She blanched, but instead of pulling away, she cupped one hand against his cheek. "Oh, Jack." Tears glistened in her eyes.

He wanted to pull her against him and savor her warmth, but this wasn't the time. It was more important to keep her talking, for he was finally making progress. "Think, Marianne. I've touched you countless times in the last month. I'm holding you right now. You've leaned on me more than once and always take my arm when we are walking. Yet I've seen no evidence of fits."

"You don't understand."

"Then tell me about it." He led her back to the bench, then resumed his own seat to keep his libido under control — today's cloak hid her lack of stays, but he knew all too well what lay beneath.

71

"It began in France," she said slowly. "At first I was too numb to do anything but follow wherever Francine led."

"Who is Francine?"

"Mama's maid. You knew her as Clarisse. I'm surprised that she did not reveal her name once we were safely back in England."

"But why change her name when she was so obviously French? Did she fear being connected to your family?"

"No, to her own. Her father was the Comte Dubois. He was killed during the Terror. The rest of the family barely escaped with their lives. Francine never forgot that flight and swore that *aristos* remained unsafe in the countryside despite Napoleon's overtures to the émigrés." She drew in a deep breath, twisting her hands in her lap. "We would never have reached the Channel if not for your help. Francine didn't know where we were — she'd been seven when they fled. I was too numb to spot danger. I suppose that is why you seem so safe now. You helped us when it would have been easier to look the other way, yet you demanded nothing in return."

"Not true." Jack couldn't let her turn him into a hero — not with his breeding. "I would not have made it to the Channel myself if not for Cla-Francine. No French-man would ever mistake my accent. If she had not done all the talking, we would have been arrested."

"Then I needn't apologize for endangering your life." A spark of humor danced briefly in her eyes. "I remember little of that trip. Fog encased my mind until we reached Barnett Court. When it dissipated, I was surrounded by people I'd never met."

"But they were family!"

Her head shook. "Lord Barnett was Papa's brother, but he and Papa were estranged. I had never seen the house or anyone in it. When I realized that even Francine was gone, the screams I'd kept inside escaped. Laudanum finally put me to sleep, but that was the only prolonged sleep I managed for weeks. Every time I closed my eyes, nightmares jerked me awake. My screams disturbed the entire household — and it was a huge house. Lady Barnett demanded that I control my outbursts, but I couldn't. The day I attacked one of my cousins, Lady Barnett moved me to an unused wing to protect her family."

"My God. But where was your uncle?"

"At Halworth, settling Papa's affairs. Once he learned how disturbed I was, he brought me here, hoping I would heal faster in familiar surroundings. He posted gatekeepers so I would not have to deal with condolence calls or curious neighbors. It helped, to a degree. I slept better in my own bed, and no one bothered me during the day. But the problem remains. I cannot tolerate people. Whenever someone calls, I fall apart."

"I thought the gatekeepers turned away callers."

"Not those sent by Barnett. At first, he came himself, but now he sends his secretary. Despite seeing Mr. Craven dozens of times, I still cannot endure him. He looms over me in the most threatening fashion, and a simple touch is enough to trigger a fit that sends him fleeing for his life."

He didn't like her description of Craven. "That may be a habit, or perhaps he is simply unlikable. I've met such men. But you could never relax with me if you were mad. Nor could you tolerate your staff." He smiled as her eyes flared blue. "Perhaps you should experiment. Are there any neighbors that you liked in childhood?"

She cocked her head in thought. "Mrs. Dingle. She ran the linen draper's shop in the village and always gave me sweetmeats when we called — my governess insisted a walk to the village was excellent exercise, though her real purpose was to flirt with the apothecary."

"Perhaps we should walk that way tomorrow."

But she was already shaking her head. "My uncle would be furious if I disobeyed his orders. He is a terrifying man."

"That is the impression of a frightened child suffering an excess of grief," he said firmly. "By your own admission, you've not spoken to him in years. I did not see him at Barnett Court, but I've heard nothing against him. My only quarrel is that he failed to send a governess who could have helped you put the grief behind you."

"I could not have accepted such a person."

"Certainly, you could. Not the first day or the second, but even the wildest creatures calm in time. And it is not too late. You know that to take charge of your inheritance, you must meet with Crane and others. It would be better to practice on someone you know."

She frowned, but finally nodded.

"We can discuss it tomorrow," he said, drawing her to her feet and giving her a quick hug. "Any trepidation you feel arises from lack of practice. Believe me, were you truly mad, I would see it."

The corners of her mouth twitched.

Jack caught his breath at the sight. She'd nearly smiled, tumbling his heart into a gallop and sending excitement surging into his loins. If even a half smile made him dizzy, what would happen if she ever laughed?

Chapter Five

Lord Barnett glared as his wife sailed into his study. Age had thickened her waist and expanded her bosom, inviting comparisons to battleships. He knew the look in her eye all too well. She was determined to change his mind about attending the Styles house party.

He suppressed a sigh, wishing yet again that he'd had the courage to refuse this match. He should have known that Maude would be just like her mother, an unscrupulous harridan who ignored any opposition in pursuit of her goals. If Maude wanted to entertain, she did. If she wanted to bring the girls out in London, nothing stopped her. If she wanted wealthy titles for each daughter, London lords had better protect themselves, for she would do anything to make it so.

Which was one of many reasons for sending regrets to Lord and Lady Styles. Devonshire's heir would be one of the guests. Maude had set her sights on snaring him for Catherine. The only way to succeed was through trickery.

Another shiver wracked his spine when he recalled his daughters. Catherine had come out six years earlier at age seventeen. But despite a dowry of ten thousand guineas, she'd not attracted a single offer. Nor had she done better the next year.

Charlotte and Elizabeth had followed in her footsteps. He'd warned the girls that smiles and flattery would improve their chances, but they wouldn't listen. Not for them the art of flirtation. They scorned the cubs whose admiration could raise a young lady's credit. Like Maude, they were single-minded in their pursuit, insulting anyone they considered inferior, clearing the decks so they could concentrate on the object of their greed. None of them believed that their sharp-tongued cuts repelled every-one, especially the men they wanted to attract.

And every Season was worse than the last. The expense of outfitting a growing number of females meant he could no longer offer large dowries. Reduced por-tions, average looks, and increasing haugh-tiness had made the girls laughingstocks. Poor Anne wouldn't stand a chance when she joined them, despite being the sweetest and prettiest of the group.

Not that she would have that opportunity. There would be no more London Seasons. His financial crisis was another reason he had refused Lord Styles's invitation. Maude was already demanding new clothes, but he couldn't afford them — not after Harold had lost ten thousand guineas playing cards with Alvonley's set. The boy should know better than to sit down with men renowned for deep gaming.

But it was all of a piece. Harold had inherited Maude's lack of sense, her disregard for money, and her belief that she was superior to the highest in the land.

Barnett clenched his fists. Only two choices remained — mortgage Barnett Court or sell unentailed land. Neither was acceptable. Selling land would reduce his income to subsistence levels. Yet repaying a mortgage would have the same effect. And mortgaging the estate would remove the last buffer against future disasters.

"Catherine must have a new ball gown for Lord Styles's party," Maude announced, berthing her bulk in front of his desk. "And you must inform him that Anne will accompany us. She needs to mingle with society before going to London in the spring."

"I told you that we are not going to Styles's gathering — or anywhere else. There is no mo—"

"Of course we are going. This is an opportunity we cannot miss. Aside from Devonshire's heir, the guest list includes the Earl of Westlake, Colbein's heir, Glendale's heir, and Lord Bankhead, though his fortune is questionable. I accepted the invitation two days ago."

"Then you will look exceedingly foolish. Lord Styles already received our regrets, in which I made it clear that we have other plans."

"How could you!" Her face purpled. "This is a chance to attach a duke's heir. Hartington never attends the same entertainments we do in London."

"Which is ample evidence that he would never look at our girls."

"Of all the —"

"No more, Maude. I may be a viscount, but dukes do not wed so far beneath them — not even a duke who houses his mistress and by-blows under the same roof as his wife and children. How can you wish a connection to Devonshire House? It would cast doubts on the chastity of all the girls. As for this party, we cannot afford it. Harold's losses have put us so far in debt that I have to sell the London house simply to pay the Court's staff this quarter."

"You wouldn't!"

"I must. The alternative is to sell the Strowbridge farms, but they produce a third of our income. I only hope the house will bring a reasonable sum, for it is not well situated." Another of Maude's perennial complaints.

She slammed her fists onto the desktop. "You unfeeling, unnatural cad! I won't let you continue this campaign against us. What sort of father hates his own children?"

"I don't," he protested, then kicked himself for arguing with her. She was a master at deflecting attention from facts she wished to ignore.

"You do!" she countered. "Your parsimony will condemn your daughters to spinsterhood. If you gave them decent dowries, they would have found matches years ago."

"Hardly. Catherine qualified as an heiress her first two Seasons. It was her own misbehavior, compounded by your public megrims, that drove away potential suitors. How many times have I told you that society expects politeness, especially toward those of higher rank? How can you be stupid enough to think that your aspirations remain secret? No one of means will go near a fortune hunter, especially one who has used dishonorable ploys in the past. Your reputation is so bad that men flee if they so much as glimpse you coming. After six years of squandering a fortune on London Seasons, your only achievement is a notoriety that makes any match impossible. I doubt I could buy a simpleton for the girls, so we will remain here. Your antics have embarrassed me enough. If you can teach the girls to smile and keep their tongues between their teeth, then perhaps we can attend assemblies in Colchester this winter."

Maude's mouth opened, but fury choked her words.

"Go. I must attend to business, or there will be no money for even a modest social calendar. But don't think to go behind my back," he added, seeing a spark in her eye. "I've given orders that you are not to leave the estate. And your dressmaker knows that I will not pay for new gowns."

He exhaled in relief as she stormed out. His edict would not keep her quiet for long, but at least she would not be back today.

"Damn that boy!" he muttered. If only

Harold had inherited his sense instead of Maude's selfishness.

"Can you find an heiress for him?" asked Craven. He'd remained unobtrusively in the corner during Maude's tirade.

"Hardly." Barnett snorted. Harold was barely one-and-twenty and in no mood to wed. "Who in her right mind would ally herself with us?" The Barnett name had become infamous.

Craven coughed discreetly. "With all due respect, sir, Miss Marianne is not in her right mind. Nor can she appreciate her wealth." He extended the latest statement from her trustees.

Barnett flinched at the figures. It was the first statement he'd seen in years — he tried to forget the wench existed. Now he stared. The trust had doubled in value since its inception. Damn Richard to hell for his betrayal. Halworth and Richard's investments should have come to him.

Richard had been another who'd not been in his right mind. The man had been as prissy as an aged spinster, so enamored with dead civilizations that he'd ignored the usual gentlemanly pursuits.

Barnett shook his head. He should have suspected that Richard would do something stupid like leaving his estate to his daughter. Even that damnable trust would terminate soon, putting everything into her incompetent hands. One of the most productive estates in Dorsetshire would be at the mercy of a madwoman. "It's tempting to propose such a match, but it would never work. Even if Harold agreed, no vicar would perform the ceremony. You've seen her condition for yourself."

"If I may be so bold, I was not suggesting a match. But she will never recover. It is time to place her in an asylum."

"But she's family!"

"True, but what will happen to Halworth when she takes possession? Who would care for its tenants? It is unconscionable to expect her staff to keep her in line."

Barnett sighed. He had taken Marianne to Halworth after her family perished, hoping that familiar surroundings would hasten her recovery from shock and grief. But the plan had failed. Women were simply too fragile to endure trauma.

Pride had stopped him from revealing her loss of reason. Maude's abrasive tongue had already threatened his credit, so tarnishing his name with madness would have caused new whispers — never mind that Marianne must have inherited the weakness from her mother's family. By leaving her at Halworth, he had hidden her problem from the world, giving his daughters a chance to make good matches.

Now the situation had changed. His daughters were unmarriageable even without the stain of madness, and Harold's profligacy threatened very public ruin.

"Forget your pride," murmured Craven. "As I was saying when Lady Barnett arrived, you cannot cover your debts. Without new income, you will lose everything. Your only hope now is Marianne's trust, so put her in an asylum where she belongs. The court will then extend your guardianship to include her property."

Barnett frowned, but the idea made sense. Craven understood finance better than Barnett ever had. And this would be good for Marianne, too — he had done her a disservice by denying her the treatment she needed; she might have improved by now if he'd taken better care of her in the beginning. In the meantime, he could borrow enough of her funds to put Barnett Court back on its feet.

He nodded as a weight slipped from his shoulders. It was the best course for everyone. Halworth's tenants deserved a master capable of understanding their needs. And Halworth's staff deserved release from a burden they should never have been asked to carry.

She would want for nothing — her fortune would cover the finest care even after the loan. She would surely agree to help with his other problems, too. After buying husbands for his daughters, he could banish Maude to a remote cottage. A reasonable revenge for forcing him into marriage. If only he'd known . . .

Jack stared at the wineglass in his hand. Three days had passed since Marianne had claimed insanity. At every meeting he had urged her to visit the village. But while she agreed that such a test had merit, she continued to balk, claiming that she could not defy her uncle.

Her reluctance didn't make sense, for Barnett couldn't object to proving her sanity. Mrs. Dingle was warm, caring, and nonthreatening — a perfect test. Marianne was understandably nervous after twelve years of isolation, but three days was plenty long enough to gird her loins. Was she too terrified to put the question to the test? How could he help her if she refused to take his advice?

It was frustrating, for without her cooperation, he could prove nothing. Declaring him safe indicated that she trusted him. Yet that trust could not overcome her fear of Barnett. What had the man done? There had to be more than locking her up.

He'd considered appealing to the gate-keepers, for they could arrange a more private test within the confines of Halworth. But they gave him no opportunity.

"Miss Barnett is not at home to visitors," the man at the main gate had said the moment Jack arrived. He looked like a pugilist, his bent nose and scarred face looming half a foot above Jack's eyes, the massive head attached directly to the shoulders of a hefty body. Both appearance and attitude made it obvious that he was a guard, not a servant. Without the massive gate between them, Jack might have felt a frisson of fear.

Jack hadn't argued, accepting that there would be no assistance from that source. So he must solicit help from the neighbors.

Emptying the glass, Jack checked his uniform, then headed for the door. Squire Jenkins had invited him to a christening ball. With luck, he could discover more about Marianne's history from the other guests.

Jack cursed to find Jenkins and his wife still receiving. He needed someone to introduce him. A hundred people crowded the ballroom, none of them familiar.

But his uniform made his own identity clear.

A matron wearing a fussy gown and too much jewelry rushed to his side, dragging her equally fussy daughter with her.

"Welcome, Colonel Caldwell. I'm Lady Paine, wife of Sir Thomas Paine and cousin to Mrs. Jenkins," she said through a predatory smile. "And this is my daughter, Priscilla." She presented a giggling girl of about eighteen.

Jack nearly groaned. He had forgotten that his uncle's death had transformed him from the impoverished scion of a scandalous house to a landed gentleman of means. In other words, a matrimonial prize.

"We are delighted to have you at Seacliff," Miss Paine said with a giggle. "It is a marvelous house. And huge. I've often admired it." Giggle, giggle. "Will you be staying here now that the war is over?" She rapped his arm with her fan as another giggle escaped.

"Hardly. I must return to duty," he said stiffly, cursing himself for accepting this invitation. His common sense must still be on the casualty list.

"They cannot possibly need you back just yet. There is no one to fight." Still giggling, she grabbed his arm. Lady Paine smiled and headed for the refreshment room.

Jack frowned after her. Country manners might be more relaxed than in town, but not this relaxed. Miss Paine had a death grip on his arm and was pulling him toward the terrace.

"Miss Paine!" His attempt to halt resulted in a tug-of-war over his arm.

"Did you say something?" She turned a too-bright smile on him and nodded toward the door. "The crowd is so loud I can barely hear myself think. Let's move outside so we can talk in peace."

"No. I need to greet the other guests. Introduce me." As long as he was stuck with her, he might as well use her.

She pouted, then sighed, and finally used her fan to point out her relatives. "That's Uncle Lester in the brown jacket — Mama's brother. And Cousin Hortense next to him. Cousin Jeremy in the blue . . ." She recited names and relationships so fast that Jack's head spun. She had covered most of the room before he caught up.

"The man in the shabby green waistcoat is Uncle Darwin, from Bath," she was saying. "He's barmy. His son Jeremy — the one waving the quizzing glass — is nearly as bad. And stay away from Aunt Clare — the woman trussed up in gray." She giggled. "She loves to talk, but she's deaf as a post. Even her whispers can be heard in London."

The woman resembled a pudding, bulging around oddly tied ribbons. Her skirt drew in at the bottom and ballooned around her hips. Jack winced. "I'm more interested in my neighbors. I understand Mr. Turlock is here." Turlock owned the third estate that bordered Seacliff.

"Card room," she said shortly. "He is a prosy old bore. You would prefer to meet Cousin Oswald. We can catch him in the refreshment room." Again she dragged him toward the door.

He resisted. "I need to see Turlock. Business." He rescued his arm and turned toward the card room, but another chit barely out of the schoolroom stepped into his path, foiling his escape.

"Introduce me, Pris," demanded the newcomer.

Fury flashed in Miss Paine's eyes. "Colonel Caldwell, this is Abbey Hofstone. It is her first ball, so you must forgive her for being so forward."

And you aren't? But Jack didn't say it, unable to be rude even in situations where most gentlemen would condone cuts.

Miss Hofstone grabbed his other arm, batting her lashes as she smiled up at him. "Pay no heed to Pris. She is sulking tonight because her beau isn't here."

"Abby!"

"Well, he *is* your beau — or so you claim, though we haven't seen him in ages." She smirked. "Personally, I think he bought colors to escape your pursuit. He always was rather bright."

Jack tried to spot Jenkins, but failed.

"Are you going to dance?" demanded Miss Paine with another giggle.

"Not tonight. Injuries . . ." He let his voice trail off, unable to lie even to these two. At least Miss Hofstone's arrival curtailed Miss Paine's attempt to reach the terrace.

But that wasn't much of an improvement. Her manners remained deplorable. She monopolized the conversation, talking over Miss Hofstone and ignoring his attempts to change the subject. Jack tried several times to break away, for her incessant giggling grated on his ears, but both girls clung to his arms. No matter how hard he tried, he could not order them to perdition or shove them aside. Honor demanded proper manners. He might have disgraced himself at Waterloo, but he could not abandon the standards he'd revered all his life.

Relief finally arrived in the form of his host.

"Stop monopolizing the colonel." Squire Jenkins glared at each girl in turn. "You are embarrassing me."

Surprisingly, both girls meekly released him and left.

"Forgive them," said Jenkins. "And me. I should have expected something like this. They are incorrigible — distant connections of my wife whom I usually avoid." He shook his head. "Congratulations on your recovery," he added.

"Thank you. And for the invitation. I appreciate the opportunity to meet my neighbors."

"Do you plan to stay here, then?" Jenkins asked bluntly.

"When I can. My plans remain unsettled."

The squire nodded, then asked about Waterloo. Jack ducked the question by claiming he had seen little of the battle, then switched to his own concerns.

"Miss Paine mentioned that Turlock is

in the card room, but I don't know who owns Halworth — I think it is Halworth. The estate west of mine."

"You'll not meet Miss Barnett here or anywhere else," Squire Jenkins frowned.

"The owner is a lady?" He let his voice show surprise — an expected reaction, for few women owned land.

"Yes. Sad story, that. Whole family died, leaving only her. She hasn't spoken to a soul since, more's the pity."

"Surely she has servants."

"Of course. But they won't discuss her — or Lord Barnett, if it comes to that. He's her uncle and guardian, though he's not been in these parts for years — probably avoiding the cuts. Folks hereabouts despise him. Richard Barnett was a real gentleman, beloved by everyone, so it didn't sit well when Lord Barnett petitioned the Chancery Court to overturn Richard's will. He failed, of course — it was right and tight — but the memory lingers."

"Who oversees the fields if Miss Barnett sees no one?"

"She has a good steward, though most wish he was more forthcoming with information. Whatever her eccentricities, she commands enormous loyalty from her staff. Not one of them will discuss her, so it's no surprise that rumor runs rampant."

That was all Jack learned from the squire, but others added tidbits. He didn't even have to ask. The merest mention of Halworth prompted effusive soliloquies on the elusive Miss Barnett, or mad Miss Barnett. She was the area mystery.

Several men commented on the guards, whose arrogance annoyed all and sundry. It was the consensus that they overstepped their positions often, but without seeing Marianne, no one could complain.

The matrons were miffed that Miss Barnett snubbed local society, for they had loved her mother and would have taken her to heart had she given them a chance.

Gathering information was complicated by his determination to avoid Miss Paine. Now that the squire was again occupied, she was stalking him, joining any group that included him. He couldn't help but compare her to Marianne, who wouldn't dream of ignoring proper behavior, though her solitude gave her considerable leeway.

He finally ducked into the card room, allowing himself one vicious glare before shutting the door in her face.

A chat with Turlock produced nothing — he was indeed a prosy old bore whose interests did not include his neighbors. But he was so avid to exploit a new audience that Jack needed a full hour to escape. And he only managed it then by draining a wine bottle and volunteering to find another.

He emerged into a cauldron of rumors. Miffed by his lack of interest, Miss Paine had childishly retaliated by swearing that he had tried to seduce her. Her family knew her too well to listen, but the neighbors were another matter. All knew tales of Deerchester, Wilcox, and other Caldwells. Now they rehashed the old scandals, looking askance at Jack all the while.

Jenkins was appalled. "Absolute lies, and so I've told everyone," he declared, shaking his head. "Priscilla needs a good walloping. My wife was a Paine, so I can't avoid her — especially at a family christening. But I would never have allowed her into the room had I known what she'd do."

Jack accepted the apology, but that didn't mitigate his pain as old rumors whisked through the ballroom. Every tale reminded him of his breeding. Thirty-two years of honorable behavior couldn't begin to counter centuries of infamy. And once his own crimes surfaced . . .

He reached home half an hour later, but the unpleasantness made sleep impossible.

Nightmares pounced the moment he closed his eyes. He finally adjourned to the library to think.

Brood was a better description, he admitted two bottles of wine later. Thinking was a productive activity. But Miss Paine had loosed too many demons for him to accomplish anything positive.

Attending the ball had been a serious mistake. He'd learned nothing new about Marianne beyond speculation on the extent of her fortune, and nothing new about Barnett except that bit about the Chancery suit, but that was twelve years old.

He frowned. Barnett's treatment of Marianne called the man's honor into question, so it would be a mistake to assume that he had shrugged his shoulders and walked away after losing that suit. He must have believed that Halworth and his brother's fortune belonged to him. Had he found a way to circumvent the trust?

A sunbeam slipped through a crack in the curtains, setting a troop of rough-shod infantry armed with bayonets rampaging through his head. It was morning, and he'd consumed enough wine to finally sleep.

You can't. Marianne is expecting you.

"Devil take it!" he swore, wondering how

96

he'd lost track of his wits. He rubbed his eyes to realign his thoughts.

Marianne.

Whatever the truth of Marianne's incarceration, she possessed a fortune that Barnett had already tried to claim. Why the hell hadn't he considered that sooner? If Barnett's purpose was venal, the man would have to act soon. Once Marianne took control of her inheritance, she could take steps to protect herself.

His head throbbed worse than ever, so he yanked the curtains shut and downed a glass of brandy to quiet it. Again, his wits scattered.

Danger lurked nearby.

Instinct had saved him so often that he'd learned to pay attention to it. This time it was Marianne who was in danger. He had to save her.

He stifled the voice asking why he felt so strongly. The law might not give him authority over her, but she'd been his moral responsibility for twelve years. Besides, she had become a friend.

More than a friend.

No. He could not afford an attachment. But he owed her for leaving her with strangers. Never had he considered that she hadn't known her closest relatives. He knew all of his, though he'd never wanted to meet any of them.

His eyes sagged shut.

Half an hour passed . . .

Marianne's golden curls fanned across emerald grass. The sky seeped into her eyes — or maybe it was passion that turned them so blue. She moaned, writhing as his hands opened her gown to caress her perfect breasts, plucking the nipples into hard red berries. He sucked them deep into his mouth as her fingers touched him, teasing, inciting, tugging at his hips, forcing him closer and closer until he buried his shaft —

"No!" Jack leaped to his feet, panting.

Gulping wine did nothing to banish the nightmare — a disturbingly erotic fantasy worse than reliving Waterloo . . .

"No!" he repeated, pressing against the buttons on his falls so the force of his erection didn't tear them loose. He called up images of war, of murder, of dishonor. Slowly his shaft softened . . .

"Friends. Just friends," he reminded himself as he drained the glass and stumbled to his feet. "Have to protect her. Danger." A glance at the clock sent him out the door. He was late. He usually reached the cliff by now.

★ ★ ★

"Nice day," Jack slurred when he caught up with Marianne halfway to the folly. She hadn't been on the cliff, which was good. His balance was too unsteady to risk standing near the edge.

"You've been drinking." She frowned.

"Christening at Squire Jenkins's last night. Heir's heir." He meant to stop, but his tongue kept wagging. "You should have been there. You'd have been the belle of the ball."

"I wasn't invited."

"Would you go if you had an invitation?"

"No."

"Why not?" Suddenly furious, he grabbed her shoulders, turning her so she had to look at him. "Why not, Marianne? I don't care what threats Barnett made. You have to test it sometime. Quit hiding. You're a grown woman, not a child terrified by thunder. How can you hope to take up the reins of Halworth if you cannot even walk to your own village?"

"I dare not leave the estate until the guards are gone. I can't dismiss them until the trust ends."

"Poppycock! What can they do? Shoot you? Come home with me. I can drive you to the village or the squire's house or anywhere else you wish to go. Once you prove that you are recovered — and I would bet my last shilling that you have been well for years — you will be able to handle anything."

"You cannot be sure. Uncle's secretary —"

"— means nothing," he insisted. "If he incites fear, then the fault lies with him." He suspected that Craven had tried to seduce her. God knew Marianne could trigger lust without even trying, and not everyone was honorable. Marianne would have sensed danger even though she was too innocent to discern Craven's purpose.

"Don't push, Colonel Caldwell." Her eyes flashed, bringing a flush to her face. Her lips parted, hesitating over her next words.

Jack's heart leaped. Heat joined the wine flowing through his veins. And electricity. Sparks sizzled from her shoulders into his hands. Anger made her more beautiful than ever. Her eyes blazed blue. Much like in his dream. She'd left her cloak at home this warm morning, so her tantalizing breasts pressed hard-tipped against her gown, begging to be touched and tasted. A light tug on the ribbon nestled daringly between them would open the gown and release them.

His loins clenched in frantic need.

He fought his lust, cursing himself for meeting her when he was three sheets to the wind. She was innocent, unaware of how she affected men, ignorant that her clothing invited advances. Only a saint would fail to notice her charms. "I'm not trying to hurt you," he managed, wrenching his thoughts from her body. "But if you wait until you are comfortable with the idea, we will still be arguing about it when you are old and gray. Once you walk into the village with a smile on your face, even Barnett must agree that you are well. Sometimes you have to take a chance."

"But I can't. Not yet." Tears shimmered. "Jack, I — I'd love to take that chance, but not while Barnett's guards are here to report it. I must remove them first. If Barnett hears of my disobedience, he will lock me away. Only after my birthday can I truly take charge of my life. I haven't the courage to press sooner. What if I fail your test?"

"You are the most courageous woman I know." As her first tear spilled, he stroked her back, groping for the control he needed. "Few could have held together long enough to escape France, especially at age twelve. You can do this, too. I know you can."

"You have more faith than I do," she said, staring up at him, her eyes fading to gray. "But you don't understand the consequences. He has long threatened to lock me in an asylum if I don't render him absolute obedience. With Craven's testimony, he could do it in a trice, no matter how I manage in the village." Her hand cupped his cheek.

Blood whooshed through his ears, drowning her voice. Bad blood that for generations had taken what it wanted regardless of convention. Recognizing the danger, he tried to pull back —

She traced his jaw. "It's only a few more days, Jack. I can dismiss the guards on —"

As her finger touched his mouth, his control snapped. He cursed even as his lips swooped, claiming the kiss he'd wanted since first seeing her on the cliff.

She gasped.

He took advantage of her parted lips to plunder deep, grinding her against an erection that screamed for a release only she could provide.

For one glorious moment she melted, twining her tongue with his, clasping her arms around his back, pressing closer as if she would crawl inside his skin. Her moans were the sweetest music in the universe, raising passion higher than he had ever experienced. His fingers groped for that tempting ribbon —

She suddenly froze.

He jerked back, but it was too late. All color drained from her face as her arms moved to ward off a blow. Her eyes widened in terror, staring beyond him to something only she could see. Shudders chattered her teeth. Breaking into gulping sobs, she fled into the trees.

Jack tried to follow, but tripped, falling facedown in a mound of leaves. The most unearthly wail he'd ever heard battered his throbbing head, drawing the first tears he'd shed in twenty years.

Dear God, what had he done?

Chapter Six

Marianne reached the edge of the forest before she realized that no one was chasing her. Leaning against a tree, she let the tears fall.

What had she done?

The terror had burst out of nowhere, overwhelming and unexpected — this sort hadn't happened in years. Jack was so familiar that she had dropped her guard. So when memories suddenly engulfed her, she'd reacted without thought. But Jack would not know that.

He must be disgusted beyond all measure, furious to have wasted his time on her. Never again would he look at her in friendship, for this proved beyond doubt that she was mad. It might not be an everyday sort of madness, but it prevented her from living a normal life. Why else would she flee in terror from a simple kiss?

Her knees gave out. Sliding to the ground, she let her tears fall faster — not gusty sobs this time, but silent, hopeless sorrow.

Jack had gotten his test. She'd failed it. There was no point in going back to apologize. He would be gone by now, never to return.

Pain increased her tears.

It would have been better if she had never seen him again. Before his arrival she had convinced herself that she was merely cursed with a callous guardian. Now she had to accept that she was flawed. She would never be normal again. Yet memories of this month would make settling for her usual activities difficult.

If only she could forget walking with Jack, laughing, arguing, and especially touching. She'd been content with a life of study and gardening. But now that Jack had shown her companionship, that life seemed barren. Halworth would never be the same. It was no longer a refuge, but a prison.

He had done more than ignite a longing for people. A forgotten part of her heart had blossomed under his attentions, baring needs she had never acknowledged. Having come to rely on his company, the future promised nothing but loneliness.

Weary, she mopped the last tears from her face, then leaned her head against the tree.

If she'd had more experience with people, she could have handled the past month better — or if she'd been sensible enough to avoid the pitfalls of fantasy.

Jacques had been her hero long before they had met on the cliff. Invoking his memory had helped her overcome terror that first year. He was calm, competent, able to face any danger with equanimity. She'd tried to copy that. But it had worked so well that she had exaggerated him, building him into a god, using the fantasy as a model whenever Craven incited a new fit. Jacques controlled his terror and saw his duty through to the end. She could do no worse.

The fantasy had affected other aspects of her life, too. Hutch had urged her to organize her father's papers and educate herself, but it had been Jacques who had prodded her to begin. He had been her mentor and protector since France.

Dangerous, she admitted wearily. Talking to Hutch was one thing. In their seven years together, Hutch had lectured on every subject imaginable, making it easy to know what she would say. But Marianne had known Jacques for less than a week under trying circumstances in which she had been too grief-stricken to talk at all. The only time he'd paid her much heed was the night he'd held her, sheltering her from a hailstorm. So using him as a mentor was dangerous.

It was her fantasies, not their brief acquaintance in France, that explained her instant rapport — bad enough if he hadn't been as honorable as she'd pretended. But confusing dreams and reality had pushed her beyond friendship. Jack incited excitement, warmth, and an effervescence she couldn't name. He was the only person in twelve years whom she could touch without fear, and the only one who could touch her, so she had used him unmercifully as she explored sensations beyond her usual reach.

Dangerous, for he was a real man, not a figment of her imagination. And his insistence that she was normal had reinforced her fondest dream.

I warned you to be careful, said Hutch.

"So you did, but I was blind."

Her dreams had been a trap, for in the end, she was not normal. As long as they had stuck to her requested conversations, everything had been fine. But she had pushed for more, forgetting that this was Colonel Jack Caldwell, the melancholy warrior, not Jacques, her dream companion.

Her curiosity about the odd sensations he raised must have sent him the wrong signal. And opening her heart and mind as she tried to help him had breached her defenses, allowing the madness to surface.

It was the only explanation for her sudden panic. All he'd done was kiss her — an act she had wondered about for days and must have invited. She'd felt many strange yearnings lately, and her nightmares had given way to odd dreams about Jack. She had wondered how it would feel to kiss him — had lain in bed thinking about it, touching her lips to test their response.

His kiss was nothing like that test, though.

Was that why she'd fled? His lips had unleashed heat and a host of unexpected sensations. And his tongue . . .

She shivered recalling the delicious taste of the wine he'd been drinking mixed with an odd sweetness that must be Jack himself.

And his body! Her fingers curved into the remembered shape of muscular shoulders, strong arms, and a broad back. She was accustomed to her own supple body, but Jack's was hard, an unyielding rock. And she lacked —

Her face heated at the memory of that hard ridge. She'd seen woodcuts of Greek statues, but none that hinted at such size. Not that she would ever feel it again . . .

It was over. And her flight condemned Jack, too. Melancholy still lurked in his eyes. Now that he knew she was hopeless, nothing would stop him from staging a new accident.

Pain released new tears. She'd driven him off by losing control of herself. Not only would she never see him again, but she would never hear about his end. Mrs. Hastings rarely shared neighborhood gossip and never mentioned death.

Are you giving up? asked Hutch. *Will you sit here wallowing in self-pity instead of fighting? Surely Jack is worth fighting for!*

"But what can I do?" she demanded crossly. "Until Halworth is under my control, I can't leave. If I called at Seacliff, Barnett would lock me up."

You can start by sending Jack an apology. Describe your cowardice as a setback, then beg for another chance. A soldier should know that no campaign is easy. Twelve years of weakness cannot be overcome in a single month.

"And how would I deliver such a letter?"

Send it with Hastings, of course. Must I think of everything? You know Hastings would walk on water if it would make you happy. He never approved of your solitude. And though he might question the propriety of meeting Jack alone, he would welcome the acquaintance of so honorable a man.

"Very well. I'll grovel on paper."

Sighing, she headed back to the house. It was worth a try. Anything was worth a try. Imagining Jack dead froze her soul, so if a written apology didn't work, she must call at Seacliff and pray that his staff would keep her visit a secret.

Mrs. Hastings was hovering outside Halworth's side door.

Even without a mirror, Marianne knew her eyes were red from weeping, and her cheeks must be blotched. Speaking would reveal a hoarse voice, raising questions, so she circled around to the front.

Another mistake, she realized the moment she opened the door. A man was in the hall. For one glorious instant, she thought Jack had come after her, but this man was shorter and thicker.

Terror welled, but she fought it down. This was no time for fits. Something was dreadfully wrong.

"Hello, Marianne."

Lord Barnett. The guards must have discovered Jack's visits. His voice shredded another layer of her defenses, reviving twelve-year-old fears. That voice had assailed her for days, demanding, admonishing, and threatening until she'd feared for her life.

"Don't you recognize me?" he continued.

She nodded dumbly. He had put on weight and lost some hair, but little else had changed, including his scent. She'd never liked musk.

He shook his head, examining her from head to toe, his eyes gleaming brighter at each sign of dishabille — wild hair, puffy eyes, stained gown, muddy half boots. "Craven is right. You are hopeless, Marianne. Come along." He motioned to the entrance.

"What?" She gathered her scattered wits.

"I had hoped that time would heal you. Since it hasn't, we must take stronger measures."

"What are you talking about?" She backed against the wall.

He grabbed her arm, shoving her toward the mirror that had always hung near the door. "Look at yourself! Running wild like a red Indian. Howling for no reason at all."

"I —" she began.

But he talked over her. "Grief should

have abated years ago. Since it hasn't, I must seek help. It is my duty as your guardian. I've found a doctor who specializes in disorders of the mind. His facility is nearby. The staff can send your things later."

"No." She tore her arm free, loath to go anywhere with him. His touch raised memories of the journey to Halworth — dodging plunging horses as Barnett dragged her across a reeking stable yard, tiny inns choking with smoke and ale, hulking strangers leering from all sides, hands clutching at her gown . . .

Terror swelled her throat until she couldn't breathe. Pain constricted her chest, radiating down her arms. Her heart battered against her ribs, too fast to count the beats.

"Yes." His voice turned hard. "I have been far too lenient. It is time to accept my responsibilities."

"No!" She backed, trying to hold the nightmares at bay. Jack. She must think of Jack. Without her help, he would die.

But Jack no longer wanted her. She was mad, disgusting, pitiably weak. She'd ruined any chance for salvation.

Lightning blazed through her mind, bursting the cages that held her demons.

"No! Don't touch me!"

Barnett swooped closer, breathing hotly in her face, his fingers splayed like talons poised to carry her off to an aerie of death.

She struck out, shoving, clawing, shouting for help. A blow jerked her head back. He pinned her arms, but she fought harder, kicking and biting.

"Bind her," he snapped.

Two burly men jumped forward. Screaming, she bucked, twisting away from their greedy hands.

Fight! ordered Jacques. *You have to escape!*

She freed an arm, smashing a fist against someone's chin, clawing another's face. One man went down, but victory was impossible. Three against one, the three too strong. Fog grayed her vision as they threw her to the floor. Renewed struggling couldn't dislodge them. Reeking breath singed her face and neck. The fog thickened until she could see nothing.

Her screams echoed, deafening her to other sounds.

Hands pinned her as cords wrapped her arms until she was helpless, raising fear to heights she had not felt in twelve years. As the men tossed her into a carriage, the last of her senses shut down, leaving only terror.

★ ★ ★

As the carriage approached a village, Lord Barnett pulled the blind so no one could see the animal that had once been his niece. He wished he'd brought a second carriage so he needn't share with her. Craven was right. She should have been locked away years ago.

She lay on the opposite seat, quiet for the moment, though he doubted she would remain so. This journey was worse than the one to Halworth twelve years ago. Then she'd merely screamed if anyone approached her. Now she fought like a wildcat, screeching until she gagged, then wailing until she swooned. Within minutes she would awake to start the process over. Her clothes stank of vomit. His carriage would never be the same.

Holding a scented handkerchief to his nose, he waited until the village was behind them, then reopened the window. Surely they were nearing the asylum. Craven swore it was only fifteen miles from Halworth. But the rutted lanes made the journey seem interminable.

Morden Heath stretched to the horizon. Sheep wandered a distant hillside, but most of the land was empty. Carey's asylum was isolated enough to discourage visitors — not that anyone would call on Marianne. Halworth's elderly staff would move to retirement cottages within a fortnight. No one else knew her.

Half an hour later, the carriage drew up before a stone manor. Bars blocked its windows. A chill permeated the air, icier than October generally produced. But what had he expected? Asylums by nature were cold, comfortless places full of inhuman beasts.

Suppressing a shiver, he climbed down from the carriage.

"No visitors allowed," said the porter, cracking the door in response to Barnett's rap.

"I'm not a visitor. Tell Dr. Carey that his new patient has arrived."

His words produced a flurry of activity. Two attendants carried Marianne inside while a third raced to fetch the doctor. The porter led Barnett to a small parlor.

Barnett had time to empty two glasses of wine and a plate of cakes before Carey finally appeared.

"Lord Barnett," he said, bowing low. "My apologies for keeping you waiting, but we had to settle your niece. A difficult case, but she is resting comfortably now. When did her problem begin?"

"Twelve years ago. Her family succumbed to disease while traveling abroad. The trip back to England was arduous. She has been unable to live with others ever since."

"It happens." Carey steepled his fingers over his nose. "She undoubtedly suffered a milder form of their illness. Disease often weakens the mind, which would have magnified her loss and made the perils of her journey more frightening."

"Can she be cured?"

"Improvement is rare, especially after so many years. Usually all we can do is make the victim comfortable."

"I understand. I will expect a formal report within the week. If she is incurable, there are legal steps I must take."

Bidding Carey farewell, he headed for Bere Regis, hoping the village inn would have a decent room — and a bath.

Jack shoved the decanter aside. Overindulgence had caused enough trouble already. He should never have visited Marianne when he was the worse for wine. She was too innocent to handle a passionate assault — and too wellborn to dally with anyway.

He smashed his fist against his desk.

Would she meet him again?

While stumbling home from Halworth, he'd worked his way through every curse he'd heard in fifteen years of warfare. How could he have been so stupid? It was bad enough that he'd kissed her, but terrifying her was insupportable. He'd thrust his tongue deep into her mouth, pulling her against an erection that must have felt like a club. He couldn't blame her for fleeing.

Even worse, she would interpret her reaction as proof of madness.

The pain doubled him over.

After years of being told she was mad, she would never believe her fear was rational, though a virgin who didn't run when attacked by a lust-crazed man was abnormal. Especially one as isolated as Marianne.

Without anyone to instruct her, she remained a total innocent. Most of society's daughters knew what went on between men and women long before they reached London, even if that knowledge arose solely from warnings on what constituted unacceptable flirtation.

But Marianne knew nothing.

He forced his feet upstairs. Guilt made it impossible to think clearly. Wine and exhaustion didn't help. He needed sleep.

Only then could he devise a way to repair the damage he'd caused.

Three hours later, his butler shook him awake. "Mrs. Hastings to see you, Colonel," announced Barton. "She swears it is an emergency."

"The Halworth housekeeper?" Jack's gut clenched as he bounded from bed.

"Yes, sir."

"Put her in the library. I will be down in five minutes." He was dressing as he spoke. There was no time to summon Jones.

Marianne might have sent her housekeeper to demand that Jack stay off her estate, but he doubted she would bother. Avoiding the cliffs for a few days would send the same message. Besides, such an errand could hardly be considered an emergency.

It was more likely that the housekeeper was here to castigate him for upsetting her mistress. He clung to that hope, though his heart feared a catastrophe. The certainty that danger lurked remained.

But whatever the errand, he welcomed the chance to question the woman. Who would know more about Marianne than her housekeeper?

When he arrived in the library, his heart hit the floor.

Mrs. Hastings was backed against a bookcase, hands white-knuckled as they gripped her reticule, eyes wide with fear. He'd seen panicked horses who looked calmer. Emergency, indeed.

"You have to find Miss Marianne," she said through a sob. "He's taken her away."

"Who?"

"That demon." Her voice rose in hysteria. "The master always said —"

"Calm yourself, Mrs. Hastings," he ordered. "Take a deep breath and sit down." He escorted her to a chair and poured her a glass of sherry, refusing to allow another word until she had emptied half of it. "Now, start at the beginning."

"I know you and Miss Marianne have been meeting in the woods," she began.

"As friends only."

"I know. And we approve — Hastings and I. It's done her a body of good to talk to someone. She is more interested in the world since you arrived. But now he's taken her away. You have to stop him."

"Who?" he asked again.

"Lord Barnett." She sniffed into a handkerchief. "He came while Miss Marianne was out this morning. Just walked in like he owned the place. He had both guards with him, so we knew something was wrong. Hastings tried to put him in the drawing room, but Lord Barnett searched the house in case Miss Marianne was hiding, then stayed in the hall so he could pounce the moment she returned."

"Dear Lord," murmured Jack under his breath. She had already been upset. What would an ambush do?

"Hastings stayed with him — he hoped to ease him into the drawing room, for we didn't expect her back for an hour or more."

Jack cursed himself yet again. If he had behaved . . .

"I slipped away, hoping to warn her — I thought she was in the woods, so I watched that direction, but she must have come the other way. The next thing I knew, the poor girl was screaming worse than when that beastly Mr. Craven calls."

Jack gritted his teeth.

"Hastings saw it all. Lord Barnett slammed her against the wall the moment she walked through the door. When she screamed, he slapped her. She tried to escape, but he held her down while the guards trussed her up like a Christmas goose. When Hastings protested, one of them struck him."

"Did they hurt her?"

"How could they not? Everyone knows she can't stand being touched. He deliberately used that against her. Hastings says Lord Barnett goaded her until he triggered a fit. He was gloating as they threw her into his carriage — she was retching by then, so what would he have to smile about?"

"Did Barnett say where he was taking her?"

"A doctor, though she's not ill."

Jack suppressed his fury — and his terror; even the strongest mind could break after such mistreatment. He had to think rationally if he was to help. "She claims that Lord Barnett thinks her mad. Why?"

"She's not mad, but there is no denying that she's been fragile since her family died. And who can blame her?"

"What did she say about her trip to France?"

"Not a word."

"Damnation," he muttered. France was the key, yet he knew no more today than he had twelve years ago. But her trauma was too intense to have come from an accident or illness. "How did her family die?"

Mrs. Hastings frowned. "Lord Barnett told us they died of plague — he's the one who fetched her from Paris — but I've always suspected an accident."

"He claimed to have fetched her?" Jack stared.

"Of course. And a dangerous business it was, what with the French breaking the peace, and all. They barely escaped with their lives."

"He lied. I doubt he's ever been out of the country. I first met her when she was fleeing France. The danger was true enough, but Miss Dubois was her only companion. They had no luggage and said only that Miss Barnett's family was gone. I brought them back to England and delivered Marianne to Barnett Court. She stayed there for a month while Barnett came here to settle her father's estate."

Mrs. Hastings was shaking her head. "We didn't see him until he brought Miss Marianne home."

The Chancery suit. Barnett had lied to everyone. The moment he'd discovered the contents of his brother's will, he'd gone to London to overturn it. But that wasn't important at the moment. Fury had replaced fear in Mrs. Hastings's eyes, making her stronger.

Jack returned to business. "If I am to protect her, I have to know what happened in France. Are you sure she said nothing?"

"Not directly, but she suffered horrible nightmares for months, often screaming in her sleep. I sat beside her bed and prayed for her, though I quickly learned never to touch her. If the screams contained words, I couldn't understand them. But she often shouted for Jacques."

His heart contracted. "That was the name she knew me by."

"She kept imploring Jacques to save them. I thought she meant her family, which is why I assumed there had been an accident that only she survived."

"That may be, but she said nothing at all during that trip home." Her reaction to his kiss hinted that she'd been raped. Her nightmares added evidence of an attack on her family. *Save them!* It made today's assault even more despicable.

"But why would Lord Barnett lie? He swore he'd collected Marianne from Paris — made quite a tale of it. Their landlord had taken her in after plague killed the rest, hiding her from the police when they picked up other English travelers, then sending a messenger to bring Barnett across the Channel." She sounded bewildered.

"I've no idea." Unless Barnett suspected

that his wife had added to Marianne's woes — in which case, he might have pretended a heroic rescue to account for the month she'd been at Barnett Court. "Do you know where Barnett might have taken her today?"

"No, but there are only two decent roads out of this area. Someone in the village would have seen which one he followed."

"Did he take the guards with him?"

"They returned to their posts, so his only servant is the coachman." She shook her head. "I don't understand this. He's ignored her for years. The only visitor he allows is that disgusting secretary. The man watches her far too closely. There is a gleam in his eye I cannot trust."

As he'd feared. "She told me that Barnett never writes."

"True. Except for sending Mr. Craven, he leaves her alone."

"Very well. I will try to find her. But Barnett is her guardian, which gives him authority over her. I have no legal standing, so the only way to rescue her will be kidnapping. I won't be able to bring her back to Halworth until I discover Barnett's purpose and dissuade him from trying again."

She nodded her understanding. "Just

keep her safe, Colonel."

His stomach clenched. His instincts had known that she was in danger. Her inheritance trust would revert to her in a fortnight. But he'd been so caught up in atoning for the mistakes he'd made twelve years ago that he hadn't considered Barnett an enemy until last night.

Only the most honorable paragon would agree to place a fortune in the hands of an untried, mentally fragile female. Even decent men would find a way to supervise her affairs so she couldn't squander her inheritance.

Today's actions proved that Barnett was far from decent. And his motives went beyond preserving her inheritance. By declaring her insane, he could take charge of everything she owned. Chancery Court might assign a judge to audit the records every year, but with a lord involved, they might not exert even that much control.

He bade Mrs. Hastings farewell, then called for his horse. Hopefully, Marianne's exercise program had restored the stamina he would need. By his calculation, Barnett had at least a four-hour lead. It would be dark before he could catch up.

Chapter Seven

Ignoring the throb in his thigh, Jack slid silently into the shadow of a rhododendron and studied Carey's asylum. One window was lit — the one next to the front door, which raised hope that Carey employed a night porter. It was past midnight, so the day porter should be asleep. Jack didn't want to meet *that* fellow again.

It had been painfully easy to track Barnett's carriage. Everyone who had seen it reported screams, moans, and wails coming from inside. It made his blood run cold. He had heard of people losing their reason with far less provocation. Marianne must know that Barnett meant to incarcerate her for life — once he took over her inheritance, he could never let her go.

Jack had pushed his leg to the limit of endurance, arriving at Carey's less than two hours behind Barnett. The place was a converted manor house, dark, isolated, and brooding. Even in sunlight, it was melancholy. In cold rain or creeping fog it would be intolerable. The employees must risk madness themselves if they remained for long.

But as cold and unwelcoming as the building seemed, the porter had been worse.

"No visitors allowed," the man had repeated to Jack's third demand for admittance. A heavy chain prevented the door from opening more than a few inches.

"You don't understand," Jack had insisted desperately. Every refusal had increased his fear. "I am her husband. She was abducted by an unscrupulous relative who is demanding a fortune in exchange for her freedom."

"No visitors allowed."

"Must I fetch a magistrate and charge you with conspiring in an extortion scheme?"

"No visitors allowed."

Jack had finally given up. The man outweighed him by at least four stone and had the look of a bruising fighter. Breaking the chain would be difficult — and useless; three equally hulking staff members had passed through the hall during his confrontation with the porter.

After promising to return in the morning when the doctor was available, Jack had left. Not that he had given up. Every minute that Marianne remained in this place increased the risk of permanent damage. But Wellington had taught him that a tactical retreat was sometimes necessary if one hoped to win the war. So he would return at night.

He used the hours to rest, eat, and devise a tale he hoped would win cooperation. Victory demanded that he wait until everyone was asleep, for there was no way he could overpower multiple attendants.

Again he berated himself for not questioning Marianne when he'd had the chance. He should have demanded facts instead of assuming that her problem was a lack of confidence. If he'd used the last month to address her real problems, perhaps she could have handled Lord Barnett.

Taking a deep breath, he clamped down on guilt and concentrated on logic. Battle required a clear head.

But he could not forget Marianne's nightmares. *Save them!*

Napoleon had arrested every Englishman he could find after the peace collapsed in 1803. Some were eventually released, though not in a timely fashion — despite having diplomatic immunity, Lord Elgin had not reached England until 1807, for instance. Many died during their years of mistreatment. Others had remained incarcerated until Napoleon abdicated in 1814.

French mobs had carried out the arrest orders with the same zeal they'd shown during the revolution — and with much the same result. While many Englishmen landed in prison, others met their fate on the guillotine or worse. Jack had seen the results of two such frenzies as he made his way to the coast. Had Marianne survived another? It was too easy to picture a mob raping English prisoners before hauling them before the authorities. Marianne might have escaped in the confusion, and the shock would explain her silence.

For the first time, he pondered Francine's exact words — *they are gone*. It was he who had assumed that meant they were dead. But it could also mean that they'd been arrested. Maybe Marianne's nightmares grew from uncertainty.

He kicked himself for jumping to conclusions — another failure of honor, especially if his assumption had left them languishing in a French prison.

Save them! What if she had known they were under arrest? Jack had told Lady Barnett that Marianne's family was dead.

If Lady Barnett had been the first to tell Marianne, it would have further distressed her, for the harridan would not have broken the news gently. Marianne would blame herself for abandoning them.

His gut twisted at the thought that he might have left her family to rot in jail because he'd been too busy saving his own neck to ask the necessary questions. How had he dared call himself honorable? His life had been a lie long before Waterloo.

For now he could only pray that Marianne could talk about it once she escaped. He had to know the full story if he hoped to help her. Freedom was merely the first step. She would not be safe until she was out from under Barnett's thumb, which meant convincing the Chancery Court to rescind his guardianship.

But that was for later. He checked the asylum's windows one last time. The bars and locks designed to keep patients inside also kept intruders out, and the building was large, making his job more dangerous. The unbarred wing probably housed the doctor. And the servants and staff doubtless slept in the attics — those windows also lacked bars. But that left three floors of two wings to be searched. And since he could hardly enter through the doctor's quarters, he must pass the porter.

All he could do was pray that no one else was awake.

He glanced over his shoulder to make sure that his horse remained out of sight. Renting a carriage in Bere Regis would have been easier for Marianne than riding pillion, but he needed the flexibility of an overland escape. His route would depend on how quickly the asylum staff organized a pursuit.

Just do it!

Exhaling, he wrapped his cloak around his uniform, then strode to the door. As expected, it was locked.

He knocked, loudly. If anyone but the porter was awake, he was in trouble.

The door creaked open. "No visitors allowed."

"I'm not a visitor," swore Jack. "Lord Barnett forgot to give the doctor some vital information."

"Come back in the morning." The porter pushed on the door.

Jack shoved his foot in the crack to keep it open, then flinched as the weight of the door pinched his toes. "Lord Barnett insisted that I deliver his message immediately. It's not worth my life or yours to thwart him."

"Life?"

"Lord Barnett does not tolerate delays."

The porter frowned. "Dr. Carey doesn't like interruptions," he countered.

"Perhaps not, but a lord wields more power than a country doctor."

Silence stretched, ending in a heavy sigh. "I'll fetch him." The porter sounded resigned to a tongue-lashing.

"Can I wait in the hall?" asked Jack. "It's cold out here." He held his breath while the porter again paused. The man's thought processes were slow. It gave Jack an advantage.

"I suppose," the man grumbled, unfastening the chain.

Jack hid his relief. Keeping his posture humble, he took the proffered chair. The porter hesitated outside the day porter's room, then shrugged and turned toward the hall.

Jack flung his cloak aside as he sprang. Covering the porter's mouth, he delivered a blow to the neck with the side of his other hand — another skill he'd learned from that Chinaman.

The porter slumped, unconscious.

Silence settled over the hall. Jack shut the front door, leaving it unlocked and unchained — he might need a quick exit — then dragged the porter into the lighted room. The man was older than he'd seemed in the darkness — thin gray hair, furrowed face, arthritic hands roped with bulbous veins. Nothing like the bruising day porter.

He stifled guilt. Attacking a harmless old man was the only way to find Marianne. And the porter was merely unconscious. He would recover in an hour or two.

To prevent him from sounding an alarm if he awoke too soon, Jack tied and gagged him, laying him on a bed in the corner. The one drawback of this plan was that unconscious men could not reveal information. He had no idea where Marianne was. Nor did he have keys — an asylum would lock the patients' rooms.

But the staff would need ready access, and he doubted that everyone carried rings of keys. Either the keys would be in the locks, or a single key would open every door. Tugging the key from the porter's door, he locked it behind him, then headed upstairs, moving as quietly as possible.

The key worked, though the first three rooms held only sleeping strangers. The fourth made his skin crawl, for the occupant was crouched in the corner, naked, dark eyes glittering in the moonlight flowing through the barred window. The man's muscles tensed as though to spring. Jack shut the door so fast it banged.

He waited until his heartbeat returned to normal, but the man made no sound, and no one came to investigate the noise.

The next room was empty. Another was so full of dolls that he nearly missed the occupant. Another empty room. Two men, one of them strapped to the bed. A locked door that did not accept his key. It probably led to Carey's apartments.

Fighting down a growing sense of urgency, he climbed to the next floor.

Three rooms with women, an empty room, two more women, an unlocked —

His fists clenched in fury. Marianne lay tied to the bed, a gag in her mouth. But she had again fallen into catalepsy. Despite open eyes, she did not move. It was worse than that last day in France.

A man stood over her, unbuttoning his breeches as his free hand fondled her breast. With a feral growl, Jack whirled the man around and landed a solid kick to the crotch.

The man howled.

Jack jerked him up by the hair, slapped him twice, then planted a fist in his jaw to knock him cold.

Shoving him aside, Jack untied the knots that held Marianne's hands and feet. "Sweetheart, can you hear me?" he whispered. "It's Jack. I've come to save you."

She didn't move.

"It's all right now," he murmured, removing the gag. She wore only a thin shift. "You are safe. No one will ever hurt you again."

The room contained only the bed, a chair, and a small table. There was no wardrobe and no sign of her clothes.

"Damnation," he muttered. He could hardly take her outside in a shift. She would freeze in an hour. The wind had veered while he'd tracked her down, bringing icy air from the north.

"Marianne, sweetheart." He massaged her wrists where the cord had cut into the flesh. "Wake up."

He thought she flinched, but that was her only movement.

He was running out of time. For all he knew, they had poured laudanum down her throat to stop her from screaming.

Wrapping her in a sheet, he set her gently by the door, then heaved the attendant onto the bed, replacing the ties and gag so he couldn't raise an alarm. Cradling

Marianne against his chest, he locked the door behind him, then hurried downstairs.

The porter remained unconscious.

Jack closed Marianne's eyes, then dressed her in a shirt and breeches from the porter's chest. Shoving her feet into oversize boots stuffed with extra stockings so they wouldn't slide off, he wrapped her in a cloak and carried her to his horse.

At least he could touch her for the moment without igniting terror. Her traumatic day might leave her unable to tolerate him.

He suppressed a new burst of fury. To achieve victory, he must stay focused on the battle plan. The next step was finding a refuge.

He had intended to take her to Seacliff, but that was now impossible. He had stupidly given his name to the day porter. The man might already have reported the encounter to Carey. That would be the first place the doctor would look when he found her missing.

An inn would likewise be impossible. He could not change their appearance enough to escape recognition. And the bustle of an inn could push her into real madness.

If she isn't there already.

"No," he said aloud. "She'll be fine." He

would see to it — as he should have done twelve years ago.

For now, the asylum remained silent, so he stayed on the road, holding Marianne in front of him with his cloak surrounding them both. He needed a refuge by dawn. His thigh was protesting the fifteen miles he'd already ridden that day, and even his warhorse would eventually tire from its extra burden. Changing mounts would leave a trail Carey or Barnett could follow. His uniform was too obvious.

He pressed Marianne's head against his shoulder as a gust of wind slammed into them. His plans hadn't anticipated her being unconscious. Where could they go? Renting a cottage would take time and cause talk. Deerchester Hall was forty miles away — but Jack would never beg asylum from his family, especially with Marianne in tow. Deerchester was too corrupt to ignore so tasty a morsel.

Wyndhaven.

Of course. Devall Sherbrooke, Marquess of Blackthorn, was a friend from his school days. Even after Jack had bought colors, he and Devall had stayed in touch — until Waterloo. His dishonor made facing friends impossible, so he'd not opened recent letters. But Marianne was more important than his pride. And even if Devall scorned Jack, he would still help Marianne. Devall had long aided victims of abuse. His wife Angela was equally fierce when protecting innocents. They would spring to Marianne's defense in an instant.

Devall's estate was twenty miles away. It would be a hard journey, but his horse could manage it at a walk. Jack would have to force his thigh and arms to hold out. October nights were long enough that they should arrive before dawn, but only if he kept moving.

"We are going to Wyndhaven, Marianne. You will be safe there. And I guarantee that you can trust Devall and Angela. They would never harm you."

He repeated his assurances every step of the way, reminding her often who he was and that she was safe. But when he staggered up Wyndhaven's front steps, she remained unconscious.

God, he hoped it was laudanum!

Chapter Eight

"How is she?" asked Devall when Jack limped into the library an hour later.

"Sleeping — I think." Jack rubbed his gritty eyes and accepted the wine his friend offered.

He'd been right to bring Marianne here. Devall had taken one look at her white face and led the way to a bedchamber. No questions. No raised eyebrows that she was dressed in male garb or traveling alone with a man. He hadn't even mentioned the eight unanswered letters lying on Jack's desk.

Jack had been grateful. He'd wanted to settle Marianne before she awoke, lest his touch do further harm. Taking the time to explain first might have made that difficult.

He also needed to be with her when she awoke. She would be disoriented enough without having to deal with strangers. And without him she would assume she remained at Carey's. But before he could closet himself with her, he must talk to Devall.

He drained the glass, hoping wine would soothe his throat, which was hoarse from murmuring reassurances for six hours without pause. "I asked your housekeeper to remain in Marianne's room. She will fetch me if Marianne begins to stir."

Devall frowned. "Aside from propriety, you need rest yourself."

"It can wait." He caught Devall's glance at his leg. "It is improving. The limp only returned because I pushed it too hard. But that is merely weariness."

"Very well. Now suppose you tell me what is going on."

"I don't know." He accepted more wine. "I have a few facts and many suspicions, but until I can talk to Marianne, I won't know whether my guesses are correct. And talking may take time. Something in the past terrifies her. Yesterday's trauma will make her more fragile than ever."

"Let's start with the facts." Devall stretched his legs toward the fireplace.

"Twelve years ago I met a woman and child trying to escape France. The woman was a French émigré who'd taken a position as a lady's maid. The child was her employer's twelve-year-old daughter —

140

and the family's sole survivor."

"What happened?"

"I didn't ask. I assumed that they had died of disease — there had been an epidemic in Paris a month earlier. Now I suspect that they were either arrested or killed when the peace collapsed. But I won't know until I talk to Marianne."

"I presume you escorted them back to England."

Jack nodded. "I delivered the child to her uncle, Lord Barnett, took the maid to relatives, then went about my business. The next time I saw Marianne was a month ago. She owns the estate next to mine."

Devall's eyes gleamed with speculation. "Convenient."

"It's not like that," snapped Jack. When the gleam intensified, he swore under his breath. But he could not tell Devall about his plans. "The little she revealed raised alarms. Her nightmares had disturbed Barnett's family, and she apparently fell into hysteria whenever a stranger approached. To reestablish peace in his household, Barnett banished her to her own estate a month after her return, setting guards to prevent any callers."

"It is not unusual to put children in the

care of a governess."

"True, but there was no governess, no nurse, no companion. As near as I can tell, her entire staff consists of a housekeeper and butler, now well past seventy, and a couple of elderly maids. She has been incarcerated there ever since."

"For twelve years?"

"Exactly. Barnett decided she was mad, so he made no attempt to train her or to bring her out, though she is nearly twenty-five. She accepted the verdict, though I do not."

Jack relaxed when Devall shuddered, for he knew the reaction was to Marianne's treatment and not her mental state. He and Devall had faced a madman two years earlier, so Devall knew Jack could recognize insanity.

"How did you meet if she is so isolated?" asked Devall.

"There is a patch of forest between her park and mine. The boundaries are not marked, so I wandered onto her land one day. When I learned who she was, we became friends." His tone closed the subject.

"So why bring her here?"

"Lord Barnett turned up yesterday, bound her, and locked her in an asylum.

When I reached her, one of the guards was preparing to rape her. She needs a safe harbor until I determine Barnett's purpose."

Devall's fist clenched so tightly, his wineglass cracked. He set it aside, wrestling his fury under control. "She is welcome."

"So I thought. I am hoping that she knows enough that I will not have to leave her here while I investigate."

"That would be convenient, but you must have some suspicions."

Jack nodded. "Money is the most likely motive. She inherited an estate and fortune from her father. It is currently in trust, but will come to her outright in a few more days. Barnett tried to overturn the will twelve years ago, but failed. Now he has another chance to claim his brother's wealth. He can lock her away, then have himself appointed administrator of her affairs."

Devall scowled, reviving the satanic look that had put off most of society before his marriage. "I cannot abide greed."

"I know. That's another reason I brought her here."

"Are you sure she is sane? Some madmen can appear normal much of the time — Atwater did, as you recall."

"Marianne is no Atwater. I've spent hours in her company every day for a month." He ignored the renewed gleam in Devall's eyes. "Her initial problems were a natural reaction to the events in France. They abated along with her grief. Since then, she has suffered a recurrence only when Barnett's secretary arrives to check on her. From her descriptions — and those of her housekeeper — I suspect Craven's goal is seduction. Her fortune casts a powerful lure."

Devall's face twisted into a more frightening scowl. "I have unfortunately met Barnett's wife. She hails from the merchant class. Most people believe she trapped Barnett into marriage, seeking his title and wealth. She overspends every year and is described as an avaricious, unscrupulous matchmaker."

"Why?"

"Too many people rank above a viscountess. She could acquire more status as mother of a duchess."

"Good God!"

"Exactly. She has three daughters out and another at home. An astute lady might have tried to snare another viscount or an earl for the first, then worked upward."

"To where? A prince?"

"We have enough of them. Fortunately, she is too stupid to hide her goals, so none have received offers — eligible gentlemen look at Lady Barnett, assume the daughters will emulate her, then run as fast as possible in the other direction. Even now the girls are sharp-tongued harridans with minimal looks and diminishing dowries — each year the figure wanes, which suggests that Barnett may be suffering financial woes."

"Making Marianne's fortune even more enticing." That explained the discourse on Lady Barnett.

Devall nodded. "How large is it?"

"I've no idea, but a neighbor claims that Marianne's father had fifty thousand when he died — plus the estate. Halworth is larger than Seacliff and must produce at least as much income."

Devall whistled.

"Richard Barnett had a golden touch for investing," continued Jack. "He was a scholar whose only indulgence was books, so he rarely spent more than a portion of his income. The trustees have taken a more conservative approach, but again most of the income must be reinvested. Marianne cannot have spent a tithe of what the estate alone earns each year."

"I will dispatch my secretary to London to discover Barnett's circumstances. Fitch has a knack for uncovering a man's darkest secrets."

"Barnett is bound to petition the Chancery Court to become steward of her affairs now that a doctor will certify Marianne insane. We need to know his plans."

Devall nodded as a knock sounded on the door. "Enter," he called.

"She is stirring," reported the housekeeper.

With no more than a nod in Devall's direction, Jack raced upstairs.

Marianne was stirring, but not to consciousness. She thrashed wildly, fighting the quilt, her face twisted in terror.

Nightmare.

"Damnation," muttered Jack as he locked the door behind him — if she started screaming, he did not want intruders.

"Relax, sweetheart," he murmured, carefully freeing the quilt so it did not bind her. "You're safe now. I will protect you."

Her agitation grew worse. *"Baisez la putain anglaise!"* she mumbled.

Jack gasped.

"Save them, Jacques! Save them! No!

146

Help! *Baisez la putain anglaise! Baisez la putain anglaise! Baisezlaputainanglaise!*" The words ran together into a scream.

"Marianne, wake up!" Jack shook her, trying to keep his hands gentle even as he fought to break through her terror. The guard at the asylum may have triggered this dream, but the memories were far older. "Wake up, Marianne. It's only a dream. You are safe."

Footsteps sounded in the hall.

"Nightmare," called Jack when Devall demanded to know what was going on. "Send everyone away." He turned back to Marianne, who had lapsed into heartbreaking sobs. "Wake up, sweetheart. I won't let anyone hurt you."

Her eyes fluttered open, widening when they spotted him. She cringed into the bed.

"It's all right, Marianne. It's only Jack. You are safe. I won't hurt you."

"Jacques?"

"That's right. You're safe now." He released her shoulders so he was no longer touching her.

"Jack." Tears flooded down her cheeks. "What happened?"

"You were having a nightmare."

She blinked several times, then focused

beyond his shoulder, staring until her eyes showed a white ring around the gray. Scooting to the far edge of the bed, she huddled into a tiny ball. "Uncle — Where am I? What are you doing here?"

"Relax. You are safe. I am the only one here, but I won't touch you."

"Jack?" Her voice shook.

"Right. I'm Jack. We need to talk, but you have to stay calm. Can you do that? I promise no one else can come in here."

She inhaled deeply several times, then nodded.

"Mrs. Hastings came to me yesterday after Lord Barnett abducted you."

Shivers wracked her from head to toe, but she bit her lip and nodded.

"Do you remember that?"

Again she nodded. "He — He was in the hall when I returned home." Her hand flew to her mouth, and he knew she was recalling their kiss.

"I'll apologize for kissing you, if you like. I'm not truly sorry for the kiss, but I would never have knowingly frightened you."

She nodded. "He — He said I had to see a d-doctor about my t-terrors. I tried to send him away, but he loomed over me, breathing in my face and g-grabbing at me like before. I c-couldn't help it. I started screaming. Then I couldn't stop. I tried to escape, but they were too strong. The hands —"

"Shhh. Relax, Marianne. It's all right. Your reaction is perfectly normal. Mrs. Hastings described the scene. I would be suspicious of anyone who docilely followed his orders. Fighting back is the natural response of a sane mind. Believe me, I know. I've seen how a madman reacts."

"You have?"

"I have. It was my duty to escort the fellow to Bedlam. He was docile as a lamb and no more aware of his surroundings than a stone. So do not regret fighting. It proves your sanity." He nearly broke into tears as hope spread across her face.

"I don't recall much after that," she said in a firmer voice. "They bound me and tossed me in Barnett's carriage. The last thing I remember is vomiting all over him."

Her mind had ceased working, he decided, for she had not been unconscious. Too many people in too many places had heard her screams. But she didn't need to know that.

He would prefer to let her rebuild her composure before questioning her, but there was no time. All he could do was pray that her newfound hope and her inner core of strength would see them through the next hour.

"Put it behind you, Marianne. There are other things we must discuss." He kept his voice soothing. "I know you would rather wait, but time is too short. All right?"

She nodded.

"Good. We'll start with what I know. Raise your hand if you need me to pause."

"That sounds ominous."

"It is. But the truth will make you stronger."

Again she nodded.

"I was able to track Barnett's carriage, but I was still two hours behind when I reached Dr. Carey's asylum on Morden Heath."

"Not Carey's!" Her face paled.

"That's where Barnett left you. What do you know of it?"

"Very little, but stories when I was a child claimed it was filled with vicious beasts and blood-drinking ghouls who roam the heaths at night looking for victims."

"Exaggerations meant to frighten children, especially those who try to sneak out after dark." That drew a hint of a smile. He tamped down a new surge of lust. "Its occupants are just people, but it is not a place I would leave anyone I cared about. They do not allow visitors, and I was not impressed with the staff."

"If they don't allow visitors, how did you get in?"

"I waited until the servants were asleep, then overpowered the night porter." He paused, but she had to face it. "I found one of the attendants preparing to rape you."

"No! No, nonono . . ." The words merged into another scream.

"Marianne! Stop this," he said firmly, daring to grasp her hand. "He did not touch you. You are safe. Safe."

His words must have registered, for she quieted. "He failed, Marianne. You are fine." He refused to consider whether the man was the first to attack her, or even if he might have visited her room earlier. If evidence surfaced later of such an attack, she would have to deal with it, but it was too soon.

"I'm sorry. The terror appeared too suddenly."

"There is nothing to apologize for. You have been through a nerve-wracking experience. If we had more time, I would not need to push you so hard, but I have no choice."

"Thank you for saving me — again." She inhaled deeply. "Tell me everything. I need to know that there is nothing else waiting to pounce."

"I suspect that they had given you laudanum to stop your screams. And they had tied you to the bed, both arms and legs."

She glanced at her wrists, still red from the ropes.

"That is all I know about the asylum. You were there only a few hours — six at most. I might have recovered you sooner if I'd brought a magistrate with me, but I have no standing under the law. Without strong evidence of fraud, confiding in a magistrate could have done great harm. Since Barnett is your guardian, there is no question of abduction, no matter how brutal his methods. And I know nothing against Carey, who was merely conducting his business."

"Then what am I to do? Barnett can demand I return."

"First he has to find you. We will remain out of sight until I learn what is going on."

"Here? Is this your house?" She gestured at the room, which was pleasantly appointed in rosewood furniture, with green silk on the walls and gold velvet at the windows.

"No. In tracing Barnett's carriage, I left a trail that anyone could follow. Once Barnett discovers your escape — which could already have happened — he will go to Halworth. His next stop will be Seacliff. Knowing that, I brought you to the house of a friend — the Marquess of Blackthorn. You can trust him and his wife completely."

She flinched, but said nothing.

"Is there anything else about yesterday that you need to know?" he asked.

She shook her head.

"Good. Time is very short, and I must learn everything possible about Barnett. I can think of only one reason for his actions — to assume control of your inheritance. Devall — the marquess — suspects that he is suffering from financial reverses."

"Do you mean he's kept me hidden for twelve years because he wants my money?" She bolted upright in bed, eyes blazing.

"I doubt it. That need might be recent, so don't jump to conclusions." He forced stillness over hands that longed to soothe her. "Blackthorn is sending his secretary to investigate Barnett's affairs. Until we have facts, we cannot mount an adequate offensive. So tell me about him."

"I know very little," she said, frowning.

"Shocking, now that I think of it. I had never met him before you left me at Barnett Court, and didn't see him until a month later when he returned from settling Papa's affairs. I never would have recognized him, for he looks nothing like Papa." She paused to inhale several times. "He escorted me to Halworth, but that journey remains a blur. I do recall that he was very angry, though having his household so badly interrupted might explain that." She bit her lip before continuing. "He visited three or four times that first year, but spent only a few minutes in my company. Yesterday he said only that I must seek help."

"What did you know of him before?" he asked, appalled at Barnett's aloofness. The man was her *guardian!* Yet he'd all but ignored her for more than a decade. Even if she were truly mad, such treatment was unconscionable. "Why did your father leave his estate to you instead of to his brother?"

"They didn't get along. He never said why, and beyond knowing that Papa's brother was a viscount, we never discussed him." She pursed her lips. "It might have had something to do with Lady Barnett, but that memory may be false — overheard servants' gossip at best. At any rate, Papa expected Nigel to inherit one day. The trust would have contained only our dowries if Nigel —" She sobbed.

"Nigel?"

She sucked in a deep breath. "My brother. He and my sister Cecily died in France."

Jack set aside France for the moment. "Do you recall the provisions of your father's will?"

She nodded. "I overheard Papa and Mama talking about it — he revised it just before we left for France. Cecily and I were to get ten thousand guineas each as dowries. There was a generous allowance for Mama out of estate funds. The rest went to Nigel. Papa stipulated trusts for anyone under twenty-five. Our shares were to go to Nigel should we die while the trusts remained in force. If he died without an heir, we would share his inheritance. That's how I wound up with everything."

"What if you had all died?"

"I don't know. I never actually saw the will. But Papa could not have hated Lord Barnett, for he was named co-guardian with Mama."

Jack nodded. Blood always counted in the end.

Shaking off the reminder of his own blood, he returned to business. "To take charge of your affairs, Barnett must convince the Chancery Court that you are mad. And he must do it before the trust terminates."

"Why?"

"To prevent you from squandering the funds. What you have to do is convince the court that you are sane."

"How?" She sat up, scooting closer so she could lower her voice. Talking seemed to hurt, as if yesterday's hysterics had sprained her throat. "What if he's right, Jack? I cannot tolerate people."

"You have no problem with me," he reminded her. "And your aversion has nothing to do with madness." When she tried to protest, he put a finger over her lips. "We've discussed this before. Yesterday changes nothing. Your problem began as a natural reaction to grief and trauma, but it soon became a habit sustained by isolation. If you were truly incapable of tolerating people, you would have fallen into hysterics when you encountered me on the cliff that day — or any of the dozens of times we have met since then."

"But I know you would never hurt me."

"Exactly. The problem is not people,

Marianne. The problem is trust, expectations, and confidence in yourself. To protect yourself from the few people who might harm you, you have turned all men into demons. By avoiding everyone, you eliminate the need to judge others — and thus prevent mistakes. But that does not really protect you, for those who are truly dangerous won't wait for an invitation — Barnett, for example. And holding the world at bay eliminates the friendships that could sustain you in times of trouble."

Like you've been doing? demanded his conscience.

But he ignored it. Dishonor was different. He couldn't ask his friends to condone his infamy.

Marianne was frowning. "That sounds easy when you say it, but it's too late. Even if my fears are habit, they are too ingrained."

"Not at all." He stretched his legs, feigning relaxation. "Anything that is learned can be unlearned."

"How?"

Jack drew a deep breath, for if he was wrong, his demands might truly send her into madness. "The first step is to tell me what happened to your family."

"They died."

"Details, Marianne. You have to bring the memories out into the light of day. It is the only way to reduce their power."

"I can't." She was shaking.

"You must. I can guess at much of it, for I was there. I know what happened to travelers caught in France when the peace collapsed. I had to fight off the soldiers sent to arrest me in Paris. And I heard the words that form your screams when nightmare strikes."

Her eyes widened.

"They are not true screams, you know. They are words — parroted French — repeated so rapidly that they sound like screaming. *Baisez la putain anglaise.*" He stripped the words of inflection, rendering them impotent. Yet she blanched. "You were caught by a mob, weren't you?"

Her mouth worked, but nothing emerged.

"Did they rape you?"

Her head jerked in shock. "N-n-no."

"Then it could have been worse."

Her eyes widened.

"They raped your mother, though, didn't they?" He kept his voice matter-of-fact.

"Sh-she was sick. My fault. All my fault."

"No!" Leaning forward, he tipped her head up, forcing her to meet his gaze. "It was *not* your fault."

"But it *was!*" Tears smudged her eyes. "I contracted an ague in Paris — I'd run off in the rain after being told to stay indoors. I was always a disobedient child. Mama nursed me for days, insisting that we delay our departure until I was well. We hadn't been on the road two hours before she fell ill. By afternoon, she was too sick to continue." Her teeth chattered. "The next day, Cecily fell sick, then Hutch — our governess — and Nigel. Everyone was furious with me for causing such trouble. I always caused trouble, you see."

"It wasn't your fault," he said soothingly. "Agues were common that year, for it had been a wet winter and cool spring. I swear half of Paris was sick. I had a touch of it myself."

She shrugged. "Papa was furious. I heard him arguing with Mama the third day, insisting that she pull herself together and finish the journey. She refused, calling him tyrant and worse for ignoring her distress. I wonder if he knew what was coming."

"Perhaps. A scholar would be more aware of possibilities than others might be.

And he must have heard the news by then."

Marianne twisted her hands together. "Mama was so fretful that day. I was reading in her room, but even the noise of turning pages bothered her. She finally ordered Francine to take me for a walk so she could rest. We were gone when the men arrived."

She paused as if steeling herself to continue. Jack remained silent. He knew what was coming, and it wouldn't be arrest — her nightmare words made that plain enough. But he could not spare her this recital. She had to remember everything, then set aside her guilt if she hoped to recover.

"We were coming around the stable when two men dragged Mama into the yard. Others followed. Francine recognized what was happening — a similar mob had killed her father. She whisked me into the stable and up into the loft, covering me with hay in case anyone came up there. No one did. The stable boys were in the yard, sh-sharing in the fun." She choked.

Jack drew her into his lap, holding her while she cried.

"I c-couldn't see, but nothing muffled the sound. Everyone was outside. Papa.

Mama. Nigel. Cecily. She was only eight, but they r-raped her and forced Papa to watch." Tears soaked his jacket. "Hutch was there, too, and poor John Coachman. Ted. Rob. And Papa's valet. I don't recall his name."

"Shhh, Marianne. You are safe." He stroked her cheek. "Did they torture the men?" He knew they had.

She nodded against his chest. "They goaded each other to new atrocities. My French wasn't good enough to understand everything —"

"Thank God!"

"— but it was obvious that they were daring each other to prove — what? Manhood?" She shivered. "By midnight, they had passed out from drink, so Francine and I crept out. We t-tripped over Mama in the stable yard."

"That's enough." He recalled the scene all too well. It was the second he'd seen — and by far the worst. The brutality had turned his stomach. The corpses had been at least a day old by then, but men still slipped out of the taproom to add new desecrations.

"I've seen similar incidents," he continued, refusing to admit that he had also seen hers. "Your impressions were right.

The men were probably strangers, met on the road as they answered the call to arms. They would have been boasting of what they would do to France's enemies, and then they had to prove it. War can turn men into beasts. I am thankful that it did not touch English soil." He shuddered, recalling the sack of Badajoz. "But you cannot let a few drunken fools destroy your life. You will always grieve for those you lost, but you should also rejoice that you survived. And no matter how much pain your family suffered in that stable yard, it would have been worse if they had been arrested. Too many were mistreated for eleven years before finally achieving their freedom."

She seemed not to have heard him. "It would have been better if I had died, too."

"No. You are strong, Marianne. The attack left you feeling helpless, and terror increased that helplessness, but it has not defeated you. It is time to set it aside once and for all."

"I can't."

"You can." He thrilled when her arms moved around his waist, though he knew she sought protection rather than passion. "You must," he added firmly. "If you remain in thrall to the fears of that night, then those men will have harmed you even more than the others. Will you hand them that victory?"

"Victory?" She straightened to look him in the eye.

"Exactly. Wittingly or not, they waged war on you, assailing your senses, stealing your confidence, laying siege to your reason. Will you let them win, or will you fight back by proving that you can live a full life?"

"It seems impossible." But uncertainty had crept into her voice.

"It is not. You are a lady, Marianne, far superior to cowardly cads who attack unarmed men, women, and children. You are strong. And with a little effort, that strength can build the confidence that will set the past truly behind you."

She laughed — bitterly.

"Truth. If not for your innate strength, they would already have won. And they may yet. If you allow Barnett to confiscate your inheritance and lock you up, then you will have given that mob of cowardly fools the ultimate victory."

"My God!"

"Exactly. You must honor your father's memory by seeing that his last wishes are carried out. But to protect your inheritance and remain free, you must prove your sanity to a judge. You will have to walk into a courtroom, endure questioning by men you have never seen before, and perhaps even allow them to touch you."

She shuddered.

"I only mention it so you know what is coming. Are we agreed?"

She nodded, stiffening her shoulders. "But how will I manage?"

"One step at a time. We will start with something simple. Barnett will know if I summon your servants, so you will have to use one of Devall's. And since you lack even the rudiments of a wardrobe, you must borrow clothes from Angela for a few days."

"Angela?"

"Devall's wife, Lady Blackthorn. You will meet her soon. She is every bit the angel that her name implies. If you trust yourself, you will become good friends. Her husband is equally angelic, though that is not the impression one draws at first meeting."

"What's wrong with him?"

"His looks have been described as satanic, brutal, and cold, and those are just the repeatable words. He is tall, with black hair, nearly black eyes, and brows that rise to incredible peaks. Even his name sounds devilish — Devall. When he scowls, he could pass for Beelzebub himself."

"I can't face him, then."

"You can. He has spent his life rescuing people from brutality and oppression, often sacrificing his reputation in the process. You will not find a kinder man in England, nor a better champion, so bear that in mind when I introduce you. You can trust him with your life."

She stifled a shudder by stiffening her shoulders. "I will try."

"Excellent." He set her on the bed, passed her his handkerchief, and stepped back. Her eyes were red from crying, but already she seemed calmer. "Angela loaned you a dressing gown. There is also a morning gown on that chair, but the fastenings are complicated and require the services of a maid. I will be in the hall. Let me know if you wish a maid. Once you are dressed, I can order a breakfast tray or accompany you to the breakfast room."

"I will think about it."

Hoping she would find the courage to face the breakfast room, he left. Time was fleeing. She needed to meet Devall and

165

Angela today if they had any hope of winning in court. Barnett must bring his case to trial within the week.

Chapter Nine

As Jack left her bedchamber, Marianne bit her tongue so she couldn't call him back. She did not want to be alone. But he was right. Time was precious. She had to dress, eat, and face the day. And within the week, she must face a judge and prove that her wits were intact despite Carey's medical opinion. If only she'd spent as much time fighting Barnett's perceptions as she'd spent learning estate management . . .

Swallowing hard, she climbed down from the bed to examine her borrowed clothes. Dressing gown or morning gown? She wanted desperately to choose the dressing gown, order a tray, and spend a few hours regaining her composure. But such cowardice would play into Barnett's hands.

Again, Jack was right. She had chosen the easy course twelve years ago — the lazy course. Avoiding people might have seemed the best way to mitigate her fears and protect her from harm, but it had prevented her from living. And in the end, she had failed, for harm had found her anyway. Now her weakness could be used against her.

Imagining a judge and jury raised new terrors, but she thrust them aside. That was tomorrow's problem. Today she must hold herself together long enough to meet Lord and Lady Blackthorn.

Fifteen minutes later, she nearly changed her mind. Going down to breakfast meant donning Lady Blackthorn's complicated gown. Even leaving off the stays — a garment she had never worn — she couldn't dress without help. The ties were in the back, and pins anchored the shoulders — odd, curly pins she wasn't sure how to fasten.

Her own clothes were simple round gowns with drawstrings at the neck and bodice. She'd designed them so the drawstrings tied in the front, allowing her to dress without assistance. It had been easy to modify her mother's gowns to fit her. They had been Grecian — simple muslins draped over a minimum of underclothes. Judging from this gown, fashion had become more elaborate.

"This is ridiculous," she muttered as she twisted, trying to reach a tie. She'd thought that if she could fasten the basics, Jack could do the rest. After curling in his arms while she bared her soul, she could surely remain calm while he fastened a few pins.

But she couldn't reach the ties.

If you can't deal with a maid, how do you expect to meet your hostess? demanded Hutch.

"Jack promised that the Blackthorns were trustworthy."

Yet their servants aren't?

She cursed. Her fears were ridiculous. Did she honestly think a servant would slit her throat or brand her with burning coals? This wasn't France.

"Jack?" she called, opening the door a crack.

"Yes?" He stood outside as if on sentry duty.

"Can you summon a maid?" Her voice shook.

"Immediately." He signaled a footman at the end of the hall.

Relief washed over her. Jack was not going to leave her unprotected for an instant. She thanked him, then practiced deep breathing until the maid arrived.

Expecting a stern harridan, she was surprised to see a cheerful girl of fifteen. Marianne barely had time to wonder if

Jack had chosen her, before chatter diverted her attention.

"I'm Daisy, Miss Barnett. It's wonderful, it is, to see you recovered. Lady Blackthorn asked me to look after you, but she wasn't sure when you would feel well enough to rise."

"Is she up, then?" It couldn't be much past eight. "I hope I haven't disrupted the household."

"Oh, no. Her ladyship keeps country hours at Wyndhaven, though I've heard tell she sleeps as late as any in town. But here, she's up with the sun."

"What is she like? I've never met her."

Daisy hesitated. "I've only been in service for a year," she admitted, "so I don't know the lady well. But she keeps a close eye on the staff. Knows our names and families. Shows appreciation for our work. My cousin Kate is at Dobson Grange, and her mistress is quite different. Looks right through the staff without seeing them, never has a kind word about anything, and turns off anyone who displeases her, no matter how minor the fault."

"Which probably makes it difficult for your cousin to care about her position."

"A truer word I've never heard." Daisy pinned a tuck in the bodice to improve the fit — Lady Blackthorn had a more generous bosom. "Kate swears she's going to next month's hiring fair."

"I wish her luck." Marianne wondered if Jack needed any servants, but the thought fled when Daisy's hand brushed her neck. Only biting her tongue stopped a scream.

The girl continued to chatter as she pinned and tucked, but Marianne no longer heard the words. Not until Daisy stepped back, head tilted as she studied the gown, did Marianne relax.

"That should do for now, miss. If your own clothes don't arrive today, I will take up that hem so it don't brush your feet. This year's fashion bares the ankle."

Heat washed Marianne's face. She could hardly alter Lady Blackthorn's gown, yet she had nothing else to wear. There was no sign of her own clothes — considering yesterday's illness, that was hardly surprising. If Jack was wary of sending for her servants, he would be even less willing to fetch her wardrobe.

But that was for later. She had survived Daisy's touch without drawing attention to her problems. It might seem a small matter, but it was more than she'd thought possible. Jack's voice echoed. *A little effort will build the confidence to put the past truly behind you*. He was right. Her fears were mostly habit. The prospect of being locked in an asylum staffed by rapists made most of them fade into insignificance. She would conquer the rest and convince a judge of her sanity. Only thus could she honor her family.

"Shall I do something less severe with your hair?" asked Daisy. Marianne had pulled it into a knot low on her neck.

"Perhaps tomorrow. For now, I need some breakfast." She had not eaten since breakfast yesterday, and she'd lost much of that.

Drawing in a deep breath, she opened the door and took Jack's arm.

Jack kept one eye on Marianne as he escorted her to the breakfast room. She was pale — even more than when they'd spoken earlier — but she seemed calm. Her minutes with the maid had actually steadied her.

Tension seeped away. He hadn't realized how fearful he'd been. Urging her to call on a villager she'd liked as a child was one thing. But taking her to a strange house and thrusting her amid people she'd never met . . . His actions could have hurt her beyond redemption.

So far that hadn't happened, but they'd chosen Daisy because her cheerfulness and youth made her nonthreatening. The next step would be harder.

"Ready?" he murmured, pausing with his hand on the breakfast room door — the footman had been sent away this morning.

Marianne nodded, though fear flashed through her eyes.

"You will like Angela," he added. "She is not the least bit haughty — Lady Barnett's opposite in every way." He opened the door.

Angela was alone, by design. She jumped up when they appeared, hugged Jack in greeting, then motioned them to the table and served loaded plates that had been kept warm above steaming water. By the time she resumed her seat, Marianne had relaxed.

So had Jack. Each new hurdle was as much an ordeal for him as for her. Though instinct had sent him to Wyndhaven, he no longer trusted it, for even his intuition was tainted by bad blood and could be led astray. But this time he'd been right. Angela was a perfect mentor for Marianne.

Which was good, for another problem loomed large. His eyes were so heavy with fatigue that he could barely keep them open.

"Thank you for your hospitality, Lady Blackthorn," said Marianne softly. "I can't think it is easy to have a stranger arrive without warning."

"Nonsense. Two guests are no trouble at all. Besides, I would do anything for Jack. He supported me when everyone in society turned their backs."[1]

"Fustian!" snorted Jack. "I did nothing but dance with you a few times. Devall's investigation and your own angelic character turned the tide."

"Not fustian. Who was it who rallied so many officers to my defense? Who convinced Brummell to support me? And who turned his influence to redeeming Dev's reputation?"

"What happened?" Marianne's voice was stronger.

"My mother," said Angela shortly. "When I came out two years ago, she tried to force me into a match with a brutal madman — who happened to be wealthy, titled, and loved by all."

"Society loves brutality?"

Jack scowled at Angela. Atwater's face

[1] See *Devall's Angel*, Signet Regency 1998

had fooled many, which was not a subject Marianne was ready to handle.

Angela ignored him. "Few looked past his pretty face until I turned him down. He nearly drove me from town, but Jack and Dev exposed him as a scoundrel, saving my reputation and teaching the London gossips a lesson. Jack is very good at such campaigns."

Jack's face heated. "I'm no saint, Angela. They would have reached the same conclusion without me. Besides, that is ancient history." He deliberately changed the subject. "Marianne asked me about Locke's treatise on the effect of agricultural reform on the tenant class. I haven't had time to read it, but I'm sure you have."

The ploy worked. Angela had indeed read the paper — she and Marianne were much alike. Both had unusually broad educations. Both had spent years secluded in the country. And they were the same age.

The discussion grew spirited as it moved to other topics. Jack relaxed as Marianne forgot her nervousness in the joy of finding someone as well-read as she. Her eyes were bluer than he'd ever seen them, and though she didn't yet smile, she willingly debated the merits of Peacock's most recent novel, *A Headlong Hall*. It was like watching a flower unfurl for its first day in the sun.

He thrust the image aside and concentrated on suppressing another wave of lust. Every glance recalled the feel of her cradled in his arms on the long ride to Wyndhaven or nestled in his lap as she'd cried. His thighs still felt her weight. His fingers knew her soft skin and silky hair. Her taste lingered —

This was no time for desire. If he'd kept an eye on Marianne as he should have done, he would have discovered Barnett's plot years ago. Rectifying his negligence was an honorable goal, but it could never counter murder — for which he must still atone. So he had no business lusting after her.

He set his tankard on the table and stifled a yawn. It would be time enough for sleep when he was sure Marianne was safe.

Angela noticed. "You look exhausted Jack — and no wonder. You were up all night."

Marianne's head whipped around. Her eyes widened as she examined him. "I never thought — You need sleep, Jack. You were tired enough yesterday." She blushed.

That kiss. "I slept when I returned to

Seacliff," he said.

"Not long, I'll wager. You reached Carey's only two hours behind me. Did you sleep at all last night?"

"He did not," swore Angela. "Go to bed, Jack. You are no good for anything when you are this tired."

"Yes, go," added Marianne.

He raised his brows to ask if she was sure.

"I'll be fine." She nodded firmly.

So he left.

Marianne hid her clenched fists as Jack rose from the table. He was so kind that it was easy to be selfish. But she couldn't ask that he push himself beyond endurance. It was time to manage on her own.

The trip to Wyndhaven must have been difficult. She had no idea how far they had traveled, but it would have taken hours. He would not risk remaining near the asylum. Complicating the trek were the battles he must have fought at Carey's and being burdened with a body during a long night journey. When he'd come to Halworth yesterday — had it really only been yesterday? — he'd shown all the signs of a sleepless night spent drinking. So she kept her expression calm until the door closed behind him.

Then she sagged.

Trust Angela, said Jacques. *She won't hurt you.*

Listen to him, added Hutch. *You are safe here.*

Perhaps, but emotion rarely followed logic. Taking a deep breath, she looked at Lady Blackthorn.

The marchioness was a beautiful woman whose stunning auburn hair set off moss-green eyes. Her morning gown seemed simple enough, but Marianne's newfound knowledge detected an even more elaborate system of pins and ties than on the one she wore. The gold-hued muslin set Angela's face glowing, and cunningly embroidered vines seemed demure even as they drew attention to her generous bosom.

Lady Blackthorn's character was probably just as deceptive as her gown, no matter what Jack claimed. A man accustomed to the horrors of war would think any lady harmless. Angela could undoubtedly be formidable, but today she had chosen informality, exuding an aura of relaxation Marianne had never before encountered. And discovering that her hostess was at least as well-read as she made Marianne wonder if her image of society was wrong.

To prepare for taking charge of Halworth, she had read widely about crops, commodity prices, and anything else that might affect her estate or tenants. The newspapers also contained society news, which she perused so she would know enough to venture out if necessary. But it left the impression that society ladies disdained intellectuals. It was another reason she had been content to remain at Halworth, for she would never have felt comfortable talking to people who derided her interests. Now she suspected she had misunderstood. So she asked.

"Educated women are called bluestockings," Angela said frankly. "It is not a compliment in some circles — current fashion ridicules intelligence. Thus most of us stick to gossip in ballrooms and drawing rooms."

"Isn't that dishonest?"

"No. We also attend intellectual soirées and scientific lectures, making no attempt to hide our activities. And Madame de Staël was eagerly received all over London when she visited last year."

"The author?"

"Exactly — and a renowned intellectual.

But when I sit in Lady Beatrice's drawing room, I follow her lead, which restricts my remarks to gossip and scandal. No one knows more about society than she."

"Ah. The hostess sets the tone for any event."

"Exactly. Formal balls — even subscription balls like Almack's — are other places with light conversation. When I came out, I despaired of finding a congenial husband, because most Marriage Mart events disallow serious subjects."

"So how did you manage?"

"Luck. I met Dev in a bookshop. He'd been banished from society long before — though that misunderstanding has now been rectified, thanks to Jack — so I would never have met him at a ball." Mischief gleamed in her eyes, but Marianne refrained from asking why. Learning about society was necessary if she was to prove her reason, but asking about Lady Blackthorn's courtship was too personal.

Angela laid down her fork and rose. "You will need several other gowns, Marianne — I may call you that?"

Marianne nodded.

"Good. And I am Angela. I hate formality at home."

"This gown is plenty," protested Marianne. "At home I rarely change clothes except for gardening."

"Horrors!" Angela shuddered, then laughed merrily. "You cannot appear at dinner in a morning gown. Nor can you wear the same thing for a week."

"A week!"

"At least. Dev says we will soon leave for London, but even Mademoiselle Jeanette cannot outfit you in a trice. The local dressmaker has no talent, so you cannot shop until we reach town."

Marianne's head was reeling, but she pushed thoughts of London aside. Jack would explain when he awoke. For now she must concentrate on relaxing with Lady Blackthorn.

"Come," ordered Angela. "We have much to do."

Marianne hesitated. "I cannot impose on you for more than a dinner gown," she said firmly.

"It is no imposition. I will be replacing most of my gowns soon anyway — Dev is active in Parliament, so we spend half the year in London. Thus I need an enormous wardrobe, all in the current style. Dev insists."

"But —"

Angela must have seen the shock in her

eyes. "I had trouble accepting the necessity at first, too," she admitted. "My brother inherited a pile of debts, so my wardrobe before marriage was quite limited. It was a shock to discover that a marchioness is expected to set styles, but I've become used to it. The profligacy became easier to bear once I realized that it benefits the lower classes."

"Really?"

Angela laughed. "Sarcasm! Wonderful. You are finally relaxing. I feared you would flee — Jack would hang me for sure if I drove you to such desperation."

Marianne shook her head as she trailed her hostess up a broad staircase.

"But to answer your question, yes. Replacing my wardrobe every year helps the lower classes. First, by keeping my modiste in business, thus supporting the dozens of seamstresses she employs. Second, by contributing to my maid's retirement fund — she sells my castoffs to a clothing dealer in London, then invests the income."

Marianne was speechless.

"By custom, one's maid lays claim to discarded clothing. It is one of the benefits of her position — or his; valets have the same arrangement with their masters."

Marianne nodded, but inside, she grimaced. There was much about everyday life she didn't know.

"The next to benefit, besides the clothing dealers themselves, is the merchant class, for secondhand clothing provides them with stylish wardrobes they could not otherwise afford. In turn, their old clothes go back to the dealer to be sold to the lower classes, often more than once. Ultimately, the remnants go to rag pickers to be turned into paper."

Angela's explanation had carried them upstairs to her dressing room. Marianne stared. At least fifty gowns hung on pegs or lay stretched on shallow shelves. Others were neatly folded into wardrobes. She had never imagined one person owning so many gowns. Her own wardrobe had never held more than four, even before her parents' deaths. There had been no need for more.

"You see?" said Angela. "I won't miss a dozen gowns. Have Daisy alter them as needed. And if you still feel guilty," she added as Marianne shook her head, "then give them to my maid as soon as you replace them with your own. I will be ordering at least that many when we reach London and replacing the rest for next year's Season."

Marianne remained overwhelmed, but she allowed Angela to choose two more morning gowns, three dinner gowns, a walking dress, a carriage dress, a cloak, and two nightrails. Each had matching slippers, gloves, and other paraphernalia that left her light-headed. Was this how Cinderella had felt after the encounter with her fairy godmother?

The wardrobe expedition tired Marianne enough that she returned to her room with a book from Lord Blackthorn's extensive library. It wasn't cowardice, she assured herself. The strain of too many new experiences atop yesterday's shocks and a hefty dose of laudanum had worn her out.

And she did not remain alone for long. Half an hour later, Daisy arrived to fit the new gowns and chatter away about the household. Marianne heard about Blackthorn's son, Lord Harbrooke, now sixteen months old and the apple of his papa's eye. She heard that Angela was again in an interesting condition, though it did not yet show. And she heard that Jack was beloved by the Wyndhaven staff, though his last visit had been shortly after Napoleon's first abdication. It was impossible to stay nervous in Daisy's company.

That afternoon, she donned one of the altered gowns — an elegant Indian muslin embellished with rows of ruching around the neck, hem, and puffed sleeves — then joined Angela in the drawing room. Angela was pouring tea when Jack arrived, accompanied by a satanic figure who could only be Lord Blackthorn.

His title fit him perfectly. The sharp planes of his face made her think of thorns. And he was not only dark in his own right, with black hair and weathered skin, but he dressed in black from head to toe, the starkness broken only by his cravat and linen. This was a man capable of anything.

She couldn't help herself. She flinched.

"So this is your neighbor," he said to Jack, ignoring her reaction. "I'm pleased to meet you, Miss Barnett." A smile changed him to approachable.

"Thank you for your hospitality," Marianne managed without stammering.

"You are welcome to stay as long as you wish." He turned to his wife with a question about how she had spent her day.

Jack joined Marianne on the couch. His eyes were clearer after his sleep, though next to Blackthorn, his red and gray uniform seemed almost garish.

"Are you all right?" he asked softly. "This must be difficult."

"Not as hard as I thought it would be," she admitted. "Angela is everything you claimed, and more. It is impossible not to like her." Even as she spoke, she cast a nervous eye at the marquess.

"I knew you would get on. You are very alike." He glanced at her gown. "Nice. I see you've had a busy day."

"Exhausting. Angela is far too generous."

"As is Devall. Trust him." He patted her shoulder, then turned to his friend. "Tell Marianne what we were discussing just now."

"About Lady Barnett?" Those peaked brows rose so high they nearly disappeared into his dark hair.

"Yes. She should understand that it was not her fault that Barnett Court offered her no comfort."

"Ah. You can rest easy on that score, Miss Barnett," said Devall, taking a chair near the fireplace. "I have met Lady Barnett and her unholy brood several times, thanks to these two meddling in my affairs. The moment society accepted me back, the woman sicced her oldest daughter on me. I had to flee town to escape." He scowled fiercely at Jack.

"It was time to set the record straight, and you know it," said Jack calmly, then turned to Marianne. "He had been hiding from the world for years, refusing to fight for his rights after society ostracized him for no good reason."

Marianne read the message in his eyes. Jack thought she was doing the same thing, hiding in the comfortable but lonely world she had created. And perhaps he was right. Today had been far easier than she had expected. When had she changed?

Devall shook his head. "I cannot imagine a more ill-suited person to care for a child awash in grief. Lady Barnett is cold to the bone. Having no emotion herself, she cannot abide it in others. And she is the most selfish woman of my acquaintance."

"Don't exaggerate," said Angela. "My mother is worse. Lady Barnett has worked tirelessly to find husbands for her daughters. It is not her fault that their dowries are inadequate and their characters are worse."

"I might quibble with that analysis, for their faults arise mostly from aping her, and their dowries were much larger in the beginning. But I was not exaggerating. She

187

cares nothing for the girls and wants them out of her life as quickly as possible — she bristles at snide remarks blaming her for rearing two brace of spinsters. Suitable marriages would stifle her critics and allow her to resume her quest for social power. Lacking maternal feelings for her own offspring, she would have cared even less for a girl not of her blood."

"What do you mean?"

"Jack told me that you were silent the entire time you were in France, but that you collapsed into hysteria when you arrived at Barnett Court. Is that true?"

"Yes. I knew no one at the house. My father and uncle had long been estranged, so I had never met the man."

"And Barnett left immediately?"

She nodded.

"I suspect that Lady Barnett shoved you out of the way the moment you started crying. Did she banish you to a remote part of the house?"

Again she nodded.

"And if you did not obey when ordered to be quiet, she undoubtedly punished you."

"She has a heavy hand," Marianne admitted, then blushed. She had not meant to say that. She had offered so much

188

provocation during her month at Barnett Court that she could hardly blame the woman for trying to subdue her.

"That does not surprise me. She was the worst sort of person to take charge of a grieving child. But her antagonism was not your fault." He straightened, changing the subject. "You will remain here until we discover Barnett's plans. Once he learns that you are no longer at Carey's, he will likely press for an immediate hearing on his petition, using your flight as evidence against you. We must be ready to mount a defense."

"I'm not sure I can," admitted Marianne.

"You can." His eyes bored into hers, filling her with unexpected courage. "We will leave as soon as we discover where that suit will be heard — probably London, but it is possible that he filed in Essex, or even Dorset. Use the time to speak to everyone you can. My staff is harmless, so you need not be nervous. But the more practice you have in meeting others, the easier it will be to handle the not-so-harmless men you must face in London."

"We will start in the stable," said Jack, helping Marianne to her feet.

She froze. "I ca—"

"Yes, you can. I know stables make you nervous, but the reason is obvious. The smell reminds you of France. One of the benefits of discussing that day is that it makes everything else easier. Knowing what causes the fear will allow you to separate it from the stimulus."

"Very well. I will try."

But her knees were so weak that she could barely follow.

Chapter Ten

Three days later, Devall summoned Jack and Marianne to the library.

She had become accustomed to his appearance and had learned to relax with both him and Angela, which confirmed that her aversion to Craven was not a general problem. While she must remain wary of those associated with Barnett, she needn't automatically fear other men.

It was a liberating conclusion, and not only because it promised a chance to lead a normal life. Many of her fears were fading. She no longer jumped when a servant appeared. This morning she had not needed deep breathing before she could summon Daisy.

Yet some terrors remained. Her first expedition to the stable had been a spectacular failure. Her hysteria had ended in a swoon. Jack swore that practice would help, but three more tries had elicited the same response. She couldn't force even one foot over the threshold.

The prospect of going to London wasn't much better, though at least those fears were rooted in logic rather than emotion. London was dangerous for a single lady who had no father or brother to protect her — and not just from social disgrace. The newspapers decried London's rampant crime. Footpads lurked on every street. Females who ventured forth alone could be abducted and sold into brothels. Some neighborhoods were so unsafe that ladies could not enter, even in daylight when accompanied by sturdy footmen.

It sounded too much like France, so she was praying that her sanity hearing would be scheduled in Dorset.

"Is there a problem?" asked Jack once the butler closed the library door behind them.

Devall sat behind his desk. "Nothing we didn't expect. Fitch just returned from London."

"What did he learn?" Marianne forced the words from a suddenly tense tongue.

"Many things. To begin with, Barnett sold his town house last week to cover his son's gaming debts — proof of how badly he's dipped. He submitted a petition to Chancery a fortnight ago requesting full control of your affairs, citing your unsound mind. Until the hearing, he is staying at Ibbetson's."

"He must be in trouble, indeed," said Jack, then turned to Marianne. "Ibbetson's is the cheapest hotel with any claim to gentility. It is a favorite of vicars and schoolboys."

"Oh." What a come-down for a viscount.

"Fitch discovered a number of interesting facts," said Devall, returning to the subject. "To begin with, Barnett has heard nothing from Carey."

"Nothing?" Jack's surprise was clear.

"Nothing. Carey was supposed to send a report on Marianne's condition by now. Without a diagnosis, Barnett will have to produce Marianne for examination by a court-appointed panel, so Carey's silence has moved beyond irritating. Several men commented on his snappish behavior."

"I wonder if Carey's staff is searching for her so he can hide her escape."

Devall shook his head. "I doubt it. His no-visitors policy has bothered me from the moment you mentioned it. If even family members are kept away, how does anyone know the patient's condition? He could continue collecting fees long after the patient died or ran off."

"That's awful!" Marianne exclaimed.

"Agreed." Devall's eyes flashed. "I must look into the matter. Madness should not leave anyone at the mercy of an unscrupulous charlatan. And a stupid one at that. Not writing the diagnostic report must attract attention from Barnett and the court."

"Unless he denies that she was ever there," said Jack. "If the court questions his diagnosis and demands a second opinion, Carey would have to produce Marianne. I already raised a huge fuss over her admission, then left two employees trussed up in beds. Carey may decide to wash his hands of the entire business. But we can consider him later. When is the hearing scheduled? I assume it will be in London, since Barnett remains there."

"Friday," said Devall. "I was hoping for next week. Locking you up eliminated the need to rush, for you could no longer squander your fortune."

"Perhaps he fears that Carey might claim my fortune when the trust reverts on grounds that he is now my custodian," suggested Marianne.

"Then why leave you with Carey at all?" asked Devall.

"Lack of foresight. Papa always claimed that his brother never considered consequences. Barnett probably didn't think of it until Carey failed to send his diagnosis. The new fear might be contributing to his unease." Marianne forced calm over her voice, though the prospect of going to London turned her insides to jelly.

"There is no need to debate what Barnett thinks or what Carey might have done," said Jack wearily. "Let's concentrate on the case."

"I can try to have the proceedings delayed a week on grounds that you wish to mount a defense," offered Devall. "But I may fail, for I've no official standing."

"Thank you," said Jack. "However, we can't count on a delay. Marianne must be ready to appear in three days."

She stifled a moan.

Devall spotted her distress. "He's right, Marianne. You have no choice. And court will not be the only problem. Barnett is busy shredding your character to society."

"How?" asked Jack.

"By trumpeting Marianne's madness in very exaggerated terms. Few people question his claims, for he damages his own reputation and that of his family with every word. You know how people react to any hint of insanity."

"Damned greedy bastard," muttered

Jack. "Marianne will have to face down society as well as the court. Letting this fester even a month will make it impossible to root out. Can you force him to recant?" he asked Devall.

"Not before Friday. He needs money too badly. And I've foresworn my old tactics, so would have to use reason — which takes time."

Marianne flinched. "He will never recant, for he truly believes me mad," she admitted. "And why would he not? When he accosted me at Halworth, I reacted worse than twelve years ago. He is not a man who easily admits fault, so changing his mind will be very difficult."

"I thought you did not know him," said Jack.

"Not personally, but I have been trying to recall everything I heard about him from the staff. I was rebellious as a child, often escaping the nursery to run wild in the park or eavesdrop on the servants. Thus I often heard them telling new maids or footmen about the family."

Jack shook his head, but the corners of his mouth twitched.

Marianne turned to Devall. "Two tales demonstrate the problem. Barnett arrived at Halworth one day wildly excited about an investment opportunity. He wanted Papa's support, for together they could put up enough to earn a higher return. Papa refused, claiming the scheme was a fraud. Barnett left in a huff. Within six months, he'd lost everything. Only his expectations kept him out of debtor's prison. Not until he inherited the title did he recover."

"Ouch," murmured Jack.

She nodded. "Another time Papa warned him to avoid a certain merchant's daughter. Barnett laughed at his concerns, but within a week the girl trapped him into marriage. I don't know if either incident contributed to their rift, but it is clear that Barnett clings to his own course even when others point out the pitfalls."

"That was a long time ago," said Jack. "Even if he won't admit it aloud, Barnett must know by now that his judgment is unsound."

"I doubt it," said Marianne. "While I rarely see real people, reading gives me insight into human nature. Many men refuse to accept responsibility for their problems, finding something else to blame instead — Fate, Lady Luck, a friend, a relative, their horse . . ."

Devall chuckled. "Astute observation."

"Barnett blamed Papa. And Papa's success at making money increased his fury. As did his marriage to a lady he loved."

"Envy," murmured Devall.

"Or jealousy," said Jack. "Discovering that his brother left everything to Marianne instead of him must have been the last straw. He probably transferred all his hatred to her."

"To give him his due, he could have locked me away years ago," said Marianne. "While he terrifies me, there has to be some element of honor in his heart. It would have been easy to have me declared insane when I turned twenty-one." The realization steadied her. Barnett was family, after all.

"True," agreed Devall. "But honor is no longer a factor. Even the best men abandon it when their backs are against a wall. Between them, Barnett and his heir have squandered his entire inheritance, and this time, there are no expectations to hold off his creditors. Without your fortune, he will lose everything but the entailment. According to Fitch, Barnett's debts are double this year's entire income. Selling the town house did nothing beyond cover Harold's latest gaming losses."

"We can argue Barnett's level of villainy another time," said Jack. "The immediate goal is to prepare for the hearing. Can we keep him from discovering that we mean to mount a defense?"

"I wouldn't count on it," said Devall. "We will have to file a counter-petition. Barnett's barrister is certain to hear about it."

"Then we cannot expect surprise to throw him off balance. How many witnesses can he produce?" He looked at Marianne.

"Craven will be the strongest, for he visits Halworth four times a year. I cannot spend more than a minute in his company without falling apart."

"Why?"

"I don't know, though I suspect he is deliberately provoking hysteria. He stands very close, breathing in my face — his breath is very foul — then touches my arm in a way that makes my skin crawl. And his voice hisses." She shivered.

"Is that all?" asked Devall.

"That is all I can identify specifically, though just the sight of him makes me want to flee. He feels evil. I could probably manage better with time to prepare, but his visits always occur without warning. He does not even allow Hastings to announce him."

"Mrs. Hastings believes that he wants to seduce you," said Jack. "Your combination of beauty and innocence casts a powerful lure."

Marianne stared. Was that why Jack had kissed her?

"There is also the lure of your inheritance. Seducing you would force you into marriage, giving him control of your fortune," he added. "Mrs. Hastings described him as a disgusting beast. Has he ever struck you?"

"Once." She wrapped her arms around her shoulders to warm the sudden chill. "But I hit him first. He'd sneaked up behind me and grabbed my arm." His arm had also brushed her breast, shocking her into the worst burst of hysteria she'd suffered in years.

Jack nodded. "You instinctively know he is dishonorable, so you use fits to drive him away. It's an unusual weapon, but formidable."

"Good heavens!" She stared. Could she be that devious?

"Craven has been waging war against you for years," said Jack. "The most important rule of war is that victory is all that matters — war is no place for niceties. Another rule is that the only practical weapon is the one at hand — in your case, hysteria. Your stay at Barnett Court had proved that it alienated others."

"Which is why we can't use it now," said Devall, breaking into their discussion. "The current battle is for respect. She can't win if her weapons subvert her goal. But send for her staff. If Barnett doesn't know she escaped, he will have no reason to watch them. Their testimony should discredit Craven. And it might reflect badly on Barnett for employing the man — to say nothing of his neglect."

Jack nodded.

"Who else might Barnett produce?" Devall asked Marianne.

"The Halworth guards. They witnessed last week's fit. And it's possible that Barnett will produce his family. Lady Barnett swore that I was mad from the moment I arrived on her doorstep. I attacked at least one of my cousins when in the throes of nightmare — possibly more, for I have little memory of those days."

Jack flinched, again berating himself for leaving without even speaking to Barnett. "Hardly unusual," he said. "And I doubt their testimony would carry much weight. Those events occurred twelve years ago, just after you had witnessed the butchery of your entire family."

Marianne gasped. "I said nothing of b-butchery."

Jack cursed himself for losing control of his tongue, but it was too late to recall the word. "When you described their deaths, I realized that I had seen them. I stumbled across two such scenes before meeting you in France. Do not think of their ends," he added when she paled. "By then, their spirits had moved on to a better place and had no further use of their bodies."

"You sound as if the two are separate."

"They are. One of the first lessons war teaches is to distinguish the man from the body. In life, they seem as one, but death divides them. The spirit leaves, no longer caring what befalls its former home, for the vacant body is of no more importance than a broken wheel or shattered sword. When the battle is finished, we bury the shell in memory of the man who once inhabited it, but the depredations of war cannot harm the spirit. The same is true of your family. They await you in the hereafter, whole and at peace, uncaring of the hurts inflicted on their flesh."

She nodded.

"Are those all the witnesses he might produce?" asked Devall, returning the conversation to the point.

"Unless he sends for someone from Carey's or produces his staff to corroborate my behavior. But I was barely at the Court a month. Only Craven and Barnett have seen me in the years since."

"I doubt Carey will corroborate anything. We can counter tales of those early days by explaining Marianne's distress," said Jack thoughtfully. "They attributed it to madness, because her behavior seemed too extreme for grief. But they did not know how her family died. Nor did they understand the terror she experienced afterward. Escaping France was not a simple jaunt up to town. Not until we touched England's shore did I believe we would make it."

"Are you saying that your testimony will counter everything Barnett can produce?" asked Marianne.

"It might raise doubts, but even the word of a military hero would need corroboration," said Devall.

Jack flinched. "Which means finding Miss Dubois. Have you any idea where she is?"

"I never really knew her," admitted Marianne. "She was young — not yet twenty — and had only been working for

Mama for a few months. I didn't even know about her family until after mine died."

Jack frowned. "I escorted her to an aunt's cottage, but I don't recall the direction — somewhere near Kensington, but that was twelve years ago. She didn't even reveal her true name, calling herself Clarisse."

"That attack revived her own childhood terrors." Marianne turned to Devall. "Her father, Comte Dubois, was killed by a mob when she was seven. When she saw what was happening at the inn, she feared for her life — either as a hated aristocrat or as a traitor for serving the English."

"Have you any idea what the aunt's name was?" asked Devall.

Marianne shook her head. "We rarely spoke before that day. Afterward, we said only what was necessary for the journey. She feared that someone might overhear us and ask questions."

"Fitch will find her family."

"But not before Friday," said Jack. He met Marianne's eyes. "Can you manage a hearing before a stern judge and sarcastic barristers in a room filled with strange men? Barnett's barrister will poke and prod you, hoping to trigger a fit. The judge

204

will censure him for such tactics, but if you react, he will remember."

"I don't know," she said honestly. "These last three days prove that I am stronger than I thought, but this hearing will determine how I spend the rest of my life. I will be terrified even before anyone speaks to me. And you know that some of my fears are very real. Even you can't talk me into a stable, no matter how hard I try."

He was right that odor was the problem. One whiff of hay and she was back in that loft, pelted by her mother's screams. If Barnett's barrister thrust a clump of hay in her face, she would fall apart.

"Then we must delay the hearing and make it harder for Barnett to prove his claims," said Jack.

"How?" Devall raised his brows. "I can try for a postponement, but my power is limited. Society may have welcomed me back, but my reputation persists in some circles, and my fight for reform in Parliament has made new enemies."

"A change of venue will put Barnett on the defensive and place the onus of proof in his hands rather than ours," said Jack. "Chancery handles wills and contracts and other civil matters, but it can't rule on marriage, so Marianne and I will wed immediately."

She choked.

Jack ignored her. "Marriage will terminate his guardianship, removing the legal standing he now enjoys. Chancery will throw out his petition because he is no longer an interested party. If he wishes to continue the battle, he can file for an annulment on grounds of insanity, but that case would go to the ecclesiastical court. It will take more than claims of hysteria to prove madness there. The bishop favors unions. And he does not move quickly, which gives us time to find Francine Dubois and prove that Carey is a charlatan, raising questions about Barnett's motives."

Marianne's mood changed from euphoria to shock to terror so quickly that she nearly slid to the floor. "But you c-can't want —" She stuttered to a halt when she met Jack's eyes. Determination blazed in their depths. So did apathy. Her stomach turned to ice.

"It is a novel approach, but something you should discuss in private," declared Devall, rising. "Let me know what you decide."

Marianne barely heard the door shut. Jack still intended to kill himself, so this proposal meant nothing. But the cause of his melancholy was more elusive than ever. Devall and Angela considered him the finest man they knew — honorable, caring, and a damned good soldier — which explained his offer. Hadn't he just expounded his philosophy of war? A good soldier used the best weapon available. In the battle against Barnett, that weapon was marriage.

His next words echoed her thoughts. "Marriage is your only chance, Marianne. We cannot find your witnesses before Friday, and you are too nervous to carry the day on your own. We can investigate Barnett's finances further, but finding evidence that would sway a judge takes time. Most of what we know is gossip — not compelling under law, I'm afraid. So your only hope is to force Barnett to start over in a new court. Marriage would also terminate your trust, preventing the trustees from releasing your assets to Barnett in anticipation of the court ruling."

"They would never do that."

"How do you know? Have you met them?"

"Of course not."

"How often do you correspond with them?"

"They send me quarterly statements, and they send books whenever I ask for them." She frowned. "That's odd. I should have received a statement last week."

"But you didn't. Barnett probably convinced them to pay for Carey's evaluation, preparatory to his court case. It wouldn't have been hard. Conservative bankers do not believe women can handle money. Since you never married, they would consider it in your best interests to let Barnett manage your affairs. How much is in the trust?"

"The estate and several investments."

"What investments?"

"I don't know. Consols, I expect. And possibly a few shares Papa had before he died. The statements are very simple — a list of my expenditures with the notation that the excess income was reinvested. They send money to Hastings each quarter to cover staff salaries and household expenses."

Jack stared. "That can't be right. Bankers revel in details. They should tell you to the last pence what you have and where it is. There should be a list of income by source and another list of shares bought and sold."

"Maybe it is because I am a female —

don't forget that I was only twelve when the trust began. No one burdens children with financial details — especially females — so they kept the accounts simple. I never complained, so they had no reason to change." She shrugged, though she was kicking herself. She had expected to engage a man of business to oversee her investments, but that was no excuse for ignorance. How did she know the trustees were honest?

"Write to Hastings. The staff should come to London so they are available to testify — they can corroborate that Barnett is a liar, for example. And tell Hastings to bring all your financial statements. It's time to audit your accounts."

She glared at him, though he was right. She should have demanded an audit years ago — certainly when she came of age. "Very well."

"Good. But none of this will help unless we postpone the proceedings, and that means marriage."

She shook her head. Before they could discuss his proposal, he had to understand that marriage was more than a weapon. "I know you were planning to fall over the cliff that day, Jack."

He blanched. "You can't have known —"

"Of course I knew. It would have been obvious to the most simpleminded child. If you hadn't been so mired in melancholy, you would have realized that. So don't think you can use marriage to defeat Barnett, then stage another accident. I won't stand for it. If we go through with this, you had better plan to face me across the table for at least fifty years."

He rubbed his hands over his face as he paced the floor. Time stretched. Finally he met her gaze. "All right."

"Whatever possessed you to jump, anyway?"

"Nothing that matters now," he said wearily, then added, "Don't press, Marianne. There won't be another accident."

She frowned. Both tone and eyes seemed honest, yet she sensed that something was still wrong. But he had clearly closed the subject. And he'd promised. Jack would never break a vow.

"You have two choices," he continued, deflecting further thought. "You can marry me tomorrow, or you can walk into that hearing on Friday with little chance of winning. Bishop's Court has very stringent standards for annulment suits. They hate setting aside vows. And unless the bishop truly believes you are mad, Barnett has no standing, for his guardianship ends with your marriage."

Marianne paced to the window and back. Jack's honor was getting in the way of his sense — her fault. When she had asked him for help, she'd had no inkling that the situation would explode out of hand so quickly. But having vowed his help, he would do anything to provide it — even marry an emotionally crippled stranger. War made for strange alliances — on both their parts.

She had no wish to wed where there was clearly no love. Her parents had shared a rare communion that she had dreamed of repeating. Yet Jack was right. If she appeared in court on Friday, she would surely lose. And marriage might let her help him. If it was a good weapon against Barnett, it was an equally good weapon in her war against Jack's melancholy. Surely as his wife, she would have a better chance to discover the cause.

But if she cured his melancholy, would he resent her? Being tied for life to so heavy a burden might give him a new reason for suicide. No one could want a wife as inept as she — lacking social graces, ignorant of all but basic manners, unable to function without clinging to his arm. How could she ask him to sacrifice everything to save her from an asylum?

He promised not to stage another accident, Hutch reminded her. *This isn't a whim for him.*

Which meant they would have a lifetime together. She shivered at the thought, for Jack was the dearest man she had ever known.

That's not saying much.

Perhaps not, but he was special. Few men would bother helping someone like her. And even fewer would go to such extremes.

Maybe he wants your inheritance, too.

Marianne nearly smiled at the absurdity. The one absolute was that Jack had no interest in her money — or even her estate. Seacliff had come with a fortune, and someone preparing to die had little use for worldly goods. But it was a question they must consider.

"Won't marriage give Barnett a new weapon against me? He will accuse you of scheming for my fortune, then claim that my acquiescence proves that I am incompetent to manage my own affairs. A hurried marriage will cast doubts on your testimony anyway, and charges of avarice can only make that worse."

"We can claim that the betrothal is of long standing, with the actual wedding moved up because of his abduction. And he will look foolish when he discovers that everything remains in your name. Marriage is necessary to obtain the delay we need, but I cannot deprive you of the independence you have been anticipating."

"Wha — How? Everything goes to you if we wed. The trust was established as a dowry, terminating upon marriage. It only reverts to me if I remain unwed at twenty-five. But even an elderly spinster loses control of her possessions upon marriage."

"True, but I can create a new trust, naming you as sole trustee and beneficiary with the right to appoint your successor. That will give you complete control."

"It seems you have thought this out."

He nodded. "I suspected that Barnett would take his petition to trial before your birthday. It is clear that you are not ready to face him. This is the only course that gives you more time."

He made it sound inevitable, and perhaps it was. If only he cared for her. But she doubted that he did. Jack was a warrior. Once he embarked on a campaign, he cared only for victory and would do whatever was necessary to achieve it.

Then why did he kiss you?

Her lips tingled at the reminder. But one kiss meant nothing. He had been trying to entice her away from Halworth and had been drunk enough to think that seduction might help.

Yet the hope that he might care remained. Perhaps they could build a reasonable partnership. Friendship was a good foundation, more than many couples had.

She still feared that he might circumvent his promise to stay alive, but she had to consider marriage as the serious step it was — not merely a quick solution to an immediate problem, but a commitment for life. Jack would make a good husband once he banished his demons. To be worthy, she must banish her own.

Two long breaths set her mind at ease.

"Very well, Jack. I accept. But I hope you know what you are doing. Winning in Bishop's Court means we can never annul this match."

"Thank you, Marianne. You have made me the happiest of men." He placed a chaste kiss on one cheek, then squeezed her hand and left.

Chapter Eleven

Standing at the window on his wedding night, Jack watched a carriage race around and around Grosvenor Square, its lanterns dancing wildly as it clattered across the cobblestones. He could identify with its occupants, for his life was on a similar journey to nowhere. And today had been the most bizarre yet.

After Marianne had agreed to the only counteroffensive he could devise, Jack had sent Jones back to Essex to investigate Barnett in greater depth, then dispatched a letter to Poole. It enclosed Marianne's letter to Hastings and ordered Poole to fetch her staff and send them to London without alerting the guards.

Fitch had returned to London to open Blackthorn House, procure a special license, and find Francine Dubois. Devall had sent others to investigate Carey, gather detailed evidence of Barnett's finances, and enlist the aid of his most powerful friends to counter Barnett's gossip, lest society reject Marianne before giving her a chance. Barnett was probably using the gossip to keep Lady Barnett at home. He had no need to hurt Marianne, who would never hear the stories if he was successful in court.

To avoid spending the night at an inn — something Marianne was not ready to face — they had risen well before dawn and set out for London. The journey had been arduous, making him grateful that Marianne had been unconscious the night he'd brought her to Wyndhaven.

Marianne had tensed as they'd approached the carriage, clearly bothered by the horses, though once inside, she was able to relax. But the first time they'd stopped for a fresh team, she had nearly fallen apart. He could only pray that Barnett had not recognized her aversion to stables. She had already been so hysterical from the abduction that he might not have made the connection.

Jack had stayed in the carriage with her at each stop, holding her, murmuring soothing sounds, and burying her face in his coat so his scent could dispel the memories. Twice, he had stopped well away from villages so they could walk through meadows and spinneys, as they had so often walked at Halworth. It had seemed to help.

By the time they'd reached London, both had been exhausted, but Jack had immediately fetched a vicar. Within the hour, they were wed. Come morning, he would launch the next phase of their campaign.

Jack closed the draperies, blocking further view of the still-circling carriage. He had no idea what its drunken occupants were doing, but a wager doubtless lay at the bottom of it. Number of circuits in an hour, perhaps. Waiting until the wee hours reduced competing traffic.

Marianne was asleep in the next room. At least, he hoped she was asleep. Old fears might be keeping her awake, nightmares brought on by the hard journey. But he couldn't go to her. Nor would she expect it. Claiming her would revive her terror.

He cursed. Even a kiss had precipitated flight, so he dared not consummate the marriage — not that he could risk inflicting the Caldwell weaknesses on another generation anyway. But Marianne didn't need to know that. She was still too fragile. Revealing that her white knight was a dishonorable rogue with the blood of a thousand felons flowing in his veins would destroy her growing confidence. So he would have to work harder to hide his own problems.

He couldn't believe she had read his mind so clearly yesterday. How could he have been so careless? Masking his thoughts was a habit he'd learned in childhood, yet she had known that marriage meant little because he would be gone as soon as she was safe.

The condemnation in her eyes haunted him, stripping away the platitudes to expose the ugly truth — suicide was dishonorable, even if disguised as an accident.

Yet it was necessary.

He shook his head as he poured brandy. As long as he had lived in honor, an honorable path had always been available. Now that option was gone. His own dishonor tainted everything he touched. Suicide might add a new stain to his soul, but it was better than bringing shame to the army he had served so long.

Yet marriage made suicide more difficult. He must see that Marianne was strong enough to weather the gossip his death would provoke. And protecting her was more important than protecting a name already renowned for scandal, so he must admit his guilt publicly. If anyone suspected the intention behind an accident, they might blame her, tarnishing her reputation. Confession had other benefits, too. People could rejoice at the end of the Caldwell line, for no Caldwell was worthy of life.

I know you miss Charger, Reeves had said the day he'd found ten-year-old Jack weeping in the stable. *But he broke his leg. When the problem can't be fixed, it's best to end the misery. You would not want him living in constant pain.*

He faced the same fate. His breeding couldn't be fixed, so he must end his misery.

He shuddered.

Marianne's eyes had pinned his during their brief wedding ceremony, as if daring him to make their marriage real. Something in those blue-gray depths had stirred his senses, reviving the lust he'd felt in the forest.

It was far too easy to imagine her in bed, her breasts nestled snugly in his palms as she writhed beneath him. That kiss still haunted him, her taste so achingly sweet that his soul clamored for a repeat. And the image of her clad in nothing but a thin shift was etched on his mind.

Her breasts were firm globes topped with rosy crowns that would harden into ripe berries under his lips. Her waist was slender, begging to be spanned by caressing hands. Those long legs — his mouth watered at that memory alone — met in a luxuriant pelt of tawny curls several shades darker than her hair.

His shaft swelled, pleading for a taste of what was now his.

But he couldn't. Marianne was a beautiful woman who could lighten his spirits merely by being there. He wanted her more than he had ever wanted anyone. But he could not take her. He had to stay as far from her as possible, and not just to avoid making a child. Attaching her affections would make his death more painful for her.

He finished the brandy, then reluctantly undressed. He had to sleep if he was to manage tomorrow's business. Winning the first battle meant little, for Marianne would remain at risk until the war was over and Barnett vanquished. He would need a clear head.

Which wasn't likely, he acknowledged. Nightmares were inevitable after the turmoil of the day.

Reviewing tactics had calmed him in the past, so he listed the most urgent steps he must take on the morrow. The first was to notify her trustees of her marriage and demand an audit. If Barnett had withdrawn so much as a farthing, the trustees would have to recover it or face charges of malfeasance. Richard's will forbade access to the trust by Lord Barnett — a copy of the document had been on Devall's desk when they'd arrived, compliments of Fitch's efficiency. It explained why Barnett hadn't killed Marianne after losing his original suit. The residual beneficiary was a school.

Then he must see his solicitor, set up Marianne's new trust, and revise his will so she would inherit Seacliff and his own fortune. It would not atone for the unpleasantness of his death, but it would protect her from blame and prevent his family from benefiting from his demise.

Notice of his nuptials must go to Barnett, the newspapers, and the Chancery judge. If there was time, he would take Marianne shopping. She needed her own wardrobe. Angela could choose styles and colors, but he must be at hand when the dressmaker measured her.

Few aristocrats were in town this time of year — which was a godsend — but he must introduce Marianne to society as soon as she was fashionably clad, starting with Lady Beatrice, the most avid gossip in England. Gaining her support would nullify the rumors Barnett was spreading and protect Marianne's reputation from further claims.

In the meantime, he must sleep.

Marianne lurched upright, stomach churning as she gasped for breath. What had awakened her?

"Move . . . break, damn you! . . . *Out of my way! . . . No!*" Gasps and pants interspersed the shouts and sobs, the whole coming from Jack's room.

Grabbing a dressing gown, Marianne rushed to the connecting door, praying that it was not locked.

Jack had escorted her upstairs after dinner, kissed her lightly on the forehead, then left her alone. She had known that their marriage was merely a weapon against Barnett, but his indifference still hurt. She wanted a real union with a chance for a real future. But though he'd been as caring as possible on the interminable journey to town, he'd grown increasingly aloof in the hours since they'd arrived. By the time he'd deposited her in this room, a wall of ice had separated them. Did he think her mad after all? She was beginning to think only a madwoman would have agreed to this farce.

But he hadn't been gone five minutes when the truth slammed through her head. While he had vowed not to stage another accident, he'd said nothing about deliberately blowing his brains out. He still meant to die. In the meantime, he would keep her at arm's length so she wouldn't grieve. Idiot!

Don't let him, Hutch had ordered.

"I can't watch him every second," she'd whispered in despair.

Then change his mind.

Easier said than done. How could she change the mind of a bullheaded, mule-hearted warrior?

She'd fallen asleep without finding the answer.

Now Providence offered hope. Not only was the connecting door unlocked, it stood open a crack, as if he'd checked to see that she was safe. It was a start.

Another shout filled the room. She flew to the bed where Jack thrashed in agony.

"Shh," she soothed, shaking his shoulder. "Wake up, Jack. It's only a dream."

He froze.

"Wake up, Jack," she repeated softly.

"Marianne? What are you doing here?" He blinked as she pulled the draperies open to let moonlight into the room.

"You were dreaming — and shouting."

"What — what did I say?" He was still groggy. Perspiration stood out on his forehead, though the room was icy.

"Why don't you tell me?" She pulled a chair close to the bed and sat. This might be her only chance to learn what bedeviled him. When awake, he kept his defenses up. And now that his nightmares had attracted attention, he might well move to an isolated bedchamber. Blackthorn House was huge.

"I don't remember."

"You've never lied to me, Jack, so don't start now. Talking about problems reduces their power."

"Hah!"

"That's a direct quote from you. And it worked. Telling you about that day opened the door to healing. If you had not forced me to discuss my family's death, I would still be hiding in a mental closet, terrified of everything new or different."

Jack swore under his breath. "You have enough nightmares of your own. You don't need mine."

"But yours would not affect me. You don't share my nightmares."

He said nothing.

"Talk," she ordered. "Or should I summon Devall? You cannot think he would be harmed by your dreams."

Pain ripped across his face, making her wonder if perhaps he was right. But she could not save his life until she knew what threatened it. This had to be it. Anything powerful enough to drive a man like Jack to suicide had to cause nightmares.

"You don't know what you are asking," he finally said. "I doubt that my nightmares would invade your dreams, but it would pain me to lose your respect."

"Jack." Shaking her head, she grasped his hand with both of hers. "You are the most honorable man I have ever heard of. Nothing you say could diminish my respect."

"Then your imagination is woefully lacking," he snapped, trying to retrieve his hand.

She refused to release it. "Tell me what is wrong, Jack. I do not believe for an instant that it is as bad as you think. You are turning a mote into a tree."

He snorted. "Marianne —" Another

choking sob burst out. "You don't understand."

"Then explain. I won't leave until you
do. The only way to settle this is to drag
your demon into the light and examine it."

"I can't."

"You can. I know, for I went through the
same process only four days ago."

Jack was silent for a long moment.
Marianne bit her lip to keep from crying at
the anguish in his face.

Finally he spoke. "All my life I've tried
to control the bad blood I inherited from
my father. But one cannot forever outwit
Fate. In the end, blood always wins."

"How?"

He glared. "I murdered a fellow officer,
then fled the field like the veriest coward."
His voice rasped with pain.

"No. You would never do that, Jack."

"Do not turn me into a saint just
because I led you out of France." Extri-
cating his hand, he turned his back.

"Do not allow one incident to negate a
lifetime of good," she riposted.

"You don't understand."

"Then tell me. Everything. You cannot
expect me to believe such tripe without
evidence. My God! That is less convincing
than the claim that I am mad. What hap-

pened? When? Why?"

"I don't know why," he admitted, rolling halfway back so he could stare at the canopy. "Much of the day is hazy, and some of it is completely blank."

"Are you speaking of Waterloo?" She moved to the window, knowing that Jack would speak easier if she was not watching him. Grosvenor Square was empty save for a cat slinking across the central garden.

"Yes. It was the worst battle I've faced in fifteen years of war. The carnage was unbelievable." His voice shuddered. "I spent the morning at Wellington's command post, analyzing reports and writing orders. But the battle lines stretched nearly two miles, making communication difficult. Several couriers went down in the early charges, so staff officers were often pressed into carrying messages. I hadn't worked as a courier in years and had forgotten how terrifying it is." He paused to inhale deeply several times. "About six hours into the battle, I left with orders for the 95th. They were already delayed. Colonel Morrison, another of Wellington's aides, had been killed trying to reach the 95th an hour earlier. That much I remember clearly. And the terror."

"Terror is understandable," she said

softly. "I've read accounts of the battle, all making it clear that the danger was extreme. A man who doesn't feel fear in such a situation must be very cold-blooded. I've also seen sketches of the lines, so I know that they were far from straight. You doubtless cut in front of our troops rather than circling behind, where it would be safer."

"True. Speed was essential. Wellington wanted them to move so the next French attack couldn't divide our forces. That bend made the line vulnerable. I cut across a field littered with debris."

Marianne glanced over her shoulder. He had shut his eyes, but his face twisted in pain.

"The casualties were awful — heaps of bodies, and rivers of blood that made the muddy ground even more treacherous. As usual, it had rained heavily before the battle. I can't recall Wellington fighting a major engagement on dry ground. Wellington weather, we call it. Morrison's body was there, half hidden under his horse."

Marianne shivered, but said nothing. Jack's voice had gone distant as his mind retreated to the battlefield. She dared not interrupt him now that he was finally talking.

"He was always so full of life." Again Jack sobbed. "If someone of his vitality could fall, what chance did the rest of us have?"

Marianne made a soothing sound.

"Terror was clogging my throat, but I kept going. The message was already late. I passed others I knew. That piece of ground had been fought over all day, so it was thick with bodies. And the French were massing for another attack." He cleared his throat. "I was spurring my horse when he went down. I thought he'd stepped in a hole — the field was riddled with cannon-balls and torn up by cavalry — until I saw his side. He'd been hit. The fall dislocated my shoulder badly enough that I couldn't move my arm."

He flexed his left hand as if confirming that it had recovered.

"I wanted to mourn — or at least hasten his end, for he wasn't yet dead. Charger had served me well for six years. But there was no time. I had to continue on foot." He stopped.

"What happened?" she asked after a lengthy silence.

"I don't know. The next clear memory is waking in a barn, surrounded by groaning men. The pain was incredible, and not just the shoulder. My side hurt so bad I could barely breathe." He rubbed a spot just below his ribs. "And I thought they had cut off my leg. Nothing but amputation should hurt like that. Only two images of the battle remained — stabbing a British officer in the back and fleeing the field in terror."

"Did you ask about them?" she asked, returning to her chair.

"I couldn't."

"Then how do you know they are real? They could have been the product of a nightmare or images formed from words spoken nearby."

"No. It was me. It fits too well. After years of denying my breeding, in the end it was too strong."

"Fustian!" she snapped.

"Stop ignoring facts," he ordered.

"I'm not. You are so busy wallowing in guilt that you haven't given me any facts."

"I told you —"

"You described a nightmare that came while you were out of your mind with pain. Where is the evidence?"

"In my head. Those are memories, not dreams. You, of all people, should know how memory can cause recurring nightmares. And no dream could conjure up those emotions. I've never felt such a frenzy as when I killed that man — I must have gone mad. And the terror that drove me from the field could only have been an attempt to escape punishment."

"All right. I will concede that those two flashes might be memory. But I do not believe your interpretation. There has to be another explanation."

"No."

"Did you ask anyone for the details?"

"Do you want me to tell the world what a blackguard I am?" he countered angrily.

"Jack." She again took his hand. "Don't exaggerate. You could do any number of things to find out what happened without revealing your fears. Who was the officer?"

"I don't know. All I see is the back of his uniform coat."

"Then how do you know he is English?"

He glared. "The uniform belonged to a Hussar."

"But was the Hussar wearing it?" She caught his gaze. "Perhaps it had been borrowed by a Frenchman so he could slip close."

"You read too many of those horrid novels," he snapped.

"And you are stubborn beyond belief. Have you forgotten that you were wearing a French uniform the first time we met? You apply reason to other cases — like pointing out that I was not responsible for my mother's illness, since half of Paris was suffering at the same time. Yet you refuse to apply logic to your own situation. How can you accept guilt for something that may not have happened?"

"It happened."

"But I would wager my entire trust that it didn't happen the way you think. If it wasn't a spy masquerading as an English officer, then it must have been a traitor."

"What?"

"Think about it. Why else would you kill a comrade? You are the most honorable man I know. Deep-rooted honor doesn't disappear in an instant."

"I would like to think so, but blood always tells in the end. My father is a coward, as was his father before him. Between cowardice and his scandals, his name has become a byword. Surely you've heard of the Earl of Deerchester. You've lived in Dorset all your life."

She nodded, again struck by pain over the image of Jack growing up under his influence.

"My brother is worse," he continued. "Wilcox is vicious as well as cowardly."

"I've seen no mention of him in the papers for some time," she murmured.

"Three years. It was the most dishonorable duel on record. He fired before the signal, killing his opponent, wounded the second when he tried to appease the foul, then fled to Italy to avoid arrest. There he defrauded at least two noblemen and engaged in a series of duels, the third of which was so badly done that he was run out of the country. The last we heard he was somewhere in North America, terrorizing their frontier."

"But that has nothing to do with you."

"You aren't listening. The blood is there."

"Why? Your father might be rotten to the core, but what about your mother? Her blood also flows in your veins. Remember our discussions about sheep breeding? Introducing new bloodlines dilutes weakness."

"Not always. Caldwell traits are so strong that they have survived for centuries. My ancestors were weak, scandal-ridden cowards, every one. I tried to change, but in the end, I failed."

"No, Jack." She squeezed his hand. "The only evidence of cowardice I see is your refusal to look for the truth. I dare you to investigate. Find out what really happened so you can stop torturing yourself."

"I have all the proof I need," he murmured as his eyes closed. "My thigh was shattered from the back as I fled the field." He slid into sleep, his hand going lax.

"But your side was hit from the front," she muttered, staring at the spot he'd rubbed. She tucked the coverlet around him. "Idiot!"

She had to find someone who knew what he had done between his fall and his injuries. He was too stubborn to do it himself.

The side wound countered his thigh, so neither proved anything beyond the brutality of war. By his own admission, he'd been between the allied and French lines when his horse went down. He had likely been shot by both sides.

Many people could not recall the accidents that injured them, so Jack would likely never remember. She doubted he had reached the 95th before being hit, though that told her nothing of where he had been or what he'd been doing. But a man on foot in the open would have made an enticing target, so he couldn't have gone far.

She gazed at his face, now deeply asleep with no sign of dreams.

Biting her lip, she returned to her room. How was she to discover anything useful?

The quest seemed impossible. She could barely tolerate strangers and fell apart near horses, so how could she investigate an incident that had occurred on the Continent four months ago? Yet she had to try. She owed Jack more than she could ever repay. He was her husband — warmth suffused her heart at the thought — and she would do everything possible to see that he remained with her.

It was long before she could again find sleep.

The next afternoon, Lord Barnett hunched over his hotel's poor excuse for a desk, reviewing the latest figures from his creditors. The total made his stomach churn. But tomorrow would see an end to his troubles. Maybe. If the day's mail did not contain Carey's report, he would have to postpone the hearing.

It had been a mistake to take Marianne to a Dorset asylum, he admitted. He should have rented a job carriage for her and brought her to Bedlam. Even if Carey's report arrived in time, the judge might demand an evaluation from a better-known doctor. But delay would be costly.

In another two days, he would have to leave Ibbetson's or talk the trustees into another advance.

"Craven!" he bellowed as a door opened to the adjacent room. "Where is the mail?"

His secretary instantly appeared in the doorway, two missives clutched in his hand. "Here, my lord."

"From Carey?" The question was automatic, though he feared the worst. The man had made his diagnosis before Barnett left the asylum, so his delay in writing the report could only arise from laziness.

"No, sir."

The top letter was from his solicitor. Barnett opened it and cursed. Marianne's trustees were demanding immediate repayment of the thousand guineas he had withdrawn to cover her expenses at Carey's.

It has come to our attention, they had written, *that Miss Barnett is of age and thus is the only one empowered to request trust funds. In the absence of a letter from Miss Barnett authorizing the withdrawal, we will expect repayment in three days.*

"Damnation," he muttered. "Where the devil am I to find a thousand guineas?" Five hundred had gone to Carey, with the rest covering filing fees, his two most pressing creditors, meals, and a two-room suite in this run-down hotel.

The next paragraph was worse. *Pursuant to terminating the trust, we will also need a list of Miss Barnett's most recent expenditures so we can prepare the final accounting.*

"What the devil?" They knew the hearing was tomorrow, after which he would assume full control of her affairs. He wasn't about to question expenditures. "Damn all bankers to hell," he muttered. They were far too particular — and for no good reason.

He frowned. Perhaps they wanted this letter on file as evidence that they had been winding up the trust and were not in collusion to prevent Marianne from squandering its assets. But they should have warned him.

He slammed the letter on the desktop and stalked about the tiny room, praying that their demands were merely legal double-talk. Surely they didn't think his suit was doomed. Had the judge decided to postpone the hearing or cancel it entirely?

Several minutes of reviewing the case and everything that had led to it convinced him that all was well. This was just over-zealousness from a pair of stuffy bankers.

In control once more, he skimmed the

letter a second time. The three-day deadline was the key. They knew the matter would be settled in his favor tomorrow. He had nothing to fear.

Setting the letter aside, he opened the other missive and immediately collapsed. Fury grew until red haze obscured his vision.

With cheeky informality, Colonel John Caldwell announced his marriage to Marianne. Then he thanked Lord Barnett for serving as Marianne's guardian and congratulated him on obtaining freedom from a responsibility that must have been quite onerous.

An eternity passed before shock gave way to questions. How had she escaped Carey's? Why had Carey failed to report that escape? How had a girl so deranged she couldn't function made her way to London? And how had she come to Caldwell's attention?

He cursed. *Colonel* Caldwell. Obviously a half-pay fortune hunter who had taken advantage of Marianne's madness to steal her estate. But it would be hard to prove. Euphoria over Waterloo still gripped the country. High-ranking officers were considered gods —

Caldwell.

He frowned. Caldwell was Deerchester's family name. Was there a connection? If so, the colonel's honor was dubious at best.

A rap on the door distracted him. Craven answered, then handed him yet another letter, this one hand delivered from his barrister.

Hilliard informed him that Chancery had canceled tomorrow's hearing. Marianne's marriage meant that Lord Barnett was no longer an interested party. Her trust was now in Caldwell's hands, and her mental condition was Caldwell's problem.

"He won't get away with this," Barnett growled, again prowling the room. "I'll see his fortune-hunting soul in hell. He's no better than that black-hearted Wilcox. I'll be damned if I let that family fleece me again. They've taken me for the last groat."

Caldwell's letter had been posted from Blackthorn House. Barnett hesitated, for tangling with the Marquess of Blackthorn could be fatal, but he had no choice. He'd see Caldwell in jail for fraud if it was the last thing he did.

His first step must be to recover Marianne, so she could receive the help she so obviously needed. Then he must file for an annulment of this ill-conceived marriage and have Caldwell arrested for his crimes. Caldwell must have kidnapped Marianne. How else could she have reached London? But to find her, he must have been stalking her for some time.

An hour later, Barnett glared at Blackthorn's footman.

"Mrs. Caldwell is not at home," the man repeated.

"I am her uncle and guardian," Barnett snapped.

"She is not at home to callers."

"Then take me to Colonel Caldwell."

"He is not at home."

"The marquess?"

"None of the family is at home to callers at this time. If you leave your card, the marquess will schedule an appointment at his convenience."

Barnett detected a smirk under the footman's impassive face. He wanted to force his way into the hall, but a butler and two other footmen stood in the background, as if waiting for a chance to throw him bodily into the street.

Defeated, he headed for his barrister's office. If Caldwell wanted war, he would get it, even if waging that war meant mortgaging Barnett Court. Without control of his brother's fortune, he would have to mortgage it anyway.

Chapter Twelve

Marianne spent Friday morning at Mademoiselle Jeanette's shop on New Bond Street. The first hour passed in teeth-gritting nervousness, but Jack's comforting presence and the lack of any discernible threat finally allowed her to relax.

Angela was in her element, perusing stacks of pattern cards, fingering fabrics, and discussing trims and details with Jeanette. She occasionally consulted Jack, but never Marianne. They all knew that she understood little of current fashion.

That was made more obvious when she relaxed enough to take in the procedure. There was more to ordering gowns than she'd dreamed. Even the question of color needed careful consideration.

"Not green. Blue," Jeanette insisted after Angela handed her a pattern card with the suggestion that it would look best in green Georgian cloth. "Blue turns madame's eyes the color of the sky. *Voilà!*" She draped a length of fabric around

Marianne's neck.

"Lovely," murmured Jack.

Jeanette covered the blue with a length of green. "But green turns her eyes gray. Lovely in candlelight, but not outdoors, *n'est-ce pas?* And toilinette makes a better walking dress this time of year. Save the Georgian cloth for spring."

"Very well, but you do agree that we should modify the braiding to make it less military. With the war decidedly behind us, styles will quickly soften."

"*Oui.* Excellent suggestion."

Marianne felt stupid as she sat silent as a statue. She let her attention stray to Jeanette's fashionable establishment.

Angela had described Jeanette as the best mantua-maker in London, so Marianne wasn't surprised to find the place crowded. Assistants raced back and forth with piles of fabric and trims. Maids bustled about with tea and cakes, disappearing into some inner fastness to collect wine whenever a gentleman appeared. Half a dozen customers were placing orders. It didn't take long to realize that receiving Jeanette's personal attention was a great honor, bestowed on someone of her insignificance only because Angela was a marchioness.

A baroness and her daughter sat at a nearby table choosing gowns for an upcoming house party. From their conversation, Marianne deduced that they had come to London primarily to shop. A dowager complained that current fashion bared too much of her thick ankles and was quickly assured that a flounce would distract the eye of any observers. In another corner two sisters debated the merits of lace versus ribbon.

"If Madame Caldwell is ready," said Mademoiselle Jeanette, recalling Marianne's attention, "Nicole can measure now." She gestured to a door that had just disgorged a beautiful matron.

Marianne met Jack's eyes. His smile reminded her that Jeanette's staff needed her business, so they would not hurt her. Taking a deep breath, she headed for the fitting room.

Jack had remained aloof since she'd shaken him awake two nights before — hardly a surprise. He abhorred weakness, so would regret his revelations. But at least he was here for her today.

Facing Nicole and an anonymous under-assistant alone was her hardest test yet. To keep her mind from the hands brushing her body, she focused on the voices in the

243

next room. Two young ladies were laughing together as they fitted their new gowns.

"Beautiful," remarked one. "You were right about using point lace on the sleeves."

"If only Mr. Carstairs likes it," sighed the second. "But I'm probably doomed. His eyes strayed to Miss Oberon again last evening. He will never see me as aught but Robert's baby sister."

"Stop moping, Sarah," demanded her companion. "No one could mistake you for a child in that gown. For all its propriety, it draws the eye exactly where you want it." She giggled. "But haven't you heard? Miss Oberon is in the briars this morning."

"What happened, Mary?" Anticipation lit her voice.

"Scandal, my dear." Fabric rustled. "She abandoned all manners after you left. Mr. Carstairs was appalled."

"But what did she do?"

"First she threw herself at Sir Reginald Northridge and followed him outdoors — he was the highest-ranking gentleman present, you might recall, so it was obvious that she was hoping to attract his interest and raise her consequence. She didn't return for at least half an hour. But things must not have proceeded as she'd hoped, for when her mother remonstrated with her, she lost her temper, shouting that she was no longer a child. Then she flounced off in a huff, bumping Lady Matthews and nearly knocking her into the punch bowl."

"Heavens! How could —"

Marianne lost track of the conversation as the under-assistant shoved her arm aside so she could stretch a tape around her chest. She stifled a shudder.

". . . far too cold for alfresco dining," Sarah was saying. "But Robert talked Mama into driving out to Richmond anyway — he swears the food at the Star and Garter is beyond passable. Mr. Carstairs will be there, and you must come, too."

"Only if you include Mr. Eppincote," said Mary slyly.

"Really? I never suspected a thing."

"There may be nothing, but he seems most intriguing. And very capable. I told you how he scattered those horrid dogs who attacked me last week."

"Yes, but —"

"It was the most romantic rescue. The slavering beasts were lunging as if they would make a meal of me. Mama's maid was utterly useless — all she did was cower and shriek. But Mr. Eppincote drove the dogs off with his cane, then walked me home, making me feel, oh, so safe."

"So you said," murmured Sarah.

"Well, yesterday I saw him approaching on Piccadilly and was preparing to thank him again when Lawrence Delaney's team shied — that boy has no business riding, let alone driving. How many accidents has he caused?"

"Robert swears hundreds, but he always exaggerates," said Sarah. "What happened?"

"Heroics, thank heaven. The horses were heading straight for me. I'd taken a footman along on the outing, but he was of no more use than the maid. I might have died without Mr. Eppincote. He rushed into the street and grabbed Delaney's team, calming them before they could reach the pavement. I thought I would faint from relief, and everyone else exhaled so loudly I vow they raised a breeze. Delaney was furious, of course, but he slipped as he jumped down to blister Mr. Eppincote's ears and landed face first in the gutter."

"Eewww!" exclaimed Sarah, then burst into laughter. "But I wish I could have seen that. It serves him right."

"He looked positively awful," giggled Mary. "His face — But you can imagine what it was like. Mr. Eppincote assured himself that I was safe, again escorted me home, then invited me to drive with him in the park this afternoon. I do hope Mama lets me wear this new carriage dress."

"That is the last measurement, Madame Caldwell," announced Nicole, recalling Marianne's attention. "As soon as I fasten your gown, you can go."

Marianne shivered. There wasn't an inch of her body that hadn't been pinched or prodded, but she had survived without breaking down.

Yet pleasure in that accomplishment faded as she passed the adjacent fitting room. Sarah and Mary were now speculating on Colonel Caldwell's mad wife . . .

She was still shaking when she rejoined Jack and Angela. The order had grown to thirty gowns in her absence. Dresses for morning, evening, balls — did he know that she'd never learned to dance? — opera, walking, traveling . . . It was obvious that he intended to push her into society. Her mouth dropped as he added a court dress.

"I can't," she moaned under her breath.

Jack smiled. "Of course you can. We can't formally present you, as there are no drawing rooms scheduled just now, but Carlton House is hosting a dinner for Wellington next week. Since I'm in town, I must attend, and you must join me. Think of it as practice for facing the bishop."

"You expect me to meet England's Regent?" she choked.

"You will be fine. There is nothing frightening about the man. He may be Regent, but he is also fat as a flawn, creaks when he moves, and dresses like a cub despite being well past fifty. He won't speak to you above a minute, if that, and will confine his remarks to wishing you well."

She had no choice but to agree. Yet it was the last straw for her nerves. Hysteria bubbled up until she could barely contain it.

Jack noticed. "Time to go," he announced, rising, then addressed Mademoiselle Jeanette. "Do you have the information you need?"

She nodded, then huddled with Angela while Jack helped Marianne with her cloak and bonnet.

"You've done very well, my dear," he murmured in her ear. "A real trooper.

Jeanette will collect an assortment of slippers, hats, and whatnot for you to approve later."

That was what Angela was arranging — another special service available because of her rank. Sighing in relief, Marianne nodded and tried to focus on two new shoppers, who were laughing over a tale about an obese lapdog who had tried to seduce a svelte terrier in the park that morning. But her brain was too fuzzy to follow the words.

A clock chimed as she followed Jack outside. Four hours had passed since they had arrived. No wonder she was tired.

A voice behind them made her jump.

"Jack! How wonderful to see you recovered."

Marianne turned. The speaker's tawny hair raged in a tousled mane around a tan face dominated by golden eyes. Powerful shoulders and legs added to the impression of a lordly lion. A tan coat and buckskin breeches completed the illusion.

"Damon." Jack paled, his tone harsh enough to chip ice.

Marianne tensed. Was this an enemy? Yet Damon had addressed Jack as informally as Jack addressed Devall, and his obvious pleasure indicated long acquaintance — even close friendship.

Jack visibly pulled himself together to make introductions. "Marianne, this is Damon, Major Lord Devlin. Damon, my wife. And I believe you know Lady Blackthorn."

"Wife! When? Did I miss an announcement?"

Marianne flinched. Was the idea of Jack marrying so odd?

Idiot! hissed Hutch. *They probably served together for years.*

Of course. *Major* Lord Devlin. If he was a friend, he would have expected to stand up at Jack's wedding. But Jack had doubtless cut all ties with his military friends after Waterloo. If Devlin had come to Blackthorn House, Jack might have refused to accept the call.

At least Jack looked uncomfortable at being caught out. "The announcement is in today's papers. We married Wednesday, very quietly." Realizing that his rudeness needed an explanation, he added, "If I'd known you were in town, I would have invited you, but I thought you would be home by now. How long has it been since you've seen Devlin Court?"

"Seven years, though I stay in touch with the steward." He hesitated as if unsure what to say next. "How is the leg? I've not heard from you in some time."

"How very interesting." Angela glared at Jack. "We hadn't heard from him in some time, either, until he showed up on the doorstep last week. Why don't you explain your sudden lack of courtesy, Jack." She pulled him around to face her. When he tried to withdraw, she insisted.

Marianne nodded as another fact fell into place. Jack had been cutting himself off from all friends, convinced that he was no longer worthy of their respect. But the friends would rather help than let him go.

She examined Lord Devlin more closely. He was more open than Devall, and possibly less haunted, but she sensed the same honorable core. And he had served at Waterloo. Yesterday had produced no ideas for investigating Jack's nightmare. Now . . .

The only practical weapon is the one at hand. Jack's own words. Marriage had revealed his problem, but she needed a new weapon to solve it.

Her plan was risky, but to help Jack, she must trust her instincts and Devlin's friendship. Jack was so disgusted with his family's weaknesses that he would never befriend a dishonorable man.

A glance showed that Angela held Jack's

attention, so Marianne beckoned Devlin closer. "Jack is suffering, but not from his leg," she whispered. "I need help if I am to heal him."

"What do you mean?" He, too, kept his voice low, but concern filled his eyes as he glanced at Jack.

"We can't talk here. Will you call at Blackthorn House this afternoon? Jack should be out on business."

His brows raised — even she knew that her request was unusual, if not outright scandalous — but he nodded. "I would like to know you better, for I consider Jack a brother. How long have you known him?"

"He saved my life twelve years ago, but I did not see him again until last month. His estate adjoins mine."

"Ah. I've known Jack since I bought colors seven years ago. He helped me survive the most devastating loss anyone can suffer, then became a mentor and friend. If there is anything I can do for him, I will."

Marianne relaxed.

Damon turned to Jack. "I'm late for an appointment with my tailor, but I'll be at White's this evening. My congratulations on your nuptials."

"What is going on?" asked Angela softly

as Jack bade farewell to his friend. Her snapping eyes were proof that Jack's explanation hadn't satisfied her.

"I'm not sure, but I mean to find out."

She deflected further questions by pleading exhaustion — which wasn't feigned. Climbing up and down cliffs would have left her with more energy than shopping.

Jack helped her into the carriage, the confusion in his eyes replacing the aloofness he'd maintained for two days. She nearly smiled. He'd expected Devlin to cut him on sight, so this encounter had pushed him off balance. And that was good. Devlin's ignorance gave her ammunition in her battle to prove him wrong. If Jack had fled the field, Devlin would surely know about it.

Pleading fatigue, Marianne shut herself in her room until Jack left for another appointment. The moment he stepped into a carriage, she summoned Daisy and changed into a sprigged muslin trimmed in green ribbons. With luck, Devlin would call before Jack returned.

He did. Half an hour later, a footman carried his card to the drawing room.

"Thank you for coming so quickly," she said when the door closed behind him.

"My request was scandalously forward, but you are the only one in a position to help me."

"Help with what?"

She gestured him to a chair. Though she knew he would not harm her, she remained nervous when anyone loomed over her. It had been Craven's favorite trick. Fortunately, manners should keep him seated until she stood. If Angela mentioned this unchaperoned meeting, she would claim that she was testing her progress.

"Am I right that Jack has not responded to recent letters?"

He nodded. "I had nearly decided to visit Seacliff to see how badly he was hurt. Even the thigh should have healed by now, and that was his worst injury."

"It is doing well. His limp is gone except when he is unusually tired. But that is not what plagues him." She took a deep breath, for she knew Jack would condemn her as a traitor if he discovered this meeting. "He will not thank me for talking to you."

"Understood. Jack goes out of his way to help others, even risking his life on occasion. But he has never once accepted help in return. I've never understood why."

"Needing help might be construed as weak, and he fears any sign of weakness.

His father has a reputation for cowardice."

"No one would ever accuse Jack of weakness! He's the strongest man I know, by any reckoning. I've seen him remain calm in situations that would have sent Wellington himself scrambling for cover."

The butler interrupted, delivering a tray with tea and wine. Marianne concentrated on pouring until Barnes left.

Once they were alone, she set her tea aside. "It doesn't matter what others think. Jack believes he harbors his father's cowardice — to say nothing of his brother's viciousness. So he holds himself to a higher standard than others, tolerating no mistakes. And he always assumes the worst."

"What are you saying?"

She paused. "He is plagued by nightmares — something he is unable to hide now that we are wed." Her cheeks burned as she realized what she'd said, but she forged ahead. "They are rooted in his conviction that he behaved dishonorably at Waterloo."

"Absurd!"

"Undoubtedly, but he believes it. Rather than face the world's censure, he cut his friends — you are not the only one who has heard nothing from him lately — and hid himself at Seacliff. Your greeting this morning confused him, for he expected to be cut."

Devlin's face paled. "What the devil does he think he did?"

"He isn't sure, for portions of the battle are a blank, but from the flashes that remain, he concluded that he stabbed a British officer in the back, then fled the field in disgrace."

"Preposterous!"

"Of course. He is incapable of killing without cause, but he doesn't believe that. Living under the pall of Deerchester's reputation — to say nothing of Wilcox's — has convinced him that he is prone to evil."

Devlin cursed. "Now I know what you meant by assuming the worst. Has he lost his wits?"

"No, but he is very stubborn and convinced that his bad blood has finally caught up with him. I refuse to believe he did anything wrong."

"Nor I."

"Good. Then I trust you will help me discover the truth. The nightmares are tearing him apart."

"Surely loving you will help."

"Hardly. Marriage was another of his kindnesses — it was the only way to foil my uncle." She shook her head, regretting the admission, for it raised speculation in Devlin's eyes.

But he said nothing. "What do you want me to do?"

"Find someone who saw Jack on foot during the battle. Discover what really happened. I can think of no other way to prove that his honor is intact. I have learned to know him well, for we have spent much time together since meeting again. Thus I know that honor is more important to him than breathing."

"I will try, but there is no guarantee that I will succeed. Waterloo was a hellhole that left little time to look beyond one's own battle. The chances that anyone can remember one minor incident involving an officer from a different regiment is very small."

"I understand. But I must try. Jack has already saved my life twice, and is trying to do it again. I cannot sit idly by and not repay him."

"Nor can I. If not for Jack, I would have died in Portugal, the victim of carelessness — or worse. There was a period when an honorable death was preferable to a life of pain. My closest friend died in the first battle. I was still reeling when I learned that my entire family had been killed in a boating accident."[2]

"My God! How did you survive?"

"Jack. He took me under his wing, making sure I kept my mind on business. And he sat through hours of maudlin soliloquies as I castigated Fate."

"He's very good at that." She was surprised when her tongue continued speaking. "We met in France twelve years ago. He escorted me back to England after my family was killed by a mob."

"Dear Lord. He can't have been much above twenty."

"About that, but already committed to helping others." She drew in a shaky breath. Amazingly, she had mentioned her family's death without succumbing to tears.

"I will begin asking questions immediately," Devlin said, laying aside his wineglass and further personal questions. "Do you have any clues that will narrow the search? He was wounded in the afternoon, but I've no idea when or where."

"He was sent with a message to the 95th about an hour after Colonel Morrison fell — did you know him?"

"Everyone did. Sad loss, that. His wife is

[2] See *The Unscrupulous Uncle*, Signet Regency 1997

an angel. She nursed most of us at one time or another." He shook his head.

"Jack had just passed Morrison's body, still headed toward the 95th, when his horse went down. The last thing he remembers is continuing on foot. He was in an area between the lines, or so I gathered from his ramblings."

"That sounds right. I will see what I can learn. Most of the troops remain in Paris, but many of the wounded are in London, along with some like me who sold out. If I learn anything, I will call on you. And I'm sure we will grace the same entertainments in coming days. The social calendar is rather thin this time of year."

"So I'm told. Unless you find something definitive, it might be best to meet in public."

The mention of entertainments reminded her that Jack meant to establish her in society. Listening to customer chatter at Mademoiselle Jeanette's had brought home how demanding society was. Embarrassing Jack was a far more likely outcome than falling into hysteria. She might be ostracized in minutes.

As she escorted Devlin to the door, she decided to ask Angela to review her manners.

★ ★ ★

Another day passed. Jack remained aloof, saying nothing about his business or hers. Marianne hadn't heard from Barnett since he'd demanded entry to Blackthorn House on Thursday.

But her fear of meeting people had nearly vanished, as had her concern over Barnett's next attack. Both had been overwhelmed by new fears when she discovered how deficient her training was.

Even basic manners had grown lax after twelve years of living alone, and her schooling had stopped far too soon. She knew none of the nuances of precedence, little about England's aristocracy and how its families intertwined, less about matters of dress, entertainment, and on and on. And though she knew the basics of recent scandals, she knew nothing of the minutiae of daily gossip.

Fortunately, her years of study made it easy to learn facts. Skills were another matter. She hadn't played cards since her family had died. She had never danced. But at least she sketched, did needlework, and could produce common tunes on a pianoforte.

She was studying the steps of a country dance when a footman summoned her to the library. Jack was there with a man and woman she didn't recognize.

"Is there a problem?" she asked.

"No." Jack gestured to his companions. "This is Jones, my batman. And you might recall Mrs. Halsey, who used to be the housekeeper at Barnett Court." He turned to the others. "My wife, the former Marianne Barnett."

They murmured greetings.

He seated Marianne by the fire. "I thought you should hear their story."

Jones looked uncomfortable in this Grosvenor Square mansion. His weather-beaten face belonged outdoors. She looked again at Mrs. Halsey, trying to find some flicker of familiarity, but there was nothing. Hardly a surprise. She'd suppressed all memory of Barnett Court as soon as she'd reached Halworth.

The woman's gray hair disappeared under a black cap. Her gown hung oddly from stooped shoulders. The bluish haze in her eyes spoke of cataracts — a problem giving Hastings increasing difficulty.

"You begin, Jones," ordered Jack.

"I nosed around Barnett Court like you said," reported Jones. "Most of the villagers dislike the viscount on account of him ignoring everyone and raising rents two years running. But they loathe Lady Barnett. They'll talk your ear off if you're willing to listen. The kindest descriptions are *cold, arrogant,* and *selfish.*"

"Did anyone recall Miss Barnett's visit?" Jack asked.

"Not in the village — she was never outside, so few even knew she was there. But they sent me to Mrs. Halsey." He nodded to the housekeeper. "She retired four years ago."

"Mrs. Halsey?" Jack turned to face her. "Do you recall Marianne."

"Of course. The poor mite was overwhelmed by us — screamed loud enough to wake the dead, though I, for one, couldn't blame her, losing her family in that popish place. And Lady Barnett is not one to succor others, no matter how distressed."

"But surely she understood a child's grief," said Jack. "I told her myself that the family had died."

"That may be — I was in the village the day you arrived, Miss Marianne," Mrs. Halsey said in apology. "But circumstances made no difference. I'm not one to criticize my betters, but I must say that Lady Barnett cares only for her own pleasure. And her pleasure is a quiet house where children stay hidden until they are called upon to entertain guests. There is no room for anyone who needs so much as a kind word. It's no wonder her own children are —" She broke off, recalling that her audience moved in Lady Barnett's circle.

"What did she do with Marianne?" asked Jack.

"Tried to ignore her, but the girl couldn't stop crying, even after Lady Barnett struck her."

Marianne flinched, remembering that blow. Mrs. Halsey was opening cupboards in her mind. She had never been struck before reaching Barnett Court. The shock had triggered new tears.

"We finally gave her laudanum so she could sleep, but nightmares woke her soon enough. I was with her, and I must admit, it made my blood run cold. Shouts of blood and knives and who knows what else — I couldn't understand half the words. I feared that her folks had died on one of them head-lopping things —"

"A guillotine?" asked Jack.

"That's it."

"Actually, they were killed by a mob," said Marianne, again surprised that she could say it without breaking down.

"You don't say!" Mrs. Halsey shook her

head. "You poor thing — not that it would have mattered to Lady Barnett. She swore that you were spoiled and seeking attention. Later, she decided you were the devil's spawn."

"Marianne recalls attacking one of the girls," said Jack, drawing her back to her recital.

"It was hardly an attack — one slap and even that wasn't intentional. That Miss Catherine has always been vicious. Now that she's grown, she's worse than her mother."

"What happened?"

Mrs. Halsey thinned her lips. "Miss Catherine hated Miss Marianne, in part because her arrival meant Miss Catherine was no longer the eldest, but mostly because of the attention she received — a room to herself, servants with her night and day, meals on a tray instead of in the schoolroom with the other children. By the end of the first week, Miss Marianne had calmed enough that we no longer had to sit with her — or so we thought." She shook her head. "I checked on her often, of course. But over the next week, her nightmares increased. I didn't understand why until I found Miss Catherine in her room one night. She'd made a game of grabbing an arm or a leg, then ducking out of sight when Miss Marianne woke screaming. I read her a scold, but it did no good. The next night I caught her holding a pillow over Miss Marianne's face — that was the night you slapped her, miss."

Marianne was shaking. No wonder she hated to be touched. Nightmares and torture feeding on each other.

"My God!" choked Jack. "But at least you caught her."

"Not that it did much good." Mrs. Halsey settled more comfortably in her chair. "Miss Catherine swore that she'd been waking Miss Marianne from a bad dream when the girl turned vicious. It would have meant my position to call her a liar. But I convinced Lady Barnett to move Miss Marianne to another floor — presented the notion as protecting the other children from disturbances. Then I put a maid with her all the time."

"Thank you." Marianne was amazed at how different reality was from her memories. She remembered only Lady Barnett's claims that she had attacked her cousin in a mad frenzy. And she'd assumed the maids had orders to punish her if she struck out again. Never in her wildest dreams had she suspected they were there to protect her. It was a lesson she must teach Jack.

"It was all I could do," continued Mrs. Halsey. "I'd intended to tell Lord Barnett when he returned, though it would have done little good — he can never withstand Lady Barnett's pressure. But he took you home without my prodding."

"I appreciate your candor," said Jack. He summoned a footman to show her to a bedchamber. Once the housekeeper was gone, he turned to Marianne. "We will keep her here until the trial."

"Has a date been set?"

"Not yet, but Barnett filed annulment papers Thursday afternoon, right after leaving here."

She grimaced. It was the first time anyone had confirmed it. The charge had to be madness, which, under civil and canon law, would render her incompetent to contract a marriage. Knowing he'd done it made everything seem more real. She suppressed a new wave of dread at the prospect of facing the bishop, then realized Jones was talking.

". . . told me other tales," he was saying, "though she probably thought them too harsh for the lady's ears."

"I doubt there is anything I don't

remember," said Marianne stoutly, though she'd not known about her cousin's abuse.

"Lady Barnett hated noise, so she went to great lengths to force quiet — whipping you, locking you in the wardrobe, binding you . . ."

Jack swore, creatively and long.

"It is over," she said simply, though Jones had revived other memories she'd locked away. And they explained other fears. She met Jack's eyes. "Thanks to you, I have put it behind me."

He nodded, then dismissed Jones so the man could find food and rest. Jack paced to the window and back. "It was far worse than I dreamed. I should have recognized her character and protected you."

"How? Be reasonable, Jack. You were barely twenty, and Barnett was my guardian. Even if you had recognized her character, you had no standing. And what did you know then of coldhearted women?"

"Nothing," he admitted. "I'd met few ladies of quality. I never knew my mother, and the females my father brought home were not ladies. But that is not the point."

"The point is that you are human, Jack, not a god who can see beneath people's masks on five minutes' acquaintance. You had already gone far beyond duty by taking me to Barnett Court in the first place. Many men would have left me in France. The rest would have dispatched me on a public coach the moment we reached England. I still had Francine with me."

"I'm not going to convince you, am I?"

"No. I refuse to beat you up for no good reason."

He shrugged. "At least this supports your case. Anyone hearing Mrs. Halsey's tale must believe that your fits were induced by mistreatment."

"Not necessarily." She had thought long about her situation since reaching London. There was no way to duck the truth. Marriage might have thwarted Barnett for the moment, but nothing they'd done was straightforward. "People might as easily believe that mistreatment pushed me into madness, especially after they learn how my parents died. You can accept that shock is temporary — I'm sure you've seen similar cases on the battlefield — but society believes that women are weak. Thus shock strips us of reason."

"Then what are we to do?" He sounded at a loss.

She laid a hand on his arm. "Continue

the battle. You were right, you know. I must obtain an official judgment declaring me sane. Mrs. Halsey's story — and Francine's, if we can find her — will explain my shock, but only my own demeanor can prove that it was temporary. If I can tolerate the inquisition and remain calm despite provocation, then the bishop must support me. Mrs. Hastings can describe Craven's attempts to seduce me, and Hastings can explain Barnett's ambush. No one will deny me the right to fight off an attack — I hope. But since every one of those stories can be interpreted two ways, it is my own behavior that will determine the outcome."

"You will do fine," said Jack, caressing her hand. "The key is confidence. When we met on the cliff that day, you believed yourself mad. Now you know you are sane."

"Are you sure?" she teased, meeting his eyes. They flared warm.

"Of course. No madwoman could have survived six hours at Carey's without slipping deeper into madness. But you are improving every day. You did not even flinch to discover two strangers in here."

"You did that on purpose!"

"It seemed a reasonable test of your

progress. I was here in case of trouble — but I will not be with you in court."

"I know." Her panic calmed as his hand covered hers. It would be weeks before she need face the bishop. At the rate she was improving, it would be all right.

"And since you are doing so well, we will attend Lady Potherby's musical evening on Monday."

"That sounds interesting," she lied. But at least she had two days to prepare. The sooner she faced society, the easier it would be to meet the bishop.

Jack hesitated, then plunged ahead. "You should know that Barnett is growing desperate. His rumor campaign is worse."

"How bad?"

"Actually, he has reached the point of being preposterous — he now claims that your work as a French spy stripped you of reason."

"As a child?"

"No, during the last years of the war. Devall's friends are countering his claims. Since their credit is much higher, Barnett is becoming a laughingstock. But his campaign has attracted considerable interest."

She stiffened her sagging spine. "He must know that his lies hurt him more than me, so why bother?"

"I suspect he no longer cares. Or maybe he expects his reputation to recover once you are back in an asylum. His purpose might be to drive you into a public breakdown to bolster his case. His finances are worse than we originally thought. If he cannot resolve this soon, he will have to drop his petition for lack of funds to pursue it."

Her fears dried up as she spotted pain in Jack's eyes. She'd been so wrapped up in her own concerns that she had forgotten how vulnerable he was. "He's attacking you, too, isn't he? Has he trotted out your father's misdeeds?"

He flinched.

"Jack." She gripped both arms. "You have to accept that you are strong and honorable. It is the only way to fight this."

"Of course."

But as he left the room, she knew that he didn't believe it. "What if proving my reason deprives him of his?" she whispered.

You have to protect him . . .

Jack walked back to Blackthorn House the next afternoon, furious with himself for going to White's. He'd avoided the place until now, fearing to see Damon again. But today he'd hoped someone might know more about Barnett's plans. Instead, he had run a gauntlet of well-wishers, the curious, and the snidely superior. His marriage was on every lip.

He had forgotten how bored most gentlemen were. Those he knew from school had nothing to do until inheriting their future titles except game, wench, and pry into everyone's business. Introducing an unknown in their midst was akin to waving a red flag before a bull — a gory sport popular on the Peninsula. Already they had discovered Marianne's lineage, Barnett's claims of insanity, and the annulment petition.

As Marianne had guessed, Barnett was also attacking him, worse even than he had expected. Acquaintances now looked at him askance. Whispers had assailed him from every side. Most spoke of Wilcox.

In the space of an hour, Jack heard a dozen new stories about the fraudulent investment schemes Wilcox had employed to fleece greenlings — his first big swindle had occurred when he was barely seventeen. Other men revived the tale of Lord Rolland's murder in that shameful duel. Many questioned Jack's motives in wedding a madwoman and speculated about her life span once he won control of her fortune.

It was worse than after that cheating charge eight years ago. At least then his honor had sustained him. Now Waterloo had stripped him of that last support. The Caldwell bad blood was exposed for everyone to see. Sooner or later someone would mention his crimes.

He had miscalculated, he admitted in despair. By wedding Marianne, he had burdened her with his own disgraces, tarring her with his family's reputation. How could they win if Barnett produced a witness to his infamy? His crimes could condemn her to an asylum.

Somehow he had to keep his failings out of court. And he must warn her that Lady Potherby's musical evening would be a crush worthy of the height of the Season. Everyone in town would turn out to gawk at the infamous Jack Caldwell and his mad wife. He ought to spend this evening preparing her.

Yet he couldn't. Sensual images tormented him — a fact not helped by the marital humor his friends had aimed in his direction or by the numerous toasts he'd drunk. He was well enough to go that he would likely attack her again. His control weakened further every day — added proof that his bad blood was taking over. He could not even control his body anymore. If he did not see Marianne safe soon, he would likely add new crimes to his tally — the greatest of which would be fathering a new generation of scandal-makers.

"Lord Blackthorn wishes to see you in the library," said Barnes when Jack reached the house.

He nodded. What now?

Mrs. Halsey had divulged everything she knew. The first of Marianne's new gowns had arrived that morning. Marianne's staff had arrived last night, with Mrs. Hastings starry-eyed over Marianne's marriage and Hastings anxious to repay Barnett for his cruelty. The good news had been the quarterly statements Hastings had produced. As expected, they had been sent by Barnett, not the trustees.

Jack had returned to the bank to put the fear of God into those dithering bankers. Despite specific orders and the force of law, they had sent Marianne's income to Lord Barnett rather than to her from the day the trust had started. It might have been understandable when she was twelve — her father had been sloppy in setting up the trust, not considering what would happen if he died immediately — but the bankers should have appointed an administrator to oversee disbursements until she came of age, then given the funds directly to her.

Her quarterly allowance had been ten times what she'd been spending. And the claimed reinvestments were news to the trustees. Their records showed expenditures for a full staff at Halworth, including companion, governess, groundskeepers, and stable hands. They also showed receipts for horses, two carriages, and a stylish wardrobe replenished annually. Barnett had been financing his daughters' Seasons using his niece's income.

Jack had given the bankers a week to recover the missing money, which should never have passed through Barnett's fingers in the first place. Now he admitted that pressure from the trustees gave Barnett another reason to attack him. The man would have to mortgage everything he owned to repay what he'd stolen.

"There you are," said Devall when Jack reached the library. "Any news at the club?"

"Everyone lucky enough to be in town will be at Lady Potherby's to gawk at Marianne."

"Inevitable." Devall shrugged. "Angela went through the same scrutiny, you might recall. We'd better call out the staff and practice a crowd scene tonight so she'll be ready for the crush."

Jack nodded, relaxing. He should have thought of that himself instead of wasting his time on self-pity — or on air dreams of bedding his wife.

"Fitch found Miss Dubois," Devall said, breaking into Jack's thoughts.

"Where?" Jack refused a glass of wine.

"Serving Lady Wedleigh only ten miles from London."

"Does she recall anything that might help?"

"I think so, Colonel," said Fitch from near the fireplace. Jack hadn't noticed him. The man had a talent for unobtrusiveness that often allowed him to overhear private conversations. "She recalls every moment of that journey. Watching the assault revived memories of her father's death."

"I thought she remained in the stable loft," said Jack.

"She did, but there were ventilation gaps under the eaves. That not only allowed the slightest sound inside, but it offered a view of the stable yard. She kept watch so she would have warning if anyone returned to the stable. The mob was large — eight travelers augmented by half a dozen stable hands. All were drunk. She describes them as chance-met travelers heading for Paris to join Napoleon's new army. That probably accounts for the excessive violence. Each had to prove his worth to the others."

"The monster attracted vicious followers," agreed Jack. French soldiers had inflicted many atrocities on Spanish partisans.

"So Miss Dubois actually witnessed the attack?" asked Devall.

"Yes. She has never forgotten the screams. The attack lasted from noon until well after dark. She remembers being glad that Miss Marianne did not understand gutter French — the men described in detail what they were doing, planned to do, or had already done. But the words and actions were alien to a gently bred English schoolgirl."

Jack exhaled in relief, though she still repeated some of those words in her nightmares. But her mind might have truly snapped if she'd understood.

"Anything else?" asked Devall.

"Miss Dubois's description of their escape mirrors Miss Marianne's. Miss

Dubois was shocked to learn that her charge had left Barnett Court so soon afterward. She would never have departed if she'd thought Miss Marianne would be mistreated."

"Nor would I have done so," put in Jack. "But Miss Dubois had no choice. Lady Barnett took one look at her and saw red. She does not allow beautiful females under her roof."

"I believe that Miss Dubois feels guilty now that she knows the full story," said Fitch diffidently. "And not just for leaving her there. She recalls a comment her mistress once made that implied Lady Barnett was a harridan and not overly bright. Miss Dubois regrets going to Barnett Court at all. Her last words in our interview were a wish that she had returned to Halworth and sought advice from Mr. Barnett's solicitor."

"Is she willing to testify?" asked Jack, wishing that he'd questioned Francine further at the time. He would have gladly escorted them to Halworth.

"Yes, though she would prefer not to."

"As would we all." Devall shook his head, then turned to Jack. "Is there anyone else who might have helpful information?"

Jack shook his head. The only other possibility was to look for witnesses to his own character, but he could not mention that to Devall. The best ones would know about Waterloo, playing directly into Barnett's hands. Devall must concentrate on building Marianne's self-confidence and poise.

Chapter Thirteen

Marianne slipped into a seat at the back of Lady Potherby's music room, grateful to have arrived after the program started. It was another sign of Jack's consideration — like arranging to call on Lady Beatrice half an hour before her scheduled at-home. The gossip had enjoyed meeting Marianne before her rivals did, and Marianne had been relieved to face her away from prying eyes — especially since Lady Beatrice had shown her no special consideration. The woman was as acerbic in private as in public.

"It's about time I met your bride," she had snapped at Jack. "You've been in town for five days."

"But I could hardly insult you by calling clad in a rustic gown that would shame even a servant," Marianne had dared. To test her growing social skills, she and Jack had agreed that she would answer questions as long as possible, signaling Jack to step in if necessary.

"Explain. Your father left you flush in the pocket."

Marianne nodded. "But I've lived secluded at Halworth since his death, so I had no need of a wardrobe I would never use."

"Ran mad is what I heard." Her eyes gleamed. Though well past seventy, she showed no sign of waning memory or fading sight, and she hunted scandal with the intensity of a well-trained terrier.

"It is true that I was in a state of shock when I returned from France twelve years ago." She kept her voice steady. "But I had just listened to a mob butcher my entire family, barely escaping with my own life. Without Colonel Caldwell's help, I would have perished."

"What?" Lady Beatrice stared at Jack, too surprised to control her voice — quite an accomplishment.

"It's true," he said calmly. "She was taking the air under the eye of her mother's maid when the mob arrived to punish the enemy Englishmen who dared defile a French country inn. I found her two days later and escorted her home."

"Why had I heard none of this?" She sounded aggrieved.

"Between shock and grief, I was unable

to talk about it," admitted Marianne. "Thus, my uncle knew no details. By the time grief waned, I was alone at Halworth and accustomed to my solitary state, so there was no one to tell."

Lady Beatrice bored in, firing questions so fast that Marianne had no time to think. She answered a dozen before calling a halt. "Enough, my lady, I beg of you. Rather than revive the grief and pain of that time, I prefer to concentrate on the future. Nothing else matters."

Lady Beatrice nodded, then turned her penetrating stare on Jack. "Have you seen your father lately?"

Marianne scowled.

"I've not seen Deerchester in thirteen years, as you well know," Jack said calmly, though Marianne detected strain beneath his voice. Angela had confirmed that Barnett was reviving every scrap of scandal about the family. This call was as difficult for him as for her.

Lady Beatrice quizzed him on his motives, his prospects, and his plans for the future, as if she were Marianne's father evaluating his worthiness to make an offer. She didn't miss any of Barnett's insinuations.

Marianne wanted to tear the woman

limb from limb for impugning Jack's honor, but she bit her tongue. He would not thank her for interrupting. He was quite capable of defending himself — which he did by denouncing Barnett as a fortune hunter without directly mentioning the viscount or his motives.

By the time they left, Marianne was limp with exhaustion and fearful that the rumors were driving Jack closer to suicide, but she'd learned three things: Lady Beatrice despised Lord and Lady Barnett, which worked in her favor and Jack's; to Lady Beatrice, being the first to report a new story was more important than the story itself; and Lady Beatrice would make a formidable ally. Anyone hiding the tiniest indiscretion feared her.

Jack had planned his campaign well. With Lady Beatrice on her side, Barnett could not set society against her. She doubted whether the gossip's support would allay suspicions of Jack, though. He could deflect specific charges, but he undermined his credit every time he opened his mouth. That note of guilt convinced listeners that he was hiding grave crimes. The only way to eliminate it was to convince him that he had not betrayed his standards. Only then would his voice ring with confidence.

Now she let her eyes wander the packed music room while a dark-haired lady coaxed cascades of notes from a piano-forte.

Devall had warned her that the musicale would be crowded, for Barnett's rumors had ignited rampant curiosity. But she hadn't envisioned such a crush. If this many people were in town at a time everyone described as thin of company, what would a Season be like?

Don't think about it. Concentrate on tonight.

People would have been curious to meet her anyway, for no one expected one of Wellington's heroes to wed someone un-known to society — she'd not been to school or London or even to Dorset gath-erings. Barnett's charges of madness added a ghoulish element that could easily turn cruel if she showed signs of weakness.

Jack would remain with her tonight, but she must learn to stand alone. Society frowned on wives who lived in their hus-band's pockets. They would interpret her dependence as proof of incompetence, making Barnett's claims more believable. She could hardly admit that she must stay close to Jack for his sake. Once he decided she no longer needed him . . .

Walking that line would be tricky indeed.

The music closed with a flourish that brought tears to her eyes. "I've never heard anything so beautiful," she whispered as the room erupted in applause.

"I thought you would enjoy it," Jack murmured back. "Miss Tassini is very talented."

"Who is Beethoven? The name sounds familiar, but I can't place him."

"A German fellow who's been all the rage for some years now." He led her to the refreshment room as Miss Tassini began an encore.

"He must be very good to amass a following so quickly."

"True, but beyond his musical talent, he is a canny businessman. He has an arrangement with an English publisher, who prints his music almost as soon as he writes it. That makes it more accessible than the works of other composers, even those who are long dead." He headed for a corner table, which would keep the crowd from pressing too close. "And since he writes for the pianoforte rather than the harpsichord, he is able to infuse his music with emotion."

"It shows. I've never been more moved.

It makes the pieces I know seem insipid."

"If you wish to study his works, hire a music teacher." He glanced at the door, but they remained alone. "I received some news just before we left the house. Most of the guests will have heard it by now, so you need to be prepared. Barnett filed a second petition this afternoon."

She sighed. "What now?"

"He wants an immediate hearing so I cannot squander your fortune before he has a chance to rescue you. We can contest it if you like."

She was sorely tempted, but a moment's thought convinced her that, for Jack's sake, it would be better to conclude the hearing as soon as possible. Continued repetition of the Deerchester scandals would harden Jack's resolve to kill himself. So she said, "Opposing a quick hearing would not serve our interests. There are only two reasons we could cite. The first — that I am unable to face examination yet — would support Barnett's contention. Arguing that my new trust protects me might raise the bishop's suspicions."

"That's absurd."

"Think deviously, Jack. I may be the sole trustee, but I will have to hire a man of business to handle the investments. Failing to do so would be mad. You know as well as I do that a woman cannot trade shares. And this is not the time or place to argue whether I can understand complex financial issues."

He choked.

"Exactly. If I were mad and you were greedy — and the court has not ruled on either contention as yet — then you could exert your nefarious influence on my feeble mind and convince me to appoint you or a confederate to handle my affairs, thus giving you free rein to plunder my trust at will. You have the bad fortune of possessing a brother who would do just that."

"Devil take it!"

"I think we should ignore this latest petition and let the bishop schedule the hearing whenever he wants. That will make us seem open and cooperative, undermining Barnett's claims. I am more comfortable tonight than I dreamed was possible. Talking with Mrs. Halsey explained many of my fears, which allowed me to put them behind me. I will be all right."

Jack could only nod, for the other guests were crowding into the refreshment room. Many headed straight for Marianne — soldiers, dandies, ladies, rakes, all demanding introductions and offering congratulations. Names and faces flashed by so fast she doubted she would remember more than half. She didn't like the suspicion directed at Jack — more evidence that Barnett's campaign was undermining his credit — but she maintained both her calm and her smile. All she could do was pray that Jack was thinking clearly enough to attribute the antagonism to Barnett and not to his imagined crimes at Waterloo.

It helped when Lady Debenham arrived. She was Lady Beatrice's chief rival for the cachet of "Most Knowing Gossip," so her support was also essential.

"I refuse to believe Barnett's latest tales, Colonel," she said, shaking her head. "The man is mad as a March hare if he thinks anyone could confuse you with Wilcox. You are his antithesis in every way." She turned to Marianne. "Barnett actually accused your husband of defrauding you. Of all the stupid, idiotic . . ." She sputtered to a halt, inhaling twice before she could continue. "Barnett is insane. Do you know he actually thinks Colonel Caldwell will squander your dowry on one of those rackety investment schemes Wilcox used to promote? The colonel has more sense — to say nothing of his own fortune to see after."

"Lord Barnett is laboring under considerable pressure," Marianne responded lightly. A gossip of any stature would know about Barnett's financial woes. After selling his town house, moving to Ibbetson's, and mortgaging his estate, only the dullest intellect would think him flush in the pocket.

"How true," Lady Debenham purred. "And he still has four budding harridans on his hands. But attacking the colonel is personal — which I will make sure everyone remembers. He will never forgive Wilcox for luring him to ruin twenty-five years ago, though he is barking up the wrong tree this time. A more honorable man than the colonel would be hard to find."

Jack stiffened, but Marianne ignored him. "Thank you, my lady. I am pleased to find my judgment validated. I have considered him a paragon since he saved my life in France."

"I heard about that." Her tone proclaimed pique that she hadn't first heard it from Marianne.

Marianne appeased her with details she hadn't told Lady Beatrice. The tale became easier with each repetition. Sometime over the past twelve years, her grief had waned.

She wanted a quiet word with Jack — was he upset about Wilcox cheating Barnett or about Lady Debenham's praise? — but the moment Lady Debenham left, Lady Hartford swooped in.

"I've been dying to meet you since reading of your marriage in the papers," she said once Jack left to collect refreshments — Lady Hartford was Marianne's age and as warm as Angela, so Marianne had sent him away. "Hartford and I had heard nothing about Colonel Caldwell since noting his name in the casualty lists. We were afraid he had succumbed to his injuries."

"He is fine, as you see." She gestured to where Jack was juggling plates. "Do you live in London, or are you up on business?" The question bordered on rude, but she wondered how much of this large crowd had come to town to gawk at her.

"Neither, actually," said Lady Hartford easily. "We came to hear Miss Tassini play — I adore Beethoven, and she is a master of his work."

"I've never heard anything so lovely," agreed Marianne, relaxing.

Lady Hartford sat down across the small table. "How did you meet Colonel Caldwell? He is rarely in England."

"We met in France when I was a child, then more recently when he inherited the estate next to mine."

"So the rumors are true that your family died in France." Lady Hartford shuddered artistically. "You must have been terrified. I cannot imagine losing my family at all, let alone so tragically."

"It was not pleasant," Marianne admitted in a vast understatement. "But thanks to Jack, I escaped."

"And now you are wed. It is very nearly a fairy tale. But I must ask why you lived alone for so long — I know the rumors, of course, but I prefer to ask those directly involved; gossip so often twists tales."

Marianne shrugged. She had decided to say nothing negative about her family — not only was it good manners, but showing family loyalty might help her case with the bishop. He was as attuned to society as anyone. So she said, "I suffered nightmares for some time after returning from France. They badly disrupted my uncle's household, so it was better that I returned home. And I was more comfortable with my familiar staff."

"I can read the truth well enough, for I know Barnett's daughters. They doubtless threw fits because you needed attention."

Marianne tried to protest, but Lady Hartford stopped her. "Not to put down your relatives, but I cannot abide Lady Barnett. She demonstrates the worst characteristics of the mushroom class. A more selfish harridan I cannot imagine. And unscrupulous. Last Season, she spread false tales about one of my friends."

"Why?"

"Miss Sheridan had attracted Kendall's heir, a man Lady Barnett had hoped to attach for her oldest daughter — not that he would look twice at her — or even once if he could avoid it."

"What happened?" Every new fact about Lady Barnett made her seem worse.

"Nothing in the end. Few believed the tales, knowing who had started them. The Barnetts' reputations eroded further, and Kendall's heir offered for Miss Sheridan a month earlier than anyone had expected — protecting himself, perhaps." Her smile broadened as a dark-haired gentleman approached with Jack. "There you are, Thomas. What took you so long? I'm starving."

Lord Hartford laughed, then addressed Jack in a conspiratorial whisper. "She doesn't eat for two when in this condition. She eats for a regiment."

Jack set down his plates so he could offer congratulations, then asked about the Hartfords' two-year-old son.

That set both proud parents to bragging. Young Robbie hadn't stopped running since he'd taken his second step. He'd escaped his nurse more than once — finding a nest of kittens in the stable, hauling a turtle from the pond, wriggling into an attic everyone had thought was locked. The Hartfords had hired a second nurse to help keep track of him and protect him from harm.

The boy's escapades reminded Marianne sharply of Nigel, who had also been a charming scapegrace as a toddler. But she forced her memories aside, turning the subject to the Hartfords themselves. Within moments she learned that Lady Hartford was a renowned musician in her own right, and Hartford bred the most sought-after hunters in England. But despite their accomplishments, neither seemed the least haughty.

Jack smiled.

She was learning to read his expression. He had arranged for the Hartfords to join them, knowing that they were another couple who would befriend her. He thought that buttressing her with people who cared would keep her from retreating into solitude after he died.

How little he knew her. She could not imagine life without him. Already he had become too important.

You love him, don't you?

Her mind blanked, blinding her to Lady Potherby's musicale, her companions, and even the taste of her food.

She had described her feelings many ways in the past month — Jack was safe, they were friends, she was grateful for his help and feared for his life — but she had never examined them.

Now she did. Every waking moment — and most of her sleeping ones — were attuned to him. Fears for him overshadowed all others. His touch raised heat and a longing for something she could not describe. That kiss still haunted her nights. If he died, she would truly go mad.

Hutch was right. She loved him. The attachment grew deeper and richer each day. Every new insight into his character made him more appealing. She wanted a lifetime together, children, grandchildren . . .

So she must work harder to save him. Barnett's lies were pushing him closer to the edge.

Half an hour later, Marianne stepped out of the retiring room and spotted Lord Devlin. Hoping he had news, she joined him.

"How fares your quest?" she asked once they had withdrawn into a corner away from curious ears.

"I am making progress. I ran into Mrs. Morrison yesterday — she had just returned to England."

"That nurse you mentioned?"

"Yes. She remained in Belgium after Waterloo, returning with the last of the wounded."

"It must have been difficult for her, having just lost her husband."

"I suspect the work helped her through the grief. She asked if I'd seen Jack, for he'd been quite ill when she last saw him. She also mentioned that Captain Lord Hardcastle had asked about him — apparently Jack once extracted him from a bit of a muddle, so he was upset to hear of his injuries."

"Where was the muddle?"

"I've no idea. It could have been anywhere, and not even in battle. Jack has rescued more than one subordinate from drunken brawls, including me — begging your pardon, ma'am." He looked as if he wanted to kick himself. "War isn't pretty, and military service in general isn't much better."

"I expect not," she said easily.

He relaxed. "It's possible Hardcastle knows more about Jack's movements at Waterloo than I do — I was engaged around Hougoumont all day and know little about the rest of the battle. But I think Hardcastle's unit was out toward the 95th. I will leave in the morning to visit him. Even if he didn't see Jack, he might know someone who did. Eventually, I will track down someone who saw him at the end."

"Where is Lord Hardcastle now?"

"At his father's estate in Lincolnshire — he is heir to the Duke of Streaford. Mrs. Morrison doesn't know how he is faring — he is another who left her care while still quite ill — so it is better that I interview him in person. It is too easy to ignore a letter if one is feeling poorly."

She thought of Jack's pile of unanswered letters and nodded. "Thank you. Is there anyone I can interview? I feel helpless and more than a little guilty for asking you to do all the work."

"I can't think of anyone. Most injured or retired officers are away from town. The common soldiers are not fit company for a lady."

"How about Mrs. Morrison?"

"She did not give me her direction. I assume she is returning home, but in all the years I knew Morrison, he never mentioned where home was."

"But —"

"Concentrate on your own problems, Mrs. Caldwell," he said firmly, making it clear that he knew about Barnett's petitions — stupid of her to think anyone in town remained ignorant. "If I discover anyone you should talk to, I will let you know. It is no imposition," he added when she tried again to protest. "I have long wanted to repay Jack for saving my sanity. I would never forgive myself if I didn't help him now."

Jack sat in Devall's empty drawing room, staring at the fire. With luck, intense concentration on the glowing coals would mitigate his lust. He should never have wed someone he found so tempting — or anyone at all, given his background — but it had been the only way to stop Barnett.

Marriage was unhinging his mind. He couldn't risk bedding his wife, yet he couldn't look at her without drowning in desire. The only solution was to avoid her, but that was difficult. Living in a friend's house meant few rooms were open for his use, none of them private. Going to White's meant ducking cuts or answering endless questions. And he had to accompany her every night, feeling her heat and smelling her lilac perfume. Mademoiselle Jeanette was a witch. Marianne's new clothes cunningly drew attention to her perfect body. Her growing confidence exposed new sides of her character — witty, teasing, sensual . . . He wanted to throw her down and taste every inch of her.

Which was a dangerous thought to entertain five minutes before he was supposed to escort her on another shopping expedition. If her hearing at Bishop's Court did not conclude soon, he would do the unthinkable.

The hearing.

He might already have irreparably harmed her, he admitted grimly. Marriage had won a battle against Barnett, but it might yet lose the war. The very fact that he was a Caldwell had pushed Barnett beyond greed into obsession.

Lady Debenham's careless words had knocked him on his ass, raising shock, horror, and desolation. He hadn't known that Barnett was one of Wilcox's victims, though he should have suspected it when Marianne described her uncle's youthful losses. Barnett had already been desperate because Marianne possessed the fortune he needed. Faced with another Caldwell making off with his prize had added to his fury. No wonder he was raking up every Caldwell scandal in history.

Jack suppressed a groan. It was too late to change course. And even if he'd known about Wilcox's swindle, marriage would have remained Marianne's only weapon. But he could have been prepared.

Guilt intensified. Guilt that his family had harmed Barnett. Guilt that protecting Marianne would hurt the man worse. Guilt that the old scandal would redound upon Marianne, harming her, too.

But at least guilt cooled his lust.

Angela poked her head into the drawing room. "There you are, Jack. The mail just arrived." She crossed the room, a letter in her outstretched hand. "Are you congratulating yourself on Marianne's success last night? Even Lady Debenham was singing her praises."

Jack grimaced at the frank on the letter. "I did nothing but escort her."

"Nonsense. No one but you could have turned so terrified a duckling into an elegant swan in only ten days. I wouldn't have believed it possible if I hadn't seen it with my own eyes."

"I agree, but the credit is all Marianne's."

"Not all. Without you, she wouldn't have tried."

"What do you mean?"

Angela scorched him with pity for being such a nodcock. "She's done it for you, Jack. She was content at Halworth. But you asked her to rejoin the world, so she did. She must love you very much."

Jack's jaw hit his chest.

"I'm surprised you didn't recognize it, for you watched Dev make the same transformation. How many times had you urged him to tell the truth and redeem his reputation? A hundred? A thousand?"

At least, but shock kept him silent.

"He was content enough, so he did nothing. Not until he fell in love did he make the effort." Angela smiled. "Marianne is the same." With another of those seductive smiles, she left.

She must love you very much.

"No!" His voice squeaked. She couldn't — and didn't. Her situation was nothing like Devall's. Blackthorn had deliberately courted ostracism to mask his war against those who abused their positions. It had been a calculated campaign that he'd abandoned solely to protect Angela. She was right that love was the primary factor in Devall's change of direction, but Marianne's case was different.

Marianne was driven by terror, not love. Unless she joined society, she would be incarcerated. Jack had nothing to do with it. She would have made the same choices no matter who had released her from the asylum. Freedom was the goal.

Yet he had to admit that Marianne was in danger of becoming infatuated. Her eyes brightened whenever he appeared. She trusted him to keep her safe, relaxing only when he was near. He had become her crutch, he admitted, frowning. A necessity at first, but it was time she stood alone. Proud. Fierce. Independent. She would be very much alone before long.

Removing that crutch would also guard against attaching her affections. So he would not accompany her to Hatchard's today. She could take her maid.

Stifling a pang of regret, he broke the seal on the letter, then scowled. Some things never changed, though at least the bad was tempered by good news this time.

He was again staring into the fire when Marianne arrived.

"The carriage is here," she announced.

"I can't go after all." He gestured toward the letter. "I must deal with this. But you will be fine without me. Take Daisy. Hatchard's has benches outside the door where maids sit while their mistresses shop. I have a subscription, so you need only give your name to get anything you want."

"What happened?" Ignoring the change of plans, she pointed to the letter. "Did Barnett devise a new plot?"

"No. It's from Deerchester." He couldn't prevent his disgust from showing.

"He is unhappy about me, isn't he?" Her face paled.

"He is unhappy" — furious was more accurate — "but it has nothing to do with you, Marianne." Pacing to the window, he pondered how much to say. Now that he'd involved her in his life, she must understand his family if she was to escape their manipulation. "I notified him of our wedding — strictly as a courtesy; I knew he wouldn't approve."

"Because I'm mad."

"No. It wouldn't matter if you were a

princess or a prostitute. He has been after me to wed Miss Somerson. I refused, but he never gives up. Every letter urges me to do my duty. He is furious that I wed elsewhere."

"Why would he want you to wed someone you didn't like?" The moment she heard the words, she grimaced, for their wedding had hardly been a love match.

But he ignored the undercurrents. "He gave up on Wilcox long ago — even Miss Somerson refused to consider him. So it is up to me to secure the family future."

"By getting an heir." She blushed.

"Actually, he doesn't care about heirs. It is his own future that matters. His fortune is disappearing faster than ice in a fire — vices are expensive, and mismanaging his estate has diminished his income. He needs money. Somerson promised him fifty thousand guineas if I would take her."

"My God! What is wrong with her?"

"Who knows? Needless to say, I refused, and the subject is now closed. But you need to understand his goals. The moment he discovers your fortune, he will try to talk you into a loan."

"You can handle him, Jack."

He cursed his slip. He'd as good as told

her that he wouldn't be there to protect her from Deerchester.

Marianne frowned. "If he wants the money so badly, why doesn't he wed Miss Somerson himself?"

"He can't. My mother is still alive."

"I thought you said she died birthing you."

"No. I said I hadn't seen her since then — a big difference. She and Deerchester had a blazing row when I was a week old. Some claim he threw her out. Others say she ran away. Whatever the truth, we never saw or heard from her again." He shrugged.

"Didn't you wonder about her?"

"Sometimes." Often, actually. He'd dreamed of her in childhood, imagining her as beautiful, loving, honorable — all those things his father and brother weren't. Reeves had encouraged the dreams as part of his campaign to turn Jack into an honorable gentleman. And it had worked to a point. The image had sustained him through Wilcox's worst abuse. But because the image was so powerful, he'd wondered if she had truly been a helpless victim. Had she provoked that fight to escape a man she despised, even if that meant abandoning her infant son? Or was the tale a lie to cover graver crimes?

Waving Marianne off to Hatchard's, he reread the letter. Deerchester's vitriol was worse than ever now that the fifty thousand was beyond reach. He was even more furious because word had just arrived that Wilcox was dead.

Emotion tightened Jack's chest, surprising him. Wilcox had been the bane of his existence from the day of his birth. Brutal, hateful, author of endless scandal. So why should news of his death raise any sense of loss? It was an ending devoutly to be wished. The family curse would now truly die with Jack.

Dropping the letter on the fire, he watched it turn to ash. He would leave a letter asking Devall to protect Marianne from Deerchester — the formality wasn't necessary, for Devall would do so anyway, but it would add a measure of legality if one was ever needed. Deerchester would be livid when Marianne inherited Seacliff. It was too much to expect him to suffer a fatal apoplexy when he heard about Jack's will.

Thank God there would be no more wicked Caldwells. The world would be a better place without them.

Marianne steadied her pulse and

climbed out of the carriage. She had left Jack brooding over his father's letter. Everything she learned about his family increased her awe at the strength of will it had taken to be different, a strength that made her present task more difficult.

But that was for later. Today she faced shopping alone — Daisy hardly counted; she was so awed at becoming a lady's maid that she was oblivious to everything else. Angela had agreed to let Marianne hire Daisy, then had assigned her own maid to teach the girl the finer points of personal service; Angela had even offered to hire Daisy's unhappy cousin Kate.

At least Hatchard's was a good place for her first solitary expedition. She was at home among books. And since today was her birthday, she deserved a treat.

Hatchard's held more books than she had ever imagined in one spot. The range of subjects awed her. Within minutes, she was so caught up in choosing what to buy, that she forgot her nerves. She even forgot that other people occupied the store. Thus, she jumped when a voice greeted her.

"Forgive me. I didn't mean to startle you," said Lady Hartford as Marianne whirled to face her.

"It is entirely my fault," said Marianne

with a smile. "I was so engrossed in a traveler's account of the Americas that I forgot this was a public place — I spent much of the past twelve years in my father's library."

"I knew you were special," said Lady Hartford. "My father is a scholarly vicar, so I grew up surrounded by books. You must accompany me to Lady Chartleigh's soirée next week. Her guest is Mr. Donovan, who will share the wonders that he saw on his recent trip to Egypt."

"It sounds delightful. But I should ask Colonel Caldwell if he has plans for that night."

"Of course." She smiled. "Enjoy his escort while you have it. As soon as you are established, he will return to his own interests."

"I know. Living in his pocket is bound to raise eyebrows." But her voice rang hollow, for Jack's only interest was to do away with himself — which reminded her of the letter from Deerchester. "There is something I've been puzzling over, but I don't know where to find answers."

"What is the problem?" Lady Hartford added a book to the stack in her arms, then checked to see that no one was nearby.

"Colonel Caldwell's mother." She'd heard the yearning in his voice when he mentioned her — and also the pain. "His father banished her when he was born. He has no idea why or even where she is. It is a question that has long plagued him."

"Deerchester is a frightful man. I've never understood how Colonel Caldwell managed to become so . . . so . . . respectable," she finally finished.

"Force of will and a dedication to honor."

"I could ask Lady Beatrice for the tale," said Lady Hartford. "She must know."

"I'd rather not," countered Marianne. "If she learns of my interest, the story will become common knowledge in a trice. I do not think he will appreciate having his personal affairs bandied about town. Nor do I wish to tell him of my interest if it turns out that his mother deserved to be tossed out in the cold." Suspecting that his mother had deliberately abandoned him — especially if she'd run off with another man — might explain his pain.

"True. It would hardly do to produce yet another relative who could shame him. He has too many already. I am at a loss, then, but if I think of anything, I will let you know. Only a few aged gossips are likely to remember anything about the matter — if indeed, they ever knew. Even Lady Beatrice doesn't know everything, especially about country affairs."

They chatted for a time, then Marianne collected her books and headed home.

But her heart remained heavy. Jack was using Deerchester's letter as an excuse to pull away and force her into independence. Clinging would do no good, but somehow she had to give him a reason to live.

Chapter Fourteen

The next days passed in a blur of activity. Though October was slow socially — Parliament was in recess and most gentlemen were either overseeing harvests or attending hunting or shooting parties — Marianne and Jack went out most afternoons and every evening. Barnett's claims fell on deaf ears once Lady Beatrice and Lady Debenham welcomed Marianne, but she still endured considerable curiosity. Every event she attended was a crush.

Marianne had expected that her demeanor at the musicale would quell further interest in her affairs, but she soon realized her mistake. The gentlemen remaining in town were mostly jaded fribbles with nothing to do or dandies unwilling to rumple their meticulous toilette by engaging in the usual autumn sports. Now back from a summer in Brighton, they were bored. The ladies — young or old — were starving for new scandal. So Marianne's affairs entertained them, providing interest and filling conversation. Their scrutiny created a circus atmosphere.

All eyes blazed to life whenever she did something odd — watching the stage instead of the audience at the theater, walking across Grosvenor Square to call on Lady Hartford instead of taking a carriage, avidly examining Lady Debenham's relentlessly Egyptian drawing room instead of displaying ennui.

Speculation never ceased. Was she an Original or merely rustic? How could an admitted bluestocking know so little about the world as defined by London society? Might Barnett be right?

Her one surprise was that Barnett never appeared. She hadn't seen him since Halworth. Devall believed that he was hiding from his creditors, all of whom knew he had mortgaged Barnett Court.

Marianne didn't agree. Barnett could easily have accosted her on the street, but repeated confrontations would breed ease. He was desperate enough that he no longer cared whether she was mad. His only goal was to break her composure in front of the bishop, possibly by springing at her in court. In the meantime, his rumors would keep her off balance.

It was working, she admitted on Thursday, fighting back tears as she returned from morning calls. She wasn't sure how long she could tolerate being the focus of so many eyes.

"I can't take any more stares," she told Angela, shaking her head so hard that several pins flew out — Daisy hadn't quite mastered this style. "They expect me to be more conventional than the most sedate spinster. The pressure makes me want to scream. And Jack just heard that the hearing is Monday."

"You will do fine," said Angela soothingly. "The bishop is nothing like society's dandies."

"I know that, but his judgment will determine how I spend the rest of my life. How can I not be terrified? I can manage as long as I remain calm. But that grows harder each day. People analyze my every word and deed. Court will be even worse."

"I know this is difficult for you," agreed Angela. "I was in the same position two years ago when Atwater spread lies about me."

"After you turned him down?"

"Exactly. He was mad, though no one yet realized it. One of his claims was that I'd bedded half of London's gentlemen.

You can imagine the response that raised among the rakes. Everyone who hadn't had me wanted his share." Her shoulders twitched in distaste.

"Heavens! That is far worse than being thought mad. What did you do?"

"Held my head up and pretended I didn't care what anyone thought. For a fortnight society reveled in reviling me. I was cut, berated, slapped — ladies can be vicious in private — and attacked by drunken lechers. Not until Atwater tried to kill me did anyone question his claims."

"What happened then?"

"The last of Atwater's reason snapped. Society decided that the word of a madman meant nothing, so they turned me into a saint. The same will happen to you. Once the bishop pronounces you sane, society will declare Barnett an unscrupulous rogue. He will be reviled for greed, ostracized for defrauding you, and run out of the country if his debts are as large as rumored. You will then have to endure the adoration that society bestows on those it has wronged."

"That sounds almost as bad."

"It is. But it will be temporary. Jack will take you home to the country. By the time you return next spring, this affair will have been forgotten. In the meantime, relax. The opinions of society's fribbles mean nothing — even to them. They strut and pose and parrot the latest gossip, rarely noticing that today's words of wisdom contradict yesterday's." She smiled. "The most enduring lesson of two years ago was that London society behaves like a flock of sheep, following its chosen leader blindly. The result is often ridiculous — half the young bucks sported lapel posies the size of dinner plates after a leader of fashion wore one as a joke one year. But they change course as often as they change clothes, so none of it matters."

"You make them sound like teapots, uncaring of what is poured in or out of their heads."

Angela laughed. "Keep that image in mind, for it perfectly reflects how much their opinion is worth."

Marianne felt better after their talk. She stopped fretting over the gossip, which allowed her to behave in a more natural manner. But she still couldn't relax.

The problem was her growing frustration over Jack. He avoided her whenever possible. His reason was all too obvious. He'd decided that she must face life alone, so she'd better learn how.

It had started the day he'd received the letter. Until then, he'd protected her, cared for her, and stood between her and her fears. Then the letter had arrived, and he'd immediately pulled back, turning remote and cold. Even his public smiles rarely reached his eyes.

The letter must have raised new fears about his breeding, or perhaps Deerchester had given him a new reason to die. She couldn't imagine what that might be, but it had to be more than a parental tirade over rejecting Miss Somerson — though the lady in question was not exactly a lady, according to Angela.

Then there was Saturday's dinner at Carlton House. After accepting the invitation, Jack had realized that half of the guests would be army officers, including everyone from the War Office and Horse Guards. Pain now flashed in his eyes whenever he mentioned the event. And dread. She hoped his fear arose from his Waterloo nightmare, for she was confident that Devlin would prove him honorable. But if he was hiding some new problem, her job would be more difficult. She had no defense against the unknown.

Lady Hartford still had no idea where Jack's mother was, but she had discovered that Jack's nurse had been a Miss Witt. The woman should know about Lady Deerchester's departure, but so far Lady Hartford hadn't found her direction. After thirty-two years, it might turn out to be a churchyard.

Marianne had again warned against consulting a gossip. Aside from the danger of raking up another scandal that would embarrass Jack, finding his mother would not relieve his nightmares and might even make them worse. A dishonorable mother would validate his bad blood, yet an honorable mother might make his presumed dishonor seem worse. Who could tolerate disappointing a mother, especially if he'd set her on a pedestal while growing up?

Then there was Lord Devlin. He had not written. No matter what Lord Hardcastle had said, his report should have arrived by Friday. Yet as she dressed for Saturday's dinner, she had heard nothing. Not even a note saying that Hardcastle hadn't helped.

She nearly groaned. There was no mail on Sunday, and the hearing would begin Monday morning. Win or lose, Jack would be free of his promise as soon as it was over, and she had nothing with which to stop him from putting a bullet through his brain.

★ ★ ★

Jack grimaced as he approached the dignitaries at Carlton House. Walking through the door at Deerchester Hall would be more pleasant than facing Wellington and the dozens of other officers. His dress uniform dragged at his shoulders, berating him for facing the Regent sporting a symbol of everything he'd betrayed. Imagining the condemnation in Wellington's eyes made him break into a cold sweat. His cowardice welled up, demanding that he flee.

Again.

How many of tonight's guests knew about his disgrace? Probably most of them, though few would do more than allude to it while they were gathered under the Regent's roof. Granted, Damon had said nothing when they'd met last week, but he had sold out immediately after Waterloo, separating him from army gossip. He would know by now, though. Enough officers were in London that the tale must be common knowledge. That would explain why Damon had missed every event Jack had attended. The Devlin House knocker was still up, proving that Damon hadn't left for Devlin Court.

The line inched forward. Jack had spent

the hour as their carriage crept toward the door calming Marianne. But now that they were surrounded by people, her attention was elsewhere, leaving him nothing to think about but facing Wellington. What could he say?

The question circled his head unanswered for another quarter hour, until the line delivered him to the front.

"You look better than last time we met, Caldwell." Wellington turned to the Regent, adding, "Colonel Caldwell, one of my most talented officers. You recognize the name, of course. He took several hits at Waterloo. For a time we feared he would lose a leg."

Jack's head swirled at the unexpected praise, but he managed the appropriate greetings, ending with, "My wife, the former Marianne Barnett, niece of Lord Barnett." He drew her forward. "His Royal Highness, the Prince Regent, and His Grace, the Duke of Wellington."

She curtsied. Being ladies' men, both made flirtatious remarks on her sudden marriage, but Jack barely heard them for the buzzing in his ears. Why the devil didn't Wellington cashier him and get it over with? Was he holding out for formal charges of treason?

They escaped into the crimson salon, which seemed garish tonight. Or perhaps thousands of candles flickering in unison with his pounding head exaggerated its impact. The heat didn't help.

"What is wrong?" murmured Marianne. "You look like a ghost. A lady that pale would need a vinaigrette."

"Nothing." When she glared, he shrugged. "It is always stifling at Carlton House. The prince is terrified of drafts."

Her glare deepened.

"My presence distressed Wellington," he added. "With the Regent there, he had to put a good face on it, but after Waterloo, he probably expected my resignation."

She didn't accept that explanation either, but she dropped the subject. He was glad. Talking about it was dangerous. One overheard word would force his disgrace into the public eye. Yet it might wind up there anyway.

It took him half an hour to relax. Several officers alluded to Barnett's rumors, and two mentioned Waterloo, but no one accused him of murder or cowardice. Airing regimental scandals in public wasn't done. He was beginning to think he would survive the evening, when Fitzroy tapped him on the shoulder.

"Hooky wants you, Caldwell. Now." He nodded toward an anteroom.

Jack's heart hit the floor, but he had no choice. As he marched away, fury ripped him from head to toe. If Marianne hadn't interfered, he would not have to face Wellington.

The duke would demand an explanation for that dead officer. Since Jack couldn't provide one, he might well find himself imprisoned.

Not today! he screamed silently. He had to be at Bishop's Court on Monday. Not only as a witness, but to support Marianne.

Setting his face in an expressionless mask, he entered the anteroom.

"You seem recovered, Caldwell," said Wellington when Jack shut the door.

"Quite." He would have preferred to remain at attention, but Wellington gestured to a chair. So he sat.

"Are you resigning your commission?"

Jack's heart sank. "I hadn't planned —"

"Then why have you ignored every query about your health in the past two months? And why did I learn you were in London from reading a newspaper?"

Jack flinched, recalling the pile of unopened mail on his desk. With a sinking feeling, he realized that he'd neglected to report his recovery to the Horse Guards. He hadn't expected to live this long, so duty hadn't mattered. But after postponing his demise, he'd neglected to resume the rituals of living. Damn! The last time Wellington had heard from him, he'd been ensconced at Seacliff, unable to walk.

"An oversight on my part, Your Grace. My wife —"

"Another oversight, I take it? You neglected to mention her, too."

Disgrace piled upon disgrace. Wellington hated incompetence. Heat crawled up Jack's neck. "I wish my injuries were responsible, but the truth is that I've been so concerned with protecting my wife that I neglected other matters."

Wellington frowned. "I heard enough gibberish on my arrival to make those Spanish intelligence reports seem clear in comparison. Something about madness. And theft?"

"All lies, sir. While her uncle is seeking to annul our marriage on grounds that she is mad, his real complaint is that it deprived him of her fortune."

"Indeed." His eyes brightened. "Explain."

Jack quickly related the facts. It didn't take long, for he'd prepared the synopsis for his presentation in court.

"It seems you have the matter well in hand," said Wellington when he finished. "Brilliant campaign strategy, as usual. That knock you took on the head doesn't seem to have hurt anything after all."

"Thank you, sir." Jack was bewildered at the duke's reaction. Delayed retribution was not Wellington's way. If not for Monday's hearing, he would bring up the matter himself, for being cashiered would explain his suicide, diverting blame from Marianne. But it would also undermine his testimony.

"Once the trial is over, report to the Horse Guards," Wellington ordered, breaking into Jack's thoughts. "We are nearly through in Paris, so you needn't come over. The Regent will announce my appointment as commander of all England's forces tonight, so I will be working here once this treaty business is done. Help Frasier set up my new office, then study the reports from India. I want your thoughts on the situation by next week."

"Yes, sir." Jack snapped a salute and left, but his heart had turned to lead. The stain on his soul made it impossible to serve the best officer in the army. So he must finish the business as soon as the trial concluded. There would be no time to see Marianne settled. Devall would have to look after her.

Bishop's Court nearly drove Marianne mad indeed. Jack had said little about the actual procedure, leaving her imagination to conjure scenes of horror.

The hearing was worse than imagination. Instead of the series of lies and confrontations she'd expected, she found herself confined to an antechamber where she could hear nothing. Listening to Barnett describe her fits would have been difficult, but at least it would have kept her mind occupied. And it would have held a new terror at bay. With no idea of what was happening, she expected every moment to be summoned before the bishop. The strain made her jump at the least sound.

Questions chased each other around her head. What were they saying? Had Barnett convinced people to lie about her? Was Rowland, her barrister, refuting Barnett's claims? Jack assured her that Rowland was very talented, but she wanted to hear his words for herself.

Angela tried her best to distract her, but

nothing worked. Barnett was presenting his case first. Marianne was sure the bishop would find it so compelling that he wouldn't listen to her.

She had expected the hearing to be quick — the facts could easily be stated in half an hour — but it dragged on for three interminable days. Monday was the worst. She paced the anteroom for hours, unable to sit as her imagination conjured disaster after disaster, all ending in a trip back to Carey's asylum, followed by Jack's suicide because she wasn't there to stop him. He'd been even more withdrawn since Carlton House. She suspected that Wellington had said something to increase his determination — not that she had any hope of discovering what or why. He was barely speaking to her, busy constructing a wall between him and the rest of the world. This one was of impenetrable stone instead of the ice she'd melted on their wedding night.

She tried, of course. "I wish I could see what is happening," she confided as they returned to Grosvenor Square Monday night. "Ignorance is too frustrating."

"A natural reaction," he agreed. "But Bishop's Court is no different from other courts. Witnesses and potential witnesses cannot hear other testimony."

"I don't see why."

"By knowing what others say, a man can tailor his words to either support or discredit previous testimony. That inhibits the court's ability to discern truth."

She'd tried to elicit further information about the proceedings, but having eased her main concern, he'd retired early, avoiding everyone in the house.

Rowland began presenting her case on Tuesday afternoon. Jack testified the rest of the day. He said even less that night. She knew he was not supposed to discuss the case, but his withdrawal bothered her. Had Barnett's barrister attacked his reputation? If even a hint of Waterloo had arisen, he might be beyond her reach. There was still no word from Devlin.

Marianne was the last witness. The bishop had listened to both sides. He'd heard about her fits and tantrums, heard about her attack on her cousin, heard about her family's death. Both barristers had propounded their theories. Rowland swore she had suffered a severe shock, but had long outgrown its effects. Hilliard swore that her mind, already fragile from an overindulgent childhood, had snapped, making her dangerous to herself and others and leaving her open to manipulation by unscrupulous scoundrels.

Now it was up to her.

"You are a diamond, sweetheart," murmured Jack, kissing her ear before opening the hearing room door. "Calm, competent, perfect in every way. Just be yourself, and no one can rule against you." He squeezed her hand in the greatest show of warmth in days. Her fingers tingled.

Then the door closed between them, and she was alone. Alone with the fear that he'd just said good-bye.

It was less crowded than she'd expected. The black-robed bishop sat on a raised dais, dominating the room. She forced her gaze to meet his, then exhaled in relief. Curiosity blazed in his eyes. He had not yet made his decision.

Rowland and Hilliard, the two barristers, each occupied a small table. A third table served two clerks. There was no jury or audience.

Relieved, she took her seat in the witness chair.

"We have heard others describe their dealings with you," began the bishop. "Why don't you tell us in your own words what happened twelve years ago and how those events affected your life?"

She paused to settle herself, then inhaled deeply and began.

"To understand the effect, you must first understand my family. Papa was a scholar with three loves — his wife, his children, and his books. We were happy at Halworth and far closer than is usually the case in our class. The only pain I recall from those years was a skinned knee, and my greatest sorrow was one stillborn pup in a litter of six."

"So you had never suffered?" asked the bishop.

"Exactly. Lady Barnett described me as spoiled. I have always understood that to mean undisciplined — which was not true in our family. But I was certainly untested. Despite being twelve, I was unprepared for what I experienced in France." Taking another deep breath, she described the illness that delayed their departure from Paris and her guilt when her mother contracted it, forcing further delay. Then she recounted cowering in the stable loft; fleeing through the night, certain that the mob was following; meeting Jack; her arrival at Barnett Court. "When Jack assured me that Lord Barnett would protect me, relief released the tears that I hadn't dared shed while we were in such danger. But once I started, I couldn't stop, even when Lady Barnett struck me, chastising me for such a vulgar display. Her fury worsened my grief. For the first time, I realized that other families were not loving. The knowledge sharpened my loss, for I knew then that my former life was utterly gone."

Rowland nodded. "A natural reaction."

The bishop glared, silencing the intrusion.

Marianne continued. "Any child with my background would have been overwhelmed, but even the strongest grief fades with time. In a few days I had recovered enough to look about me. I found my new life daunting. Lady Barnett despised me and resented my intrusion. Her daughters followed her lead, tormenting me whenever their governess wasn't looking. It did not help that I received treatment they considered preferential." She described her memories of that time and how those differed from the housekeeper's tale.

"You say Lord Barnett removed you a month later," said the bishop. "That must have distressed you."

"By then, I was grateful. Believe me, I have no quarrel with his decision. Since his family offered none of the affection I had lost in France, I was happier alone. Halworth was familiar, and the staff cared deeply for me. I soon recovered most of my composure, and the nightmares faded."

"Then how do you explain your most recent fit?"

"It was not a fit," she claimed, having worked out with Jack how to portray her last meeting with Barnett. She hated dishonesty, but to win this war, she had no choice. "Its origins were quite different from those childhood outbursts. If I had known of Barnett's plans, I would have petitioned the court to terminate his guardianship on the basis of fraud and neglect. He knew that, of course, so he gave me no warning. That limited my response."

"Explain."

"Knowing that I must soon take personal charge of my estate, I had been preparing for the responsibility as best I could — not an easy task, for I'd never been allowed to communicate with my steward. Barnett refused me a governess or even a companion, and he posted guards to prevent me from leaving the grounds. No one was allowed through the gates. Thus, I had to study on my own and meet friends in secret and on foot. But despite all that, I still considered him an honorable man who would carry out the letter of my father's will, so I was unprepared when he moved against me."

She shifted to a more comfortable position. "When I met Colonel Caldwell in the folly that day, he asked for my hand. I gladly accepted. The decision left me euphoric, for it marked the first of many steps that would restore my rightful place in society. I had no inkling when I returned to the house that Barnett had planned a much different future for me."

She glanced at Hilliard. "I had barely entered the house — had not even shut the door — when Barnett grabbed me, shoved me against the wall, then announced that I was mad and he was locking me in an asylum so he could take control of my inheritance. Naturally, I fought to escape — biting, scratching, and kicking. I screamed. I shouted. I cried. Those were the only weapons at my disposal. As I'd hoped, he flinched, allowing me to break free. But he'd brought the guards with him. On his orders, they overpowered and bound me. Yet losing that skirmish did not mean I had to lose the war. I knew my staff would inform Colonel Caldwell of my abduction, and that he would follow. So I tried to attract attention, making it easy to track the carriage. Through God's grace, he arrived in time to prevent the staff at Barnett's chosen asylum from ravishing me."

"Ravish, Mrs. Caldwell?" exclaimed Rowland.

"Exactly. Colonel Caldwell must have described how he found me. I cannot testify from my own knowledge, for they had dosed me heavily with laudanum before tying me to that bed. Once he rescued me, our only recourse was to wed immediately instead of posting banns as we'd originally planned. Since then, I have concentrated on preventing Barnett from twisting the law to his own benefit."

The bishop nodded. "That seems clear enough. Have you any questions, Hilliard?"

"I do, my lord."

"Then proceed."

Hilliard rose.

Marianne braced herself, for this portion of the hearing would be much harsher.

"Let us go back to the journey from Barnett Court to Halworth," said Hilliard ponderously. "If, as you claim, you were relieved to return home, then why did you scream and wail for the entire three-day trip?"

"No one bothered to tell me what was happening, so it wasn't until we actually reached Halworth that I knew our destination. It was then that relief set in."

"You distrusted Lord Barnett that much?" He sounded incredulous.

"Would you trust a complete stranger when you were still suffering grief and terror from listening as your family was butchered by strangers?"

"Stranger?"

She turned to the bishop. "A servant plucked me out of bed before dawn and tossed me into a carriage, saying not a word about what was happening or where I was going. A man I had never seen climbed in after me and signaled the coachman to move. I was understandably wary of strangers, so it terrified me to be locked in a coach with one."

"But he was your uncle and guardian," protested Hilliard.

"I know that now. But I had never seen Lord Barnett before that moment. He had not been in the house when I arrived, and he left without speaking to me. Nor did he see me when he returned. Even after joining me in that carriage, he did not introduce himself. I did not discover his identity until the next day when he treated me to a drunken rant condemning my father for leaving his fortune to a puling girl instead of giving it to him, as he considered his right. His anger was so intense that I fully expected him to kill me so he could claim my father's estate."

"Suspecting a lord of the realm of murder is mad, Miss Barnett," snapped Hilliard.

"Mrs. Caldwell," she corrected coldly, glaring at Hilliard. "I was twelve years old at the time and terrified. I will not apologize for my suspicions. If you think a lord behaves any better than the lowest riffraff when in his cups, then you are the madman. And I only learned last week that my father had protected me from such an attack by naming a residual beneficiary in his will. But as for your original question, I was also bothered on that journey by the many stable yards we entered. The smell recalled my family's murder, raising new waves of grief and terror."

"Another reaction most would consider mad, would you not agree?"

"Not at all. Smell often triggers memory, sometimes good, sometimes bad. Gingerbread and pine boughs recall Christmas.

The scent of brandy reminds me of my father, for a glass of brandy always sat on his desk when I came in to say good night. My sister's nurse broke into tears whenever she smelled snowdrops. She associated them with her brother's death — the scent was strong on his body when neighbors bore it home after a fatal accident."

The bishop was nodding. He, too, must have memories associated with scent.

Hilliard frowned. "But most people are not incapacitated by such memories."

"That is true." She met his eye and lied. "Which is why stables no longer bother me. But at the time, the wound was fresh, and I was greatly troubled by many things."

"But we have heard testimony that stables still send you into fits of madness."

"I cannot imagine from whom." Surely Devall had not been called to testify. He was the only one in London besides Jack who knew she still turned into a quivering mass near stables. "Lord Barnett had not visited Halworth in eleven years before he abducted me. His secretary is hardly competent to judge."

"He swears that you have not improved a bit." Hilliard leaned close, breathing in her face as his hand clutched at her shoulder.

"Ah. He explained that trick, I see," she said calmly, though her heart began to race. "But he obviously minimized his actions — his touches always included my breasts."

"What?"

The bishop leaned forward.

"Only recently have I discovered what a lecher he is. And Mr. Craven could hardly judge my reaction to stables, for I own no horses and had closed the stables many years ago — he was always irritated that he had to send his coach to the village."

"A pitiful attempt to cover your fear of horses," sneered Hilliard.

"Hardly. Maintaining a stable was an unnecessary expense. Since Barnett confined me to the grounds, I had no need of horses. But as to Mr. Craven, I suspect that his visits had two purposes. The first was to make sure that I remained conveniently mad by inciting hysteria at every opportunity. The second was to satisfy his lust should I ever give him a chance."

The bishop frowned. "Do you claim that Barnett wanted you mad?"

"Perhaps not in the beginning." She shook her head sadly. "Twelve years ago he believed it himself and did his best to hide it. His wife called me mad from the moment I shed my first tear. It was easier to pack me off to Halworth than call a physician. No one wants to stain his line with madness. I don't know when his purpose changed, but he must have realized quite soon that madness could give him the fortune the courts had already denied. So he made sure that no one could contradict his claims. He never provided a governess or companion, never sent me to school or presented me to society — though anyone currently in town can testify that I am quite comfortable at social affairs. What he did was divert most of my income to his own use. I received a final accounting of my trust last week and was shocked that barely a tithe of my allowance reached my hands, in blatant disregard of the trust provisions. For twelve years he has supported himself using my funds. In the end, he tried to lock me away and take charge of everything."

The bishop's lips pressed together so hard they turned white.

Marianne met his gaze. "Given what I have learned about his embezzlement and his mounting debts, I must wonder if he condoned Mr. Craven's lechery on grounds that rape would add to my supposed mental fragility."

"Preposterous!" exclaimed Hilliard. "Accusing a peer of the realm of such perfidy is proof enough of madness."

"Noble birth has never been a guarantor of noble deeds," she snapped, then drew in her temper. "But we have moved far afield. Barnett's crimes are not under the purview of this court, except as they define his motives for incarcerating me. And it is possible that Mr. Craven acted on his own initiative. Seducing me would have forced me into marriage, placing my estate and fortune in his hands." She shook her head in disgust. "The point of this hearing is my sanity or lack thereof. In my defense, I doubt that any lady of questionable reason could successfully stage a come-out in London at a time when accusations of madness, treason, and much more raise untold interest in her every word and deed. Since I have survived such suspicion intact — and have even thrived — I contend that my reason is sound."

Hilliard continued to harass her for two hours, but her responses remained firm, refuting every falsehood and explaining the rest. It was easier than she had expected. Fear for Jack left no room to fear the hearing's outcome. If she lost this battle, he would die, so she had to win, no matter what it took. Devlin still had not reported, so she was on her own.

Fear for Jack made it easy to parry Hilliard's jabs. She could feel him slipping away, retreating into a mental dungeon to brood. His will was so strong that she would be hard-pressed to stop him.

"It is utter madness to wed a virtual stranger without even consulting your guardian!" Hilliard finally shouted, his own fraying temper making her appear the sanest person in the room.

"Either the previous witnesses have been lying through their teeth, or you have not been paying attention," she countered, shaking her head in disgust. "I was four-and-twenty at the time of my marriage — far past the age of consent. Barnett was and remains a virtual stranger who cares nothing for me beyond stealing my fortune. On the other hand, I have known Colonel Caldwell for twelve years, first in France, where he rescued me from incarceration, if not death, escorted me back to England, and did his utmost to keep me safe. Later I knew him as a neighbor who shared many of my interests and applauded my determination to wrest Halworth's methods into the nineteenth century and improve the lot of my tenants.

By the time we decided to wed, I knew him as well as I'd known my family. He has always conducted himself with honor, courage, and kindness. He is a gentleman in truth as well as in name. He has land and fortune enough to satisfy all but the most grasping guardian. And he has made no attempt to hurt me. None of that is true of Barnett."

Another hour passed before the bishop excused her. Rowland summed up her testimony in a few brief sentences. His main point was that her activities and behavior in London could not be distinguished from those of other society matrons. That alone proved her normality. Whether terror had pushed her grief into temporary madness twelve years ago was irrelevant.

Hilliard was still ranting when she left the hearing room.

The moment she reached the antechamber, her legs gave way.

"I don't know why I'm shaking now," she murmured as Jack caught her against his side. One arm steadied her shoulders while the other wrapped around her waist.

"Reaction. We call it battle fatigue. When the fighting stops, men collapse, feeling far more exhausted than usual. The same thing happens after sudden danger.

You have anticipated this for days, marshaling all your energy for this confrontation. Now that it is over, your body demands rest."

"I can't rest until we hear the ruling." But she sagged against him, letting his heat warm her sudden chills — and raise hope that he was not too far removed to reach. It was the closest they had been since they had arrived in London.

"That won't be long. You were the last witness."

"Not any more. Hilliard wants to present more testimony. He is furious at his failure to rattle me, so he is demanding that the bishop summon Carey. They were discussing it when I left."

"Then you have won, indeed." His smile reached his eyes for the first time in days. "The bishop hates men who continue beating a horse long after it is dead."

Jack was right. Word arrived an hour later that the bishop refused to prolong a hearing that had already consumed more time than was reasonable. Marianne Amelia Barnett Caldwell had been competent when she contracted her marriage, so the petition for annulment was denied. He added some pithy comments about Barnett's negligence as a guardian and his

obvious avarice, then rued his lack of juris-
diction over corrupt lords and hinted that
he might raise the question when Parliament reconvened — bishops sat in the
House of Lords.

As she and Jack left the building, they
spotted Barnett across the street. It was the
first time she'd seen him since Halworth.

He looked terrible, with haunted eyes
sunk into a white face and slack jowls that
hinted he'd lost weight. Lady Barnett was
with him — she had also testified, which
may have worked in Marianne's favor.
Now the lady screeched loud enough to be
heard in France.

"What do you mean, there is no money?
The girls must attend Lord Houghington's
house party. You know . . ."

Marianne turned to Jack. "I almost feel
sorry for him. His wife is a harridan of the
first water."

"True, but she is no longer your concern. How does it feel to be vindicated?"

"Unreal, but I am glad that it is over."

His lips smiled, but his eyes remained
cauldrons of swirling emotions, most of
them dark.

Marianne struggled to suppress tears.
Despite offering comfort after her testimony, his wall was nearly complete. Once

341

it was done, she would never reach him. Winning was meaningless unless Jack stayed with her. Without him, she might as well return to the asylum.

She had to make him listen. Tonight would be critical.

Chapter Fifteen

Marianne nearly broke down as the carriage drew up before Blackthorn House. The journey home from Bishop's Court had been the worst hour of her life. Devall's satisfaction and Angela's promise of a victory celebration had sliced Marianne's soul. Couldn't they feel Jack slipping away? Couldn't they see the darkness settle over his eyes as he added the final stones to his wall of isolation? Despite uttering the same congratulations as the others, he felt nothing.

Desolation threaded his voice, evidence of the wasteland inside. Besides retreating from the world, he was walling off his emotions, his memories, and his very soul.

She prayed that it was merely a habit that allowed him to face the horrors of battle — which meant there must be a door in that wall that he could open between engagements. If only she could find it.

It is like Halworth, said Hutch. *The park*

343

walls isolated you from the world, but they only existed along the lanes. Jack entered the park through the woods, which had never been fortified against callers.

But where were the woods around Jack's mind? She had no idea how to reach him and no one who could help.

Devall had been Jack's friend for more than twenty years, yet he seemed oblivious to Jack's fatalistic surrender. Angela had a talent for sensing hidden character, yet she saw none of Jack's despair.

Not that Marianne could enlist their help. She had to save Jack, but not at the cost of his pride. Knowing that Devall or any other friend was aware of his plans would provide yet another incentive to kill himself. To an honor that demanded atonement for his crimes, abandoning atonement would be cowardly — yet another crime. He could not face friends if they knew.

She bit her lip as a footman opened the carriage door. Was that the key, perhaps? Choosing death over an imperfect life was also a form of cowardice. Could she force a delay by pointing that out?

It won't work.

She sighed. Jack demanded perfection of himself. In his mind, the small crime of suicide paled beside the larger ones of killing a fellow officer and abandoning the field. And if accusing him of cowardice stopped him, he would hate her forever. Every glimpse of her would remind him of his failure.

She had to find another way.

Jack led her inside.

"We won," trilled Angela to Barnes as they entered the hall. "You see before you the sanest lady in London. In England. In the world."

For all the good it did her, brooded Marianne as she accepted new congratulations from Mrs. Halsey and the Hastingses. If she lost Jack, her sanity would crumble fast enough. She loved him more than her family, Halworth, and her dreams combined.

At the same time, she was furious with him. How could he not see that his honor surpassed that of other men? How could he not feel that his memories were incomplete? Even as he admitted that he had no recollection of that day, he still insisted that his actions condemned him. Did he not know that humans were frail creatures who often made mistakes? Even if those images were as bad as he feared, he could forgive himself — if only he would try.

But nothing would convince him. They had argued about it on Friday. She had again dared him to investigate his nightmare, using her own misconceptions of that month at Barnett Court as proof that incomplete memories often veered widely from the truth. Yet he had dismissed her situation as typical of childhood, refusing to admit that he might be doing the same thing.

Helplessness overwhelmed her.

She reviewed her resources once more, hoping that she might have overlooked something, but the conclusions remained the same. Lady Beatrice was out of the question. Asking her to locate a witness from Waterloo would start a scandal that Jack would hate. Lady Beatrice was incapable of keeping secrets, and Jack abhorred his ancestors' scandals as much as their cowardice and brutality. Even if witnesses proved him innocent, publicly admitting that he thought himself capable of such deeds would tarnish his reputation for all time.

Devlin had promised to help, but she hadn't revealed the stakes, so he had no sense of urgency — as shown by his continuing silence. He, at least, would understand Jack's plans and forgive him — or so

346

she thought; his words hinted that he had considered suicide before Jack took him in hand — but she'd remained silent, knowing that Jack would terminate the friendship if he found out. Whether her decision had been right or wrong no longer mattered, for Devlin was gone.

Devall lacked the military access that would allow him to find witnesses, and he had already done so much. She could not beg yet another favor. If Jack found out, he would cut them both.

Wellington? She could hardly presume on the man after one brief introduction. Besides, Wellington's private meeting with Jack had pushed him further into isolation.

So she was on her own. All she could do was watch Jack closely, then pray that when the moment arrived, his wall would crack, giving her one last chance to reach him.

Somehow she managed to hide her fears during dinner, though she had no idea what she ate. But she declined to go out that evening, pleading weariness from the trial.

Jack's eyes brightened with relief, increasing her fear. He didn't want to be with people.

Everyone retired early. Marianne waited

an hour, then cracked the connecting door. Jack seemed asleep. Whether he was or not didn't matter. She knew he would wait until the household was quiet, for he wanted no witnesses and no interruptions. She left the door open so she could hear if he rose. This was not a night she could sleep.

Jack watched the fog gather in the square, still thin enough that the moon pearled its tendrils into ghosts. They drifted closer, taking on faces of the men he had killed.

Imagination, he decided, shaking his head in disgust. And stupid imagination at that. The men he'd felled in battle did not haunt him. It was the nameless, faceless Englishman who stole his rest.

But why would you kill a comrade?

He stifled the echo of Marianne's question. He didn't know. The answer lay in the dark hours he could not recall. But nothing could counter the stark truth. His hand had held the knife. His arm had felt the shock as that knife sliced deep into the man's back. His head had throbbed with a mad frenzy as he struck again and again. His eyes had fogged with terror as he fled the deed. His soul could no longer stand the pain . . .

He had awakened half an hour earlier, by plan rather than from nightmares, though his sleep had been as restless as ever. But the dreams no longer mattered. Atonement would come before dawn.

A frown creased his brow as he realized that tonight's dreams had been different. Marianne had battled those images of Waterloo, just as she'd battled Hilliard in court, driving them away and replacing them with her softness.

God, how he loved her!

He had cracked the door of the hearing room so he could listen to her testimony. She'd been magnificent. It had been all he could do to keep from scooping her up and kissing her.

But it was hopeless. He could not debase her with his dishonor. Nor could he risk passing his blood to yet another generation. And what if he turned his brutality onto Marianne? With his control shattered, his conduct was bound to get worse. Even if his infamy had escaped notice in the chaos of Waterloo, the next slip could bring scandal — or worse.

So it must end, and it must end now. Her eyes were growing warmer, seeming to beg for his touch. Whenever he spotted that look, his heart leaped. He wanted her so badly. But every day he remained with her risked attaching her affections. So far she felt only gratitude — a natural reaction, for she credited him for her successes. He must leave before that gratitude grew into something deeper. His departure would already hurt her enough.

She was the loyal sort, he acknowledged, recalling the open connecting door he'd found on awakening. She'd sensed his distress and checked on him, perhaps more than once.

How do you know the memories are real?

She'd asked the question often. She'd even used her own childhood mistakes as arguments. What she didn't realize was that officers had to be clearheaded and practical, even in the midst of battle — a far cry from a bewildered, terrified child suffering her first taste of life's cruelty.

But as a concession to her concern, he searched his mind one last time, unlocking doors he'd ignored for years. His first battle, childhood traumas, fits of fury that made him want to lash out as Deerchester and Wilcox did — it had taken determined discipline to control the Caldwell temper; without Reeves he couldn't have done it.

But his journey through the murkiest

corners of his mind turned up nothing new beyond Reeves declaiming Shakespeare's *Richard II* during a long-forgotten lesson — *Mine honor is my life; both grow in one. Take honor from me, and my life is done.*

"So be it."

The memories were real. Honor was gone, and his life with it. His blood had finally won.

In a way, it was a relief. He was tired of trying to prove that he was better than his ancestors, tired of pretending to be honorable. He had to be twice the gentleman others were before they perceived him as the same. His honor had to be stronger, his vices milder, his demeanor more perfect. It was too much.

The only remaining question was where to die. It would be bad form to inflict nightmares on Devall's staff — to say nothing of giving the maids a nasty mess to clean up. A bullet to the head was not tidy.

And then there was Marianne. She might check on him, then follow when she found him gone. He could not risk her finding his body. She had seen too much carnage in her life. But where —

The mews.

Of course. Despite her claim in court, it was the one place she could never go.

Pain slashed his heart. If only he could have helped her overcome that fear, too. But it was too late. Wellington expected him back, which was impossible.

Pulling out his writing case, he removed his final letter and read it one last time. It was adequate. He hadn't mentioned the murder, for that would reflect poorly on the military. But he was clear that the horror of Waterloo lingered in nightmares that had destroyed his mind, making it impossible to go on.

Marianne would be safe.

After buffing his boots, he donned his uniform, taking care that the braiding was straight. Then he checked his appearance one last time, slipped the letter into his pocket, and collected his pistol. It was time. The grooms would rise in an hour.

Marianne woke with a start, knowing something was terribly wrong — and not just that she had fallen asleep. The connecting door was shut.

Jack!

Leaping from bed, she threw the door open.

Nothing.

Empty bed. Empty chairs. Nightshirt on the floor.

A hand over her mouth held in her scream. Dear God! Why had she lain down?

Forcing terror aside, she scanned the room, seeking any change since she had last checked on him. Perhaps he had merely risen early.

The draperies were pulled back, revealing thick fog. His writing case had moved —

Her fists clenched as the significance hit her. He had vowed to avoid accidents, so this time he would leave a letter.

"I have to stop him," she sobbed, knowing it might already be too late.

His dressing gown hung from a peg. Wrapping it around her for warmth, she raced for the stairs.

Where would he have gone?

The library was empty, as were the billiard room, the drawing room, the dining room, the breakfast room . . .

"Think," she admonished herself. "He is an honorable man, a guest in this house."

He would not intrude into Devall's rooms. Nor would he impose on his host more than absolutely necessary.

The garden?

The door to the garden was unlocked. Shivering and terrified, she forced her bare feet outside.

Cold sliced up her legs. Damp seeped through her clothes. Only the faintest glow from the moon penetrated the thickening fog. She circled the garden twice before admitting that he wasn't there.

Tears trickled down her cheeks. She was too late.

No! You can't give up.

"But where would he go?" she whispered. "The park? The river?" She would never find him.

A horse shifted restlessly in the mews, reviving other fears. She was backing away when her eyes widened in shock.

"The mews. He knows I can't follow him there." She raced toward the house to wake Devall.

Coward!

"I can't!"

You can! He might still be alive. But if you waste time waking Devall, then explaining the problem, then waiting until he dresses . . .

Hutch was right. Squeezing her hands into fists, she forced her feet forward.

The scent of hay and horses and filthy straw engulfed her the moment she cracked the door. Voices rose from her nightmares. *Help me, Mommy . . . let go! . . . Papa! . . . baisez la putain anglaise! . . . bastards!*

Her mother's screams, her father's curses, Nigel, Cecily. Memory overwhelmed her, terrifying, threatening, drowning her in grief. She turned to flee.

Jack is in there.

She had to find him, had to stop him, had to heal him the way he had healed her.

Yes, he healed you. And this is your last chance to return the favor. You can do it. Concentrate on Jack. He needs you.

Sucking in a deep breath, she stumbled over the threshold. Only the strongest will kept her from fainting.

Horses shifted, barely seen in the darkness. Most of them were stabled to her right, so she turned left. Jack would not want to disturb Devall's cattle.

Her bare feet made no sound as she felt her way past carriages and curricles. The wide roof cast deep shadows that faded into the fog of the stable yard.

She found him in the loose box at the end. Somehow she'd known he would seek the most private spot.

He straightened abruptly when she pushed open the door. Only the faintest light penetrated the box, but it reflected from the pistol pressed to his temple. Relief turned her knees to water when his hand dropped to his side.

"Don't do it, Jack," she begged, barely keeping her voice steady.

"What the devil are you doing out here?"

"Looking for you."

"But — But this is a stable."

"You are more important than my fears." She took a hesitant step closer. "Come inside, Jack."

"It's too late. Go back to bed, Marianne. I can't live with it any longer."

He sounded so distant, she nearly burst into tears, but she forced calm on her voice. "Then let it go, Jack, but not like this."

"Don't argue." But he uncocked the pistol.

Marianne swayed, then quickly stiffened her legs. It wasn't over yet. "Come inside where it's warm, Jack." Another step brought her close enough to touch his arm. Tension thrummed through it.

He's terrified, said Hutch.

Thank God. "Come, Jack. Let me help you inside."

Pain twisted his face, but he finally nodded.

Taking his hand, she led him through the garden, then upstairs to his room.

As she closed the door behind them, he seemed to awaken from a trance to peer at her in the light from the uncovered window. "Your feet are bare. You must be frozen." He turned toward the connecting door, clearly intending to tuck her into bed.

"No, Jack. My feet are fine." *Liar.* "I'm not leaving this room until we talk, and neither are you."

He stood silently until her nerves nearly snapped.

Finally his tension drained away. Setting the pistol on a table, he tossed coal on the nearly dead fire, then touched a spill to the fresh flame and lit candles.

Marianne moved the pistol under a chair, then sat, spreading the dressing gown's skirts to hide the weapon. When Jack turned, she gestured to the second chair. "You did not kill an English officer, Jack," she vowed firmly, holding his gaze. "And you did not desert the field of battle."

"How would you know? You weren't there."

"I know you, Jack. Far better than you think. I could never have fallen in love with a dishonorable man."

He flinched. "Don't turn me into a saint. How can you know me? You've had less experience than anyone at seeing beyond the surface. You put me on a pedestal twelve years ago and don't want to let me down."

His rejection stabbed her to the core, but she set it aside. "Actually, that's not true. I have less experience at playing society's games, but I recognize them better than anyone. Those who embrace posturing become so immersed in polishing their own façades that they miss the falseness of those around them. But your façade is not false, Jack. Shakespeare put it best. *To thine own self be true . . . Thou canst not then be false to any man.* You have always been true to yourself, Jack."

"It was an act to hide my bad breeding," he snapped.

"Nonsense! I might believe such fustian if you applied honor only to important matters. A man can manage that for a time, though it inevitably slips when he is under pressure. But you are not like that. You are ruthlessly honorable every day, in every way, no matter how trivial the situation. I've seen you admit bumping a vase so a maid wasn't blamed for carelessness. Yesterday you walked around Angela's flower bed because leaving footprints in the fresh-raked soil would make extra work for the gardener. No one so particular in small matters can abandon honor in large ones. It is against human nature. Honor is so ingrained in your soul that you could not violate it if held at gunpoint."

Pain flashed in his eyes, flushing his cheeks.

Shaking her head, she withdrew his pistol. "How long did you stand there willing your finger to move?"

He flinched.

"Tell me, Jack. How long?"

"Half an hour. But I had to make sure I hadn't overlooked anything."

"No. That is an excuse, and you know it. You finished brooding before you left this room. You couldn't pull the trigger because suicide is dishonorable and cowardly. Deep inside you know that. A lifetime of honor isn't going to disappear, even if you want it to. That's why you grabbed the shrub when I startled you on the cliff that day. Inside, where it counts, you fight for survival, even if the enemy is your own self. You have not proven yourself guilty beyond all doubt, even in your own eyes."

"But you can't know that! *I* don't know that. There is too much evidence otherwise." His face twisted in anguish.

"You accused me of putting you on a

pedestal — being blinded by gratitude, I suppose." Returning the gun to the table, she reached for his hand. "One way to judge a man is by the friends who stand by him. You may be right that I have little experience evaluating people, but Devall has known you since you were both lads — long before war encased you in armor. He would know of any inclination to dishonor. Yet he describes you as the most honorable man he knows."

"He doesn't know me anymore. I've seen him only a dozen times in fifteen years."

"But you write often. And Lord Devlin has seen you constantly since you met — seven years ago, I think he said."

"How do you know Damon?"

"You introduced us, and I spoke with him at Lady Potherby's. Hartford speaks highly of him, as do others I've met. You and Devlin lived through the same battles, suffered the same discomfort, faced the same enemies. He, too, counts you his closest friend and a remarkably honorable man."

Jack pulled his hand away and walked to the window.

Marianne remained seated. Pain radiated from him in waves, bringing tears to her eyes. She longed to comfort him, but he had made it clear that he did not love her. Any gesture of caring might drive him back to suicide.

"You see too much," he whispered after several minutes of silence. "But how can I live knowing I failed my country, my superiors, and myself?"

"But you don't know that, Jack," she repeated. "You don't remember what happened. How can you justify making so permanent a decision based solely on a nightmare that might be a fantasy? Until you have evidence, you cannot accept those images as real. The only cowardly thing I have ever seen you do is refuse to look for the truth. You must investigate, Jack. I would wager everything I own that either the dreams are false or the facts are different than you imagine."

He turned from the window, his face twisted in pain. "Perhaps you are right. Since I am too weak to end the affair, I might as well court scandal by announcing to the world that I am a murderer."

The words brought her racing across the room. "Damn you, Jack. It was honor that stayed your hand, not weakness. Deep inside, you know that you must seek the truth."

"I don't know anything anymore,

Marianne." His arms pulled her against him. He laid his head atop hers. Shuddering sobs escaped.

She wrapped her arms around him, drawing him closer. Her own tears slipped soundlessly down her cheeks, but they were tears of joy. Jack's wall was breached, its stones scattered. He was feeling again. And it seemed that he needed her, at least a little. He might not want her love, but he didn't hate her.

She stroked his back, offering whatever comfort he would take.

He finally stopped shaking. She was wondering what to say when he let out a long sigh and murmured, "I'm so tired."

"Of course you are." She released him — reluctantly — and stepped back. "I doubt you've slept well in months, but you will now. Go back to bed. I will sit with you and make sure you don't dream."

Nodding, he snuffed the candles, removed his boots and jacket, then crawled into bed. His weariness was more apparent with each step. Now that he had abandoned his purpose, his body demanded rest.

Chapter Sixteen

Marianne and Jack were still eating breakfast — Jack had slept until noon — when Barnes announced callers.

"Damon," said Jack, glancing at the proffered card. "Probably come to congratulate you on yesterday's victory. The news will be all over town by now. You'd best be prepared to entertain society. They will beat a path to your door."

Marianne opened her mouth to object — he clearly did not intend to stay with her — but Barnes forestalled her.

"Lord Devlin asked to see both of you, Colonel. Alone."

Jack's brows flew up, but he nodded. "Very well." Shoving his plate aside, he led Marianne to the drawing room.

Marianne's mind was racing. Devlin must have found something. If not, he would have met her privately. She prayed that it was good news, or at least not too bad. Jack had promised to investigate, but he'd said nothing about what he would do if he really had killed a man.

"How lovely to see you again, Lord Devlin," she said when she entered the drawing room. His eyes glowed like twin suns as he raised her hand to his lips. He looked very pleased with himself. She nearly fainted at the thought that he'd almost been too late.

She didn't spot the second man until Devlin turned to Jack. The witness — for who else could this be? — was tall and thin, his eyes dark with suffering. One sleeve hung empty.

Jack spotted him at the same moment. "So you caught it," he said, shaking his head at the empty sleeve. "Marianne, this is Captain Lord Hardcastle, heir to the Duke of Streaford. My wife, Captain."

"You can drop the rank. I sold out when I returned from Belgium," said Hardcastle, accepting a glass of wine. "But you seem surprised by my injuries. Don't you remember?"

Pain flashed through Jack's eyes. "Parts of the battle remain blank."

"Just as well," said Devlin easily. "It was a vicious day."

"Damnation," muttered Hardcastle under his breath. "I should have sought you out earlier — or at least written. I owe you too much to allow my thanks to run late."

"For what?"

"You saved my life."

Jack's eyes widened.

Marianne wanted to jump for joy.

"I'm sorry, but I don't recall it," said Jack slowly. "What happened?"

"We'd been charging their artillery most of the morning — the damned French were more heavily fortified than we had expected. I'll never know exactly what happened. I went from shouting orders to flying through the air in an instant. I don't recall hitting the ground. Sometime later, I woke up, scarcely able to breathe for the weight on my chest. You met Cheney, didn't you?" He looked at Devlin.

"Decent lad, but too cocky by half."

"True, but so were we when we first bought colors."

All three men nodded. Their expressions excluded Marianne. Each was recalling experiences she would never understand.

Hardcastle shifted. "He might have made a good officer if he had lived."

"What happened?" asked Jack.

"His body was lying across my chest. I tried to heave it away, but the attempt hurt so bad, I passed out. By the time I again awoke, the sun was well past its zenith. Cheney still lay atop me. I managed to turn my head enough to see that a dead horse was pinning his legs — its rump crushed his thighs into my side."

"No wonder it was hard to breathe," murmured Marianne.

"That wasn't all," continued Hardcastle. "A piece of wood had skewered his shoulder. I never figured out what it was — a pike or a piece of a gun carriage, I expect. But it pinned him to the ground as effectively as the horse. I was trapped in the middle. My free arm was mangled so badly it would not move." He glanced at the empty sleeve. "The other arm was trapped beneath me. By the time you happened along, Colonel, I was convinced that I would die."

He paused to drink wine.

"What happened?" Jack's voice was unnaturally calm.

Jack's dream. Tremors rattled Marianne's cup, so she set it aside. Her heart raced. This had to be Jack's dream.

"You were on foot and wounded yourself," said Hardcastle. "Your one working hand couldn't dislodge that spear or pull me free. You tried shouting for help, but the French were massing for a new charge, so no one ventured out. I expected you to slip away, for staying put your own life in mortal danger. I should have known better."

"What do you mean?" asked Marianne, wondering if Hardcastle expected special treatment because of his birth.

He spotted her suspicions. "Not because of my status," he said, turning to face her. "Your husband pulled dozens of men from certain death, many of them common soldiers." He turned back to Jack. "I'll never forget your heroics, Colonel. Despite the French poised to charge, you hacked at Cheney's body until you had cut the stake loose. Several of the enemy were shooting at you, but you didn't waver. When I was free, you threw me across your good shoulder and raced back to our lines, the French close behind. Just as we reached the first square, you took a blow to the thigh and stumbled into our own fire. Hands pulled us into the square, but I feared you were dead. It wasn't until I woke from a coma a week later that I learned you'd survived. By the time they released me, you were gone. I meant to find you immediately, but I received word that my mother was ill. We buried her yesterday."

"I had not heard," said Jack. "My condolences."

Marianne could almost hear his thoughts tumbling about as they realigned themselves in this new pattern. She moved to replenish Devlin's wine. "Thank you," she murmured. "You will never perform a greater service. The dreams had grown worse."

"Things are often not what they seem," he agreed, matching her tone. "My apologies for the delay. I had hoped to return by Saturday, but the duchess took a turn for the worse."

By the time Devlin and Hardcastle left, Jack was more relaxed than he'd been in months. He couldn't believe how wrong he'd been.

"You put Damon up to this, didn't you?" he asked when they were alone.

She jerked guiltily, but he didn't sound angry. "I asked if he knew anyone who might have seen you fall. He didn't, but insisted on looking for someone. It seems he is grateful to you for rescuing him from trouble in the past."

"He proved you right." His head shook in wonder. "Yet who would have thought such damning evidence might have an honorable explanation?"

"You never considered that the officer might already have been dead, did you? Despite your own history."

"Never. I wish you hadn't heard that, though. Desecrations are hard to accept."

"Have you forgotten your own words? The body is merely a shell that temporarily houses the spirit. Once the two part, the body is of no import — especially when the damage saved a life. It is time to set the past behind you, Jack."

"This incident, certainly."

"No. All the past. Stop brooding about your ancestors. You are nothing like them, and never will be. I do not believe that blood plays a large role in forming character."

"Not true. I've met many evil men. It is a trait that runs strongly in families such as mine."

"But that has little to do with blood. Children often emulate their parents. If a father is sneaky, the son learns to be sneaky. If he is honorable, the child learns to love honor."

"My family produces vicious cowards."

"But not always. Think, Jack. If blood were the deciding factor, then all brothers would be alike. Yet you can find evidence to the contrary in nearly every family. What about Devall? Angela claims that his father was a brutal tyrant, yet Devall is a benevolent reformer because he chose not to follow in his father's footsteps. And Angela is nothing like her greedy, selfish mother."

Jack walked to the window and stared at the rain drumming on the cobblestones in the square. "Yet you said yourself that parents shape their children's character."

"Only if the parent spends time with the child. You can't emulate something you never see — which is how Angela turned out so well; her mother missed most of her childhood. I suspect that your father ignored you. You were not his heir and were much younger. And there are other role models available — tutors, friends, neighbors. In the end, we are what we make of ourselves."

"That makes no sense."

"Of course if does. You are a born leader, Jack. Like Devall, you choose models consciously and for specific purposes. You made a decision early in life to follow another path. And you have continued that habit ever since. There is a passage in *Romans* that makes the point quite well. *Hath not the potter power over the clay,*

370

of the same lump to make one vessel unto honor, and another unto dishonor? You and Wilcox started with the same breeding — the same clay. He chose to emulate the worst of his ancestors, a lazy path followed by someone of limited intellect, for it required little thought and no discipline. You chose honor, a difficult road, especially for someone surrounded by dishonor. But you had the intelligence, perseverance, and courage to make it work. Same start. Very different result. And the training that produced that result won't change, so relax. Be yourself, and you need fear nothing."

"How did you become so wise?"

"Reading and observation. I have watched people since coming to London — how else can I learn how to go on in society? It is very instructive. Many of the cubs are unsure of themselves, so they copy the dress and habits of others. Take Mr. Dawkins, for example. He apes Lord Sedgewick Wylie, down to the color of his coats, the knot in his cravat, and his topics of conversation. Mr. Dawkins chose wisely, for Lord Sedgewick avoids the foppish silliness of Lord James Hutchinson, and he disdains Brummell's growing dissipation. He also cares about his followers. He deflected young Reynolds from falling in with a cardsharp, for example, so Dawkins is in good hands. Mr. Singleton, on the other hand, is not wise, for he seems determined to follow in Devereaux's footsteps. Angela calls Devereaux the most unscrupulous rakehell in society."

"True. And his friend Millhouse is nearly as bad."

"Another instance of judging a man by his friends. You have hated what Deerchester represents since you were old enough to understand it. Who did you trust and admire in those years?"

"My tutor," he admitted. "Reeves was the opposite of Deerchester — educated, honorable, unwilling to compromise his ideals, even when doing so would have been to his benefit."

"The perfect model. You have always chosen well, as your friends prove. And I suspect that you chose Wellington as your model in military matters."

"You make it sound simple," he said, turning back to face her. "But I've seen evidence that blood also matters."

"Perhaps, but choice and custom can overwhelm even the harshest blood — as you have proved."

"But I would pass that blood to my children." He cursed himself. He had not expected to father any children, but now he had no choice. As Marianne had warned in the beginning, having won their case against Barnett, there was no way out of this marriage. What hope did he have of preventing his sons from falling prey to their ancestral breeding?

"So that explains it," murmured Marianne. "Jack, there are no guarantees in life. Every family has its black sheep — or so people claim. That by itself is proof enough that breeding has little to do with behavior. All you can do is love your children and teach them proper values, something best done through example."

Jack gave up the argument. Whatever the truth, he must take his chances. There was no way he could avoid children. Marianne's vow of love had warmed his heart — and other places. He could not hurt her.

"Forgive me, Marianne," he said, drawing her into his arms. "I have treated you shabbily. But you are right again. There are no guarantees. We can only do our best. You needn't fear for the future."

Her arms crept around his back. "I suspect some of your trouble was melancholia. It saps the energy and twists events until even mild problems seem incurably black."

"You sound intimately acquainted with it."

"I suffered from it for more than a year after returning from France. It seemed wrong that I had survived. Nigel and Cecily were far more deserving of life than I, for they were well behaved, while I was usually in trouble. But it passed in time."

"As has mine."

"Good." She smiled — a real smile that lifted her mouth as well as lit her eyes.

Jack's knees wobbled. He'd known that her smile must be potent, but this was more powerful than a battlefield rocket, spraying him with sparks of light and happiness, its fire heating his blood.

Turning her face up, he kissed her. "I love you, Marianne. For weeks I've cursed Fate for showing me the heaven I could never enjoy. Now I must thank Fate that you turned up on the cliff that day."

"You love me?"

"With all my heart."

"Then why did you flinch from me this morning?"

He traced her brow with one finger. "When you swore that you loved me, I knew I must give up my plans. The pain nearly felled me — remember, I still thought myself irredeemably venal. But I could not hurt you. I had tried to keep my distance so you would not form an attachment, so your declaration exposed yet another way I had failed."

"I loved you long before you kissed me that day, though I did not recognize my feelings for what they were until later." She flung her arms around his neck and met his mouth.

Passion exploded between them, more intense than he had thought possible. Gone was any hint of fear when he parted her lips and stroked her tongue with his own. She moaned — a song compelling enough to distract a man from all the Sirens in chorus.

He pulled her closer, tracing the lines of her back, then slid a hand between them to tease her perfect breast.

"Jack." She squirmed against him until he nearly climaxed. Her mouth slid down his cheek as he turned to nip her ear.

"Let's finish this upstairs," he murmured. "It's time you moved out of my dreams and into my bed."

Two days later, Jack and Marianne were again in the drawing room. He had reported for duty the day before, once again able to hold his head high.

He was glad that Wellington's new post would keep him in London, for it meant that he could retain his commission. If Wellington had been sent overseas, Jack would have had to resign. He couldn't leave Marianne behind, but didn't want her traveling with the army. Now he could buy a town house and start a family. They would visit Seacliff and Halworth often, but most of their time would be spent in town.

Fitch had turned up new information about Barnett. The viscount was weaker than even Jack had suspected. Rather than deal with his mad niece, he had handed the responsibility to Craven. It was Craven who had embezzled Marianne's allowance and falsified the reports to her trustees. He had also embezzled a large sum from Barnett. Craven had now disappeared, taking the spoils with him. Barnett swore that the plot to lock Marianne away had also been Craven's.

Marianne had accepted Fitch's evidence and dropped the demand that Barnett repay the missing funds. His other financial problems were severe enough to keep him from London, so she need never meet him again.

Barnes announced a visitor.

"Miss Witt!" exclaimed Jack when a gray-haired lady entered the room. "What are you doing here?"

"I saw your marriage announcement in my neighbor's copy of the *Morning Post* and had to meet your wife," said the lady.

Jack shook his head. "Marianne, this is Miss Witt, my old nurse, whom I've not seen in twenty years. Miss Witt, my wife, Marianne Caldwell."

Marianne poured tea, but said little as Jack and Miss Witt reminisced. Her mind reeled with questions, for Lady Hartford had not known Miss Witt's direction the last time they had spoken.

"There is something I need to tell you, Jack," Miss Witt said once she'd finished several biscuits and two cups of tea. "I had to remain silent at the time, but old threats no longer matter. A wasting sickness will finish me in a few months. It seems right to set the record straight while I still can."

Jack scoffed, but she held up a hand. "We won't argue. I'll not die tomorrow or even next week, but it will not be much longer. Before I go, you deserve to know about your mother. I was in the next room when Deerchester banished her. He threatened me with death should I ever reveal the truth, but that no longer matters."

"What happened?" Marianne asked. Jack seemed speechless.

"He had always been a brutal man," said Miss Witt.

"I thought him mostly cowardly." Jack's voice trembled.

"And so he was. But a cowardly man is dangerous, for he despises his weakness and goes to great lengths to hide it. Often that means exercising power over those who cannot fight back. So it was with Deerchester. You weren't his only target. He savaged many a girl, but his wife was his most frequent victim."

Jack was visibly shaking.

"Then why did he send her away?" asked Marianne softly. "Brutal men like having a handy victim."

"She betrayed him. Deerchester is not Jack's father."

Marianne gasped.

Jack's teacup fell, bouncing twice before breaking against a table leg.

Miss Witt shook her head. "The argument that day was vicious. He must have beaten her badly, for she was heavily veiled when she left the next morning. The staff had long suspected her betrayal — Deerchester had been gone when you must have been conceived — but no one knew who was responsible, and few would have betrayed her if they *had* known."

"Have you any guesses?" Jack's voice was rough.

"No. I had worked at Deerchester when Wilcox was a babe, but moved on when he turned five — he was deemed ripe for a tutor by then. She rarely left the estate in those days, and never without Deerchester in attendance, though that might have changed when he was away. I returned a fortnight before you were born, but she was ill and did not receive me until her confinement. She showed none of her usual spirit, though that was hardly surprising under the circumstances. Deerchester threw her out a week later."

"Did she protest?" asked Marianne.

"Who would dare? She knew better than anyone the cost of crossing him. But she did refuse to name her lover."

"So he beat her, then threw her out." Jack clenched his fists.

"That wasn't her punishment. She was glad enough to escape his heavy hand. But he refused to send you with her, though he hated the sight of you. You were evidence of his weakness, proof of her defiance. It is for that reason that I came to beg your forgiveness. Had I told you the truth when you reached your majority, you could have sought her out so she could see that you are an upstanding man, despite Deerchester's influence. Instead, I let fear lock my tongue. But perhaps it is not too late."

"It is never too late. Where did he send her?"

"Scotland, though I don't know where."

"I will find her. Deerchester's solicitor will know her direction. He must be sending her money — her family would have had him up on charges otherwise."

"Thank you," said Miss Witt. "I always liked your mother and tried to make her lot easier. When I returned for your birth, her laughter was gone. It pained me. I can only pray she found peace."

Miss Witt departed a short time later, leaving Jack and Marianne alone.

"I wonder who your father was," she said slowly.

"Reeves. It has to be. It would explain so much."

"Your tutor?"

He nodded. "And Wilcox's long before I was born, so he was in the house. Even before he became my tutor, I considered him a friend. He often spoke of Mother, spinning tales of her goodness — at a risk,

I must admit; no one was allowed to mention her name. And he taught me so much more than ciphering and history. Things like honor and compassion. I wish I had known."

"It is not too late."

"In his case, it is. He died ten years ago. I wonder if Mother knows."

"She must. He would have sent her reports on your progress, so their cessation would have announced his death even if his solicitor knew nothing. Miss Witt was only partially right, you know. Your mother lost you, it is true, but she left you in good hands — your father's hands." She smiled. "This is truly a week of miracles."

"Not really. You convinced me that life was worthwhile as long as we are together. Once I stopped agonizing over my breeding, Fate relented and revealed that it is no threat."

"Righ—" She froze as the realization hit.

"What?"

"No wonder Deerchester was so furious about our marriage."

"He has always hated me, and more so now that Wilcox is gone. It must grate that his heir is not of his blood."

"Precisely. But think, Jack. Have you

ever met Miss Somerson?"

"No."

"When did he begin pushing that match?"

"About a year ago. What —"

She shook her head. "You described him as sneaky, and this proves it. He tried to cut you out of the succession."

"He can't."

"Not in the short term. It's far too late to disown you. But I suspect Wilcox died more than a year ago. Furious to find himself with an heir who carried none of his blood — I don't believe for a moment his protestations of poverty, by the way; that was a ploy to garner your sympathy — he concocted a dastardly plan. He cannot wed, for his wife remains alive, so he schemed to shackle you to his mistress, someone he could trust to bear only his children. That way the earldom remains in his line, and he can take his revenge on you for not being his."

"Good God! But I can't believe even Deerchester would be that sneaky."

"Trust me. Angela recognized her name. Miss Somerson is your age, has been Deerchester's mistress for several years, and has borne him two sons. What better way to keep the Deerchester title and

382

blood together?"

Jack nearly choked.

"But that threat is now averted. With you, the earldom will start a new line, free from the problems of the past. What a legacy to leave to your children."

"Speaking of which, I feel a sudden urge to secure this new line." His eyes glinted in a way she recognized after two days in his bed.

She grinned. It was definitely a goal worth pursuing.

We hope you have enjoyed this Large Print book. Other Thorndike, Wheeler or Chivers Press Large Print books are available at your library or directly from the publishers.

For more information about current and up-coming titles, please call or write, without obligation, to:

Publisher
Thorndike Press
295 Kennedy Memorial Drive
Waterville, ME   04901
Tel. (800) 223-1244

Or visit our Web site at:
www.gale.com/thorndike
www.gale.com/wheeler

OR

Chivers Large Print
published by BBC Audiobooks Ltd
St James House, The Square
Lower Bristol Road
Bath BA2 3SB
England
Tel. +44(0) 800 136919
email: bbcaudiobooks@bbc.co.uk
www.bbcaudiobooks.co.uk

All our Large Print titles are designed for easy reading, and all our books are made to last.

384